"The Sp'thra make the following offer for what we want to buy. We will tell you the location of the closest unused world known to us, habitable by you. The location of the nearest intelligent species known to us ready to engage in intersteller communication. Finally, we offer you an improvement on your current technology for spaceflight within your solar system "

"In return for which you want more tapes and grammar books on microfilm?"

"*No*. That has been your mistake all along. We need working brains competent in six linguistically diverse languages."

"You mean human volunteers, to go back home to your planet with you?"

"No," Ph'theri retorted sharply. "That isn't reasonable."

"Then what do you mean if not live human beings!"

"What we say—language-programmed brains. In working order. Machine-maintained. Separated from the body."

Also by Ian Watson in VGSF

MIRACLE VISITORS

IAN WATSON

The Embedding

VGSF

VGSF is an imprint of Victor Gollancz Ltd
14 Henrietta Street, London WC2E 8QJ

First published in Great Britain 1973
by Victor Gollancz Ltd

First VGSF edition 1990

Copyright © Ian Watson 1973

British Library Cataloguing in Publication Data
Watson, Ian
  The embedding
  I. Title
  823'.914 [F]

ISBN 0-575-04784-4

Printed and bound in Great Britain
by Cox & Wyman Ltd, Reading

ONE

CHRIS SOLE DRESSED quickly. Eileen had already called him once. The second time she called him, the postman had been to the door.

"There's a letter from Brazil," she shouted from the foot of the stairs. "It's from Pierre —"

Pierre? What was he writing for? The news bothered him. Eileen had been so distant and detached since their boy was born—involved in herself and Peter and memories. It wasn't a detachment he found it particularly easy to break through any more—or, to be frank, that he cared to. So what effect would this letter from her one-time lover have on her? He hoped it wouldn't be too troublesome.

The landing window gave a quick hint of black fields, other staff houses, the Hospital half a mile away on top of the hill. He glanced momentarily—and shivered with morning misgivings. They often attacked him between waking up and getting to the Hospital.

In the kitchen, three-year-old Peter was making a noisy mess of his breakfast—mashing cornflakes and milk in his bowl, while Eileen stood skimming through the letter.

Sole sat down opposite Peter and buttered a slice of toast. Casually he examined the boy's face. Didn't these thin foxy features add up to an image of the Pierre who so many years ago had been photographed as a small boy in a field of marguerites somewhere in France? Already the boy had the same pointed urgency as Pierre, and the glossy brown eyes of a dog fox on the prowl.

Sole's own face had a sort of phoney distinction about

it. It was too well balanced. Slide a mirror up against his nose and he wasn't split into two different faces, like most people, but a pair of identical twins. This balance of the features was initially impressive, but the end result was a cancelling out of one side of the man by the other, more visible as the years went by.

He glanced at Eileen as she read. She was slightly taller than he was and her eyes had an in-between colour that her last passport described as grey, but which could easily be blue. They'd seemed bluer in Africa—the blue of swimming pools and open skies, which the airmail paper now briefly reflected.

Africa. Those hot still evenings when the open louvres brought no air into their flat and the beer came warm from the overloaded icebox. The brightly-lit university buildings there on the hill, and the yellow glow of the city a dozen miles away by the sea, with the sticky darkness in between syncopated by the mutter of drums. It had been good then, that rapport, that togetherness, before the sadness and the contradictions entered in. Before Pierre slipped over the border into Free Mozambique with Frelimo guerrilla fighters to study the sociology of liberation among the Makonde people on the far side of the Ruvuma river. Before Sole ever heard of the good and profitable destiny awaiting him in this English hospital unit. Before that final diffident encounter with Pierre in Paris four years ago, when Eileen had gone away with the Frenchman for a night and come back the next morning knowing how far their lives had separated and gone down different tracks.

"It seems he's living with this tribe in the Amazon," she said, "but they're being flooded—fighting with poison arrows—and taking drugs—"

"Can I read it?"

She held on to the letter a moment longer, her fingers crumpling the paper to give it a touch of ownership; be-

6

fore surrendering it with a sad lost eroticism of gesture that made him ache, since it wasn't directed at him.

"Shall I read it out?" he asked.

He suspected his voice might rob these lines of the emotional content they possessed for her, so that what had been a love letter would become a mass of folklore and politics. Why do it then? To make some kind of physical contribution to the dialogue of Pierre and Eileen —which he hadn't been able to join emotionally, though he reaped the fruits of the Frenchman's ideas? Or to prove that the ideas were more important—and compete with the evidence of love Eileen had, in the shape of Peter?

"Eileen?"

"I can't concentrate right now. He's getting milk all over the place. Read it yourself—I'll finish it later—"

Wiping the boy's mouth with a tissue, she stared at his features intently, then guided his hand on the spoon, picking stray cornflakes up with her other hand and dropping them into her saucer.

Sole cradled his hand round the letter guiltily, like a schoolboy not wanting his answers to be copied, and read.

"You may wonder why I'm using yourselves, Chris and Eileen, to vent my anger on? After so long too! But perhaps you, Chris, will understand when I say that there are some curious threads that lead through years and countries, linking dissimilar people, places and events—is this too mystical a thought for a marxist to entertain?—and that in this case it is that zany surrealist poem of Raymond Roussel's that we talked about so often in Africa that is the link between yourselves and my own discoveries here and now among one particular Amazon tribe.

"These people have Hobson's choice—doomed to be drowned if they stay where they are—or else destroyed

7

by a life of tin huts, rum, prostitution and illness, if they're 'sensible' enough to move out of the way of the flood that is even now covering up the whole surface of their world. Need I say nobody cares which option they choose.

"Issues seemed so simple in Africa, compared with here in the heart of Brazil. It was so easy to find an honourable and recognizable role to play in the Mozambique bush. Even the remotest Makonde tribesman knew what the political issues were, was aware of 'Politics' as such..."

Damn it, he thought, apprehensive at the mention of Roussel's name. Let Pierre get on trying to reform the world. Just leave me alone to discover what the world really is, how the mind of Man sees the world!

"But how can these Indians perceive any difference between the other Caraiba—that bastard Portuguese word the Indians use for any foreigners, including the European-descended Brazilians themselves—and myself? We're all outsiders, aliens. Frenchmen, Americans. Right Wing, Left Wing. It's all the same. Caraiba.

"Those who are aware of Politics, and the Politics of the Amazon Flood, seem so far away, city men occupied with city struggles. Even when they move out into the countryside to fight, what have they got to do with the Indians in their forests? What *can* they have to do, till the Indians have been destroyed as Indians and become poverty-stricken civilizados?

"So should I be in favour of a human zoo where these 'quaint savages' can linger on in their interesting savagery? How much it goes against the grain to say, yes maybe—for the Indians there can be no political reply!

"How glad the Brazilian régime is of this distraction

foisted on them by the Americans!—the glory of building the greatest inland sea on Earth, the only one of Man's works visible from the Moon.

"It *is* a political project, though its victims know nothing of politics—and *cannot* be made aware of politics without introducing a kind of virus that destroys them. That's the paradox that sickens me: my own impotence here. I can only record the death of this unique people. Mark up the indictment for the future. And to console myself, listen to my tape of Roussel's crazy poem..."

Sole shuddered. A hot African sun used to warm their talk of Roussel and it had seemed so innocent and exciting then, the dawning idea of his own research. He remembered the view of red corrugated roofs from a roof-top bar. Shining white plaster walls. Flame trees. A mosque. Peugeots and Volkswagens parked in the dusty street below. The sellers of carvings squatting in shorts and torn shirts while Moslem women passed by on flip-flop sandals, their bodies wrapped in black shrouds, with parcels balanced on their heads. The beer bottles on the tin table slimy with condensation, as Pierre and he talked about a poem that was practically impossible for the human brain to process—which a machine would have to be built to read...

Warm and innocent then—but now that Vidya, Vasilki, Rama and Gulshen and the others were learning their lessons in the Special Environments at the Hospital, Pierre's triggering of memories of that happy mood came with an accusing force.

As though Eileen had read his thoughts she looked up from the boy and said sharply:

"Chris, there's something I wanted to ask you. You can finish reading the letter later on."

"What?"

9

"Nothing very important, I don't suppose. Only, I was talking to one of the village women whose husband does gardening at the Hospital. She said something odd—"

"Yes?"

"That you're teaching the children there bad language." Shock.

"Bad language? What does she mean? Doesn't she know it's a hospital for kids who can't speak properly—who've suffered brain damage? Of course they speak bad language."

Glancing at the paragraphs he'd just read, he found himself assaulted by certain phrases that would not leave him alone.

Such as 'human zoo' and 'political project'.

The words had a faint aura round them on the paper— they blurred into a fog as though his brain was reluctant to process them. But wouldn't disappear. Their very indistinctness irritated him, brought them nagging to his attention. Perhaps rain had dripped on to the paper while Pierre was writing, smearing these particular words before they had a chance to dry.

Eileen was watching her husband calmly.

"I know what the Unit's supposed to be doing. That's what I told her, what you've just said to me. But you know how these country wives go all mysterious and confidential. She knew the Hospital was up to something else, she said—something secret and shameful. And what it was, was teaching children bad language—"

"So what does she mean by bad language then? What's her definition?" he demanded.

"I said about the brain damage and speech defects," she shrugged, "but that wasn't what she meant."

Sole drank some coffee swiftly, scalding his mouth, and laughed.

"I wonder what the poor gossipy bitch thinks we're up to? Teaching the kids to lisp out 'fuck' and 'bugger'?"

"No, Chris, I don't feel she was talking about 'fuck' and 'bugger'."

The Victorian wrought-iron pub table by the window was piled with spice jars and cook books—it had cost twenty pounds at an auction and they'd painted it white together when she was five months pregnant, imagining the child sitting at it in a high chair while Sole sat opposite, drinking a glass of beer maybe and steering the child's early efforts at speech.

"The gardener's wife! It's just a bit of nonsense."

But Eileen persisted, touching Peter anxiously as though the boy was threatened by events at the Hospital.

"You used to talk to Pierre about bad language. You didn't mean swearing then. You meant *wrong* languages."

"Listen Eileen, a child speaks bad language when its brain's damaged. It has difficulties—has to be taught by roundabout routes."

"She also said—"

"Yes?"

"There's a front and a back to the Hospital. The real work goes on in special rooms you can't get into without a pass. And it isn't curing the children at all but making them sick. That's where the bad language comes in. Or do I say bad languages, plural? Is that more accurate, Chris? What *is* going on at the Unit? Is it despicable—or something I can admire?"

"Damn it, the woman's just describing any hospital! There are always closed wards."

"But it isn't a mental hospital."

Sole shrugged, noticed the blue ghost of a 'human zoo' trying to catch his eye.

"Any hospital dealing with damaged brains is a kind of mental hospital at the same time as it's a physical hospital. You can't draw a line between the two. Language is a mental thing. Damn it, they hired a linguist in me, not a doctor."

"So they did."

Eileen watched curiously as he folded the airletter, stuffed it back into the envelope and put it in his pocket. She didn't raise any objection to his taking it away.

As he walked up to the Unit, Sole watched the sky lightening into a calm crisp blue day, sucked in the clean cold air and blew it out ahead of him as white smoke.

How about being in Alaska, where your spittle hit the ground as a tight ice ball that bounced and rolled? That would be something.

Or in Brazil?

How about being Pierre? Confident anguished idealistic Pierre.

So difficult to imagine the otherness of another person. Yet wasn't that his own task at the Hospital—to *create* otherness? Oh Vidya, and all you others: will you really tell us so much about what humanity is, through our little act of inhumanity?

Inevitable that somebody somewhere should try out this set of experiments sooner or later. It had cropped up in the literature for years. The yearning to try it out became a kind of pornography after a while, a sort of scientific masturbation. To raise children in isolation speaking specially designed languages.

He walked up a gravel drive between lofty skeletons of poplars and bushes like wire sculpture models of mind that might have been made in the Hospital and thrown out as too simple.

The Unit itself was a large country house with modern functional wings added on at the sides and rear, where it jutted back into several dozen acres of close-packed firs that stretched half a mile behind the building and along its flanks in a great green skirt that grew taller and thicker year by year.

Sole had been into the plantation a couple of times but

found it hard going. All the low interlocking branches and uneven sods underfoot. Anyway, there was nothing to see among the trees except more of the same. No dells or glades in there, no rides cutting through them.

(Fifty feet inside the green gloom, and it's another world. The traveller loses all sense of direction. The monotony and alienation of endless wastes of savage vegetation bear down on him. To journey a hundred yards he has to crawl on his belly, humping himself over fallen logs, and wriggling through a network of creepers; or hack a path clear for himself in the most exhausting and futile manner imaginable ...)

The elegant central mansion was bracketed incongruously by the concrete wings. Before it, twin stone lions thrust out their paws on to a lawn pocked with molecasts. Brown eruptions marked the turf like boils on a once-lovely complexion. Gardener, indeed!

The figure in the purple raincoat striding along the field path was the biochemist Zahl.

Sole thrust Pierre's letter deeper in his pocket, feeling otherwise it might fall out and be lost before he had time to read it.

Half a dozen cars stood parked on the gravel, and a lowslung United States Air Force ambulance.

The brass nameplate read:

HADDON NEUROTHERAPY UNIT.

He pushed the heavy door open and was assaulted by the hot dry air within. Crossing the hallway between the wards in the righthand wing and the service areas in the left, where computer room, kitchens, surgery and lab were, he paused by the Christmas tree at the foot of the great oak staircase leading to the nurses' quarters.

It was losing so many needles in this heat. What a scurf of green it was scattering on the tiles.

13

A nurse passed behind him, wheeling a trolley stacked with dirty plates from the kids' breakfast, rolling it gently on rubber wheels, the only noise to mark its passage a faint percussion of china rocking against greasy china.

Paper streamers crisscrossed the corridors and hallway. Balloons, pinned over doorways, seemed to summon different kinds of attention. Blue attention. Green attention. Red attention. Different areas of the injured brain blowing empty speech bubbles.

What would the bubbles be filled with?

Accusations? Or the key to reality? The $E=MC^2$ of the mind?

The spring door locked behind him automatically. There was a short corridor with a second door at the end of it. He chose a second key, unlocked the door and walked through into the rear wing, where fir branches reached out to brush the windows. A corridor ran right round the outside of the wing.

The window glass bore a fine mesh of wires within it, low voltage electrified, computer monitored as part of the alarm system.

To look down from the upper windows of the manor house on to this rear wing would show you great opaque skylights that lit the rooms within the circuit of the corridor—a blank aquarium.

He unlocked his office, switched on the neon strip lights to buck up the weak winter light filtering from overhead, then as he always did first thing in the morning sat before the monitor screen and switched on.

Bad language, Eileen? Oh yes—the worst, and the best!

The screen flickered and unfogged. In a large undulating playroom two naked dark-skinned children, boy and girl, were rolling a giant beachball along. They were three or four years old. Another naked girl wandered after them, dragging a coiled plastic tube, and a second boy

14

brought up the rear, holding his hands out before him, pretending to be blind and feeling his way.

Sole touched another switch and the sound of voices came from the playroom. However these weren't the children's voices.

He panned the camera—past the transparent-walled maze—to the great wall-screen that was the source of the voices. The magnified images of Chris Sole and computer man Lionel Rosson moved on it.

The voices were theirs. And yet, not exactly theirs. The speech computer had taken their voices apart and put them together again. Otherwise their words wouldn't have flowed naturally. Sole couldn't have framed the sentences he heard his recorded voice saying, without a great deal of hesitation. They were English sentences, yet so un-English. It was the arrangement of those strings of words that caused the confusion. The words themselves were simple enough. Such kids' talk. Yet organized as no kids' talk before, so that adults couldn't for the life of them follow it without a printout of the speech with a maze of brackets breaking it up to re-establish patterns the mind was used to processing.

It was Roussel speech.

Pierre had been appalled and intrigued by the arrogant way Raymond Roussel pushed his poetry past the bounds of human comprehension. The poem *New Impressions of Africa* became a sort of mistress for Pierre, one he constantly quarrelled with, but who continued to fascinate him. Her aristocratic manners repelled him. He wanted to master her, for the sake of logic and justice. If only he could know her completely, through one long night of understanding, he'd be free of his temptress. But like all great temptresses, this poem had her hidden wiles—her tricks. She hypnotized. She induced loss of memory.

The only way of getting near to the heart of her—if only to stab her in the heart and be done with her!—

was by hearing the words she spoke. Yet the maze they formed forever defeated the unaided human mind. If Logic was so easily put to flight by a poem, what hope was there for the reform of the world itself by logic? This mistress was an elegant bitch, a Salomé who cared not a hoot for the Third World and the Poor—a constant reminder to Pierre of the falsity of the aesthetic choice in life. Beauty instead of truth.

And right now, unaccountably, she was actually *consoling* Pierre in the midst of the injustices he witnessed in the Brazilian jungle!

It was this contradiction that made Sole pull out the letter again in search of a clue.

The words on the stamp read ORDER AND PROGRESS— the motto of Brazil, given a new and insistent reality by the military régime.

He chose a page where he noticed Roussel's name leering out at him.

"... I may as well write to you as to anyone else—at least you will appreciate the uniqueness of this particular tribe.

"They call themselves Xemahoa, but they may not be around to call themselves anything for very much longer, in spite of the incredible last stand of their tribal shaman, their *Bruxo*—a last stand not conducted with bows and poison arrows and blowpipes however!

"They have so little idea of the enormity of what they are up against; what pawns (oh less than pawns!) they are in their own jungle home to the Big Players! Their Bruxo's attempts to deal with the coming disaster in his own cultural terms truly have a pathetic grandeur about them. And oh what a zany similarity to Roussel's poem too! What an amazing similarity to the mind-sanctuary that our French dilettante built for himself. This is what astonishes me. When I am not livid with

16

rage, I toy with the idea of somehow translating *Nouvelles Impressions d'Afrique* into Xemahoa B.

"I say Xemahoa *B*, since apparently there's a two-tier language situation operating here—and in Xemahoa B, if in any language on this vicious globe, Roussel's poem might at last be made comprehensible.

"The essence of the Bruxo's enterprise for flood control is this—let me assure you, my dear Chris, you will be astonished too—and afterwards you will be enraged..."

Sole threw the letter down.

My poor Pierre, and so would you be astonished to see me sitting here watching my Indians.

Astonished—and afterwards? How enraged would you be?

To Sole's eyes, they were uniquely beautiful.

Their world was beautiful.

And their speech.

He adjusted the controls to filter out his own and Rosson's voices; tuned the feathermike pickups for whatever the children might be saying.

But they were silent at the moment.

He had hundreds of hours of their speech on tape, from the earliest babbling through the first whole utterances to the sentences they were making now—embedded statements about an embedded world. He had walked among them, played with them, shown them how to use their maze and teaching dolls and oracles—wearing a speech-mask which snatched the words from his lips as soon as he whispered them, sent them to the computer for sorting and transforming, before voicing them.

Strictly speaking, he had no need to listen and look in, in this doting way. Monitoring was automatic; all the children said could be picked up by feathermikes, processed and sorted and stored on tape. Interesting or unexpected word patterns would be printed out for him.

Yet he found it intensely healthy to look in on them. A kind of therapy. Already, his dark sense of alienation had largely lifted.

Sole's wasn't the only world hidden away beneath Haddon Unit. There were two other worlds with their children in them—the Logic World run by Dorothy Summers and Rosson; and the 'Alien' World invented by Jannis the psychologist.

The life support systems for the three worlds were automated as well as the speech programmes. There'd be less and less reason to go down there in person as the kids grew older and more capable of managing. It might even be less and less desirable. The Gods will have to ration their appearances, joked Sam Bax, Director of Haddon.

Competent, bouncy Sam Bax, thought Sole. Leave him to handle politics. The money-getting, the Institutes and Foundations, the military tie-up, the security. It's none of my business. Let Pierre bother himself about the politics of Brazil. Don't pull me into it. Just let me get on with my bloody work! The children of my mind are here, my Rama, my brave Vidya, my beloved Gulshen, my darling Vasilki. Don't make the Gods withdraw from the scene too soon, Sam.

On the screen, Vidya opened his eyes and stared at the shapes of Sole and Rosson. Giant lips moved silently, fleshy and foot-long—and spoke bad language at him.

By night, as the children slept, their speech would be reinforced by the whispering of feathermikes, by the hypnothrob of sleepteaching.

In the canteen at lunchtime, another vicious bitchy brush with Dorothy.

Sole sat at the same table with her, chewed a piece of gristly stew and thought how indigestible Dorothy was herself, emotionally. She betrayed little of Sole's dangerous love for his children. Fortunate for her charges that her partner in the enterprise, Rosson, was the warm human being he was.

"Dorothy, do you ever worry about when the kids grow up?" Sole blurted out rashly. "What's going to happen to them for the next forty or fifty years?"

She pursed her lips.

"Their sex drive can be controlled, I suppose—"

"I don't mean sex, I mean what about them as people. What's going to happen? We don't ask that question, do we?"

"Need we ask it? I'm sure there'll be space for them."

"But what sort of space? Outer Space? Space in a thermos bottle tossed in the cosmic sea in the direction of the nearest star? A crew for a starship?"

Dorothy Summers didn't seem to encounter any gristle or else swallowed what she did.

"I told Sam it was a mistake appointing married people," she said tartly. "I don't imagine your having a child of your own helps objectivity."

Sole thought instinctively of Vidya—before he remembered that 'his' child was called Peter . . .

"Do you have any idea how large the world's population is?" she demanded. "I mean, can you visualize it? All the children that are going to be born before today's over—or wiped out before tonight by accident! Do you think it matters one scrap that a dozen boys and girls are brought up—lavishly, I might add—in somewhat unusual circumstances? Don't come whining to me, my friend, if you get cold feet on a winter's morning."

Sole smiled uncomfortably.

"Can you visualize what the fate of these brats might have been had they not come here? Haddon is Aladdin's Cave so far as they're concerned. Instead of the rubbish heap!"

"Aladdin's Cave? May they discover the Open Sesame for us poor mortals then—"

"Indeed, Chris, yes in-*deed*. I'll tell you one thing—if they don't find it for us, then somebody else will. The Russians have some pretty queer things going on in their mental hospitals—besides using them to keep their intellectuals locked up!"

"What awful stew this is," said Sole, hoping to escape from her clutches; but she pinned him tight as a piece of meat on her fork, for she'd seen Sam Bax heading their way with his own plate of stew. Dorothy blandly reported the conversation to him as soon as he sat down.

Sam nodded sympathetically.

"Have you heard the story about the American spinster and her Venus Fly Trap, Chris?'

And Sam proceeded to tell a sick-funny story that deftly put Dorothy down as the spinster she was and Sole as the sentimentalist. The situation was glossed over—apparently Sam wanted his staff to be on the best of terms today.

"This woman lived in a New York skyscraper where they wouldn't let her keep any pets, not even a goldfish," Sam explained in a jolly, steamrolling manner, between forkfuls of stew. "So she bought a plant to keep her company. A Venus Fly Trap. The Fly Trap can count up to two so it can obviously think after a fashion—"

"A plant can count?" sniffed Dorothy suspiciously.

"Truly! One tap on the tripwire of this botanic gin-trap—say a grain of sand falls on it—and there's no reaction. But give two taps, like a fly would when it lands and stamps its feet—and the jaws snap shut. That's genuine counting—thinking, of a sort. Well, this woman's apartment was so clean and airconditioned and high above the city streets, there weren't any flies ever—so she had to feed it cat food to keep it happy. This went on for two years till one day she found a fly in the kitchen. She thought she'd give her Trap a treat so she caught the fly and fed it to it. Trap closed. Trap digested the fly. A few hours after that the Trap died of food poisoning. Live prey! It died of reality!"

"Or of DDT," sniffed Dorothy.

"Of the perils of a controlled environment, I prefer to think! There's a moral in that for us. Any danger the kids face isn't concerned with their being in those three worlds down below—but in being brought out of them."

Sam forked up the rest of his stew then sat back surveying Sole and Dorothy Summers amiably.

"More important than this little argument between you two people, however, is—tomorrow." He wiped his mouth with the paper napkin, screwed it into a ball and dropped it neatly in the centre of his plate. "We're receiving a visit from one of our American colleagues, which I gather the powers-that-be consider rather important."

He fished in his pocket.

"I've got a working paper this man's written on your subject, Chris. Would you glance through it before then?"

Sam passed the xeroxed sheets over.

Thomas R. Zwingler: *A Computer Analysis of Latent Verbal Disorientation in Long-Flight Astronauts. Part One: Distortion of Conceptual Sets.*

Dorothy craned her neck to read the title too.

"My God," she sniffed. "The pomposity of it."

Sam shook his head.

"I don't think you'll find Tom Zwingler so pompous in person."

"Where did you meet him?" Sole asked.

"A seminar in the States last year," Sam answered vaguely. "Tom Zwingler's a floater—attached to a number of agencies. Sort of experiment co-ordinator."

"What agencies?" Sole pressed, annoyed at his own recent display of vulnerability. "Rand? Hudson? NASA?"

"I gather he's on the salary roll of the National Security Agency. Communications Division."

"You mean espionage?" Dorothy raised an eyebrow sarcastically.

"Hardly that, judging from this paper, Dorothy. A communications man."

"A half-way house man," smiled Dorothy. "Like our Chris?"

Sam frowned. He rose bulkily from his seat.

"Tomorrow afternoon then, two-thirty. We'll give him a run-down on the present state of the art at Haddon. Right?"

Sole nodded.

"I suppose so," sniffed Dorothy ungraciously.

TWO

THE POLICE CAPTAIN flew in by helicopter, a war-surplus Huey Iroquois Slick, in the midst of a downpour, and wanted to interview Charlie Faith immediately.

Jorge Almeida, Charlie's Brazilian adviser, put his head round the door—a slim serious individual with hot dark eyes and a light milk chocolate skin suggesting perhaps an Indian grandparent.

"Visitors, Charlie," he called against the rattle of rain on the tin roof.

Jorge was proud with a truly Brazilian pride of this Amazon Project now opening up half of a country that was itself half a continent, but which had lain dormant for so long: had remained a subconscious landscape, peopled by fantasies of El Dorado and lost cities and giant anacondas that could outrun a horse. Jorge despised these fantasies almost as much as he despised the savages haunting the jungle like ghosts of this dreamscape. From the safe, hitherto uninvolved distance of Amazonia he tacitly supported the military régime that had sworn to tame and civilize this land. His own talents had been approved by two years at the National Civil Engineering Laboratory in Lisbon, and resentment lurked in his soul at being subordinate to a yanqui engineer, however temporary the arrangement. Charlie wasn't blind to this, but they were stuck with each other and usually made the best of it.

Charlie's head throbbed with a trace of hangover hardly improved by the drumming on the roof and he was having trouble maintaining radio contact with the Project

Control Centre nine hundred kilometres north at Santarém.

Damn visitors, he thought. More bloody priests.

He was a small, once muscular man, whose muscles had turned to flab since his days in the army; whose hair had thinned out since then, till it lay plastered stickily over his scalp in short brown fronds—a wet, serrated, dying leaf. The knobbly upturned end of his nose stood out from his features, softened with large greasy pores and slightly too large—as though he'd spent a few years with a finger up each nostril stretching them. Capillary breakdown had started to lay red spiders over his cheekbones some time ago.

His daydreams, as well as his daily radio call, focussed on that two-bit town Santarém—the exit point from this hole in the jungle. A strange anomaly of a place was Santarém: a hangover from the American Civil War. Confederate soldiers who refused to go along with General Lee's surrender settled there and their descendants lived there to this day, hard by other leftovers of American presence through the years—Henry Ford's settlement Fordlândia, now derelict, his Belterra, also abandoned: two reminders of the great rubber boom that had reared a rococo palace to opera in the heart of Amazonia, at Manáus, and brought La Pavlova a thousand miles upstream to dance for the rubber barons. Nowadays Santarém was filled with a fresh influx of Americans, to advise on the building of the great primary dam that would stretch sixty-five kilometres across from Santarém to Alenquer, with a twinbasin lock set in the hard rock, deepwater harbour, turbines and transmission lines; and oversee the construction of the dozen subsidiary dams of the future inland sea that would soon balance, on the globe, the Great Lakes of the northern hemisphere.

A vast sea would embrace the Amazon. Estimates were, it would cost half a billion dollars to map the whole region

24

adequately from the air. But only half that sum to flood it and erase the embarrassments of geography forever.

Charlie's own subdam consisted of ten kilometres of tamped-down earth faced with bright orange plastic carved out of the middle of the jungle. A lake fifteen thousand kilometres square would back up behind it, nowhere too deep for the big timber dredges to haul out the wealth of trees it drowned. A million trees. A billion trees. Who knew the number? Hardwoods, mahoganies, cedars, steelwoods. Silk-cotton trees and garlic trees and chocolate trees. Balsa, cashews, laurels. So many trees. So much land. And so much water. All useless to mankind, up till the present.

Damned rain, thought Charlie. Rots the soul. But at least it was speeding up the filling of the lake, bringing measurably closer the time when he could get the hell out of here.

"Who are they, priests from the camp?"

"No, it's a political police captain and a couple of his sidekicks. It's queer, I've never seen—"

He looked worried; flashed a quick grin of bravado.

"Careful what you say, hey Charlie? Remember, you're a long way from home."

Charlie regarded the Brazilian dubiously.

"Is that meant to be a bit of friendly advice? I guess I'm okay politically."

"They came by helicopter. Can you hurry up, Charlie? They're impatient people."

"Damn it, I'm on the air. Oh never mind, I can't hear nothing but static anyway. Santarém, d'you read me? Reception's terrible. I'm signing off now call you back later, okay? Over and out. Get a bottle of brandy, Jorge, huh? I'll see them in here—"

Jorge was turning to leave when a hand shoved the door fully open and propelled him into the room. Three men pushed their way in and looked round, at radio, dam

25

models, drip buckets, hammock with dirty sheet on it, open charts and records, stacks of *Playboys*.

The Captain wore a crisp olive uniform with a jaunty red spotted neckerchief, black leather boots, a holstered pistol. But if he had a reasonably military air about him, his two companions looked more like *capangas*, the thugs hired by landowners and developers in the Brazilian outback. A ratty vicious-seeming halfcaste. And a massive Negro with teeth almost as black as his skin and web-creamy eyes of bloodshot curds and whey. They wore the same style boots with stained khaki trousers and sweatshirts. The Negro crooked a submachine gun under his arm. Ratface had an automatic rifle with burnished bayonet attached to it.

Jorge was heading around the Negro when a sharp rap of the gun across his ribs halted him.

"Stay here and listen, Almeida—it concerns you as well. Mr Faith, I suppose you don't speak Portuguese?"

The Captain spoke good English with an American accent, but his smile held no real humour in it, only a kind of gloating chilly anticipation.

"Sorry, I understand some. Jorge usually translates for me."

"We shall speak English then."

"Jorge was just going for drinks. You could drink a glass of brandy?"

"Excellent. We shall have some brandy. But not my pilot."

Charlie stared from Ratface to Negro, confused.

"Which one's the pilot?"

"Neither of these, obviously. My pilot stays with his machine to look after it." The Captain spoke to his men quickly, they grinned broken greedy grins and the Negro let Jorge past.

"So you're wondering to what you owe this interruption of your useful work? For which we Brazilians are truly

26

indebted to yourself, need I say, and to your companions in all these filthy jungle holes. Uncivilized here—such a far cry from Rio or São Paulo?"

"Fact is, I came direct from Santarém—never saw those cities."

"That's a shame. Let's hope you have a chance to spend some of your bounty in our fine cities and enjoy real Brazilian hospitality after this vile jungle. It's wonderful that you are flooding it, Mr Faith. Minerals, civilization, the new wealth—"

Was this character and his two thugs planning to roll him for his wad of dollars and cruzeiros? It hardly seemed to merit a special helicopter trip. Yet Charlie recalled that business of customs clearance for essential technical equipment at Santarém, when officials had rolled the whole outfit to the tune of several grand under the guise of customs fees. He hoped it wasn't his turn.

Jorge reappeared with bottle and tumblers, slopped a few fingers of spirit into them and handed them round.

The Captain accepted the brandy from Jorge and sniffed it with a gesture of connoisseurship wasted on that particular juice. The Negro and Ratface drained theirs straight down then wandered about the room rifling through papers and looking into drawers and cupboards while the Captain talked.

"My name is Flores de Oliviera Paixao, Mr Faith. Captain in the Security Police. The Negro is Olimpio, the other one Orlando. Please remember their names, you may see a lot of them and need to ask their help."

Olimpio glanced round and grinned at the mention of his name, but Orlando just carried on rummaging through Charlie's things with quick furtive scrabbles of his free hand. Whenever the halfcaste's bayonet caught the light, Charlie felt a cold squirming sensation in his guts that stopped him arguing about the cavalier way they were treating his room. His mind wandered back to the Nam

27

and the same species of bayoneted rifle in his own hands as he rooted through a jungle hut. The blade had bathed in the guts of a dark-skinned rat of a youth very like Orlando, who went for Charlie with a knife thinking he was saving his sister. Ah, but the sister—cowering in a corner with big doe eyes, tiny cone-shaped breasts pushing at her shirt, the long black pigtails of a schoolgirl. Likely as not she'd never been near a school. She was beautiful. Orlando scrabbled vaguely and stupidly through Charlie's equipment like a ghost of that thin boy, who had somehow seized the American soldier's weapon from his hands in that hut a decade ago and lived on to threaten Charlie with it now, instead of dying.

"Mr Faith?"

Was it his imagination, or was the rain easing up? The outline of one of the slumbering bulldozers waiting on the cement apron outside was sharpening. Soon bulldozers and graders and rubber-rollers and tampers could all be floated downstream to Santarém; and he could be flown out of this hole...

"Yes, Captain?"

"You may be aware that not everyone in our fine cities is quite so hospitable to Americans nor so concerned with the values of civilization. There are alien beings loose in our society. You know who I mean?"

"I guess I do. The Reds. The Urban Guerrillas."

"How should that affect us?" Jorge asked nervously. "That's a thousand kilometres away from here, beyond the jungle. Terrorists operate along the coastal strip and in the cities—"

"How much you know, Almeida!"

Jorge emptied his own brandy and shrugged.

"It's common knowledge."

The Captain nodded.

"These people loot and assassinate and kidnap for ransom and plant bombs that kill and maim innocent people

—under the banner of socialism. Of caring for the common man. How do they care about people by planting bombs in crowded shops? But that's the Communist ideal —to break down civilization in blood and disorder. Then step in with the vain promise of a better world. You'll understand this, Mr Faith—I hear you're a Vietnam veteran? Happily Communists haven't done so well lately. They cannot kidnap ambassadors so easily. Their leaders are in prison. Their exploits no longer claim world interest. Failed men is what they are. But vicious in failure, like rats in a trap. It is the acts they plan in their despair that bring me here, Mr Faith."

Paixao took a thin cigar from an inside pocket, inspected it doubtfully before slipping it between his teeth. Ratface hurried to his side with a flickering lighter.

"Reliable information is in our hands that in their rage and despair, and to buy themselves some of the notoriety they hanker after, the terrorists intend attacking these wonderful dams. But we're not sure exactly which dams, or when, or how, Mr Faith. Our informants weren't sure. Or I assure you they would have told. Ilha das Flôres prison is persuasive that way."

The rain was certainly slackening off—but its fingers still tapped out a rhythm on Charlie's skull.

"Yeah, I can believe they would have told," sweated Charlie.

It wasn't so much the hints of torture which Paixao dropped with such a contemplative smile, as the spook boy with the bright bayonet that worried him, however.

"Some terrorists are certainly coming to harm the Project. But how? By damaging the lockgates at Santarém while some foreign-flag vessel is passing through? By killing some American engineers? I doubt they will try to kidnap anyone. Santarém isn't the town to hide out in. Nor the jungle either—this isn't the Sierra Maestra in Cuba. Those city men can't hope to hide with the labourers or rubber tappers along the rivers. Too stupid and venal, those. Someone would betray. Nor do you melt away into the interior of the jungle without killing yourself—unless you happen to be an Indian, and I hear they're so primitive they eat soil for supper. Indians want nothing to do with our urban terrorists. Maybe they put a few poison arrows in the backs of our road-builders—but for their own private reasons, to be left alone to eat dirt, not be inoculated with the filth of Mao or Marx."

"I heard that gangs have been attacking towns up north. What d'you call 'em—flagelados?"

Charlie was aware that the Captain might find the remark annoying—he intended it to be. The man's smoothly bullying tone irritated him.

Paixao nodded curtly. He blew out a cloud of smoke.

"Beaten Ones, yes. They attack villages for food with some degree of gang structure. That's in the north-east."

"Maybe these Beaten Ones have been organizing politically? I recollect your government didn't realize for a whole damn year you had any urban guerrilla problem. You thought they were just gangsters. Ain't I right?"

"Because they behaved like gangsters. Still do. Except that no gangster would indulge in such senseless violence. However, Amazonia is not the north-east, Mr Faith. There are no gangs here the guerrillas can infiltrate. Consider the size of the area. The lack of roads. Impenetrability of the jungle. Terrorists can't operate in this region without giving themselves away. Paradoxical, in view of the size, but there it is. We must assume they're ready to sacrifice themselves. But doing what? Murdering someone like yourself? You're vulnerable so we're here to protect you, you see. Is your dam as vulnerable as you are, in your professional opinion?"

Charlie glanced uncomfortably at Jorge. 'His' dam. The Brazilian stared back at him expressionlessly, tapping his finger on his empty glass slowly.

"It ain't my dam, Captain. I'm just here till the floods have been and gone. It's Jorge's kingdom then."

"You call this a kingdom? You must be joking. I've seen the miserable hovels clustering like flies round your construction camp."

You interfering, contemptuous bastard. Relations were touchy enough with Jorge already.

"There ain't no lock gates to damage," he said hastily. "A hovercraft ramp is all we've got here. Just a strip of concrete. Nothing could hurt the dam itself short of a nuclear explosion—"

Charlie could see Jorge suffering agonies of pride.

"Even a large dynamite bang wouldn't do much damage. The soil would absorb the blast. This is a broad earth-fill type of dam, not one of your thin concrete jobs. The danger's not from sabotage but from nature. If the dam was ever overtopped by floodwater, spillage would cut right through it then. Or s'posing the water level suddenly sank on the lake side—that's the pressure face—the saturated earth below the seepage line might slide before it got a chance to drain. That won't happen, we've got good seepage control. The whole of the lake face is covered with strong plastic sheeting—"

"I saw it from the air. Pretty."

"Then the base of the dam is concreted using the local gravel, and there's a rock filter on the downstream side for seepage to drain away—"

"Couldn't an explosion tear holes in your plastic, Mr Faith?"

"Wouldn't matter if it did. I tell you, it'd take one helluva punch to burst this baby open."

"Then it must be you they are coming here to kill. But not to worry, Mr Faith. Have faith. We shall scour the waterways till we catch our prey. They'll have to come by water, you know."

31

"Mind you, it is a kinda critical time for the dam right now, floodwise—"

"Better the death of your dam than your own death, Mr Faith? I appreciate your feelings. Don't worry—we shall be your guardian angels. Yours too, Almeida, since we have to keep you alive as inheritor of the kingdom. How many courtiers will you have, I wonder?"

"There's a staff of ten," Charlie said quickly, "and their families. They're already living here—"

"Have you a family too, Almeida? No? Then I guess there'll be consolations for the flesh down in the village?"

Maybe it was Paixao's technique to anger people deliberately to test their political loyalties? That seemed like an overgenerous assessment to Charlie's mind. Jorge, without taking time out to ask himself why the Captain might be acting the way he did—cunning or nasty-mindedness—blurted:

"I don't have to take these insults. I trained two years in Lisbon as a civil engineer—"

"Why didn't you build this dam yourself then?" shrugged Paixao. "Presumably they trained you to—"

Jorge turned his back on Paixao, stared out of the window rigidly.

Some more of the dam was visible now. The plastic-covered face cut a shocking orange slash through the dull green landscape. Along it, pairs of jaribu storks stood side by side like stiff husbands and wives on a promenade.

"Why, with all due respect to Mr Faith, the yanqui overseer?"

"Let me explain, damn it," Charlie shouted, furious. "Jorge's perfectly well qualified and skilled. It's just that Portugal's mountainous terrain made them concentrate on high arch dams—not this sort of long low earth dam we happen to have more experience with in the States. And it was our Hudson Institute drew up the blueprint for this scheme way back in the late Sixties. That's why I'm here. Not because Jorge is no good. He's damned good. Knows a damned sight more than me about some things. Like dam models. Who d'you think made those there?"

Paixao dropped his cigar butt on the floor and crushed it out thoughtfully.

"Supposing that this dam did burst, what effect would there be downstream?"

"In that unlikely event—let me emphasize how unlikely it is—I guess the millions of tons of water in the lake would just have to flood downstream as far as the next dam in line."

"If that dam bursts?"

"Supposing the impossible, Captain! It's about as likely as a visit from outer space."

"No sweat then, Mr Faith. It must be you the terrorists are after."

"I'm sorry, Jorge, truly," said Charlie humbly, when the three men had gone.

"Charlie, sometimes I think the cure is worse than the disease. Terrorists there may be, but—" He shrugged emphatically.

"I know what you mean, pal."

That blazing hut in the Nam. Smoke hovering over it in the dusk. A man with a bayonet fighting a boy with a knife. So confident that there wasn't any need to pull the trigger even. And a doe-eyed girl staring on sick with fear....

"Do I know what you mean! Jorge, let's take ourselves out on the dam and clear our heads."

Tapping fingers had fallen silent at last.

"We'll go down to the café tonight, huh? Hell, but we two people have nothing to quarrel about!"

A bitter smile was all Charlie got from Jorge, though they walked out on to the dam together, while the last of the rain drifted down gentle as mist.

They heard the chatter of the Huey Slick echoing off the water. It seemed not to be flying away in a straight line, but circling.

Soon, Charlie realized there were two distinct sounds. The noise of the helicopter and the puttering of an outboard motor across the tree-infested lake.

The two sounds coincided for a while, then the helicopter passed out of earshot as the boat moved closer.

Presently it came in sight from behind the drowning trees—a twenty-foot shallow draught boat with an awning rigged up to shelter the two white cotton-robed figures in it. One of these raised an arm in salute.

"I guess they're coming from a safe direction, those ones. Ain't nothing but jungle and Indians for a couple hundred miles that way."

Jorge looked slyly at Charlie.

"You think so?" He gave a soft chuckle.

Charlie slapped him on the shoulder with a show of playfulness that seemed phoney to him as soon as he'd done it.

"Hey Jorge, quit trying to scare me will you? I can recognize them all right. It's those two priests."

The boat reached the point where the ramp entered the water. The two figures climbed out and beached it on the concrete, then started up the long slope.

"Heinz and Pomar, wasn't it? One was full of beans. The other guy had cheeks like ripe apples..."

"What a spectacle!" Father Heinz cried as he came in earshot. "An orange banner across the world like on the flag of Brazil itself. I tell you, it's like a great festival flag in these dingy forests. Something almost miraculous. A sash of honour. A perpetual sunrise flooding the landscape."

The priest puffed from the effort of scaling the slope, but his native garrulity overcame the need for oxygen.

34

"Believe me, Mr Faith, seeing this appearing through the rain like a great frontier between savagery and civilization, it was a welcoming home indeed!"

"Oh, you remembered my name?" grunted Charlie as the men shook hands.

The priests looked white and thin and tired from their stay in the jungle. The beans had fallen out of Heinz, the red was drained away from Pomar's cheeks. Charlie reckoned it must be two or three months since he saw them setting off.

They weren't quite home yet. 'Home' was ten kilometres further downstream—the complex of concrete-floored tin-roofed huts, the kitchens and dispensary, church and school, made ready to receive whatever exodus of Indians there might be from the drowning jungle.

To date, the resettlement camp only held about a third of the number that had been predicted from aerial surveys of the thousands of square kilometres being flooded. The planes had dropped bags of fish hooks and knives and pictures of the Safe Village and the Great Orange Dam, with photographs of the faces of contact men like Heinz and Pomar.

Charlie was about to say something else—ask how they'd got on—when he heard a jeep engine further out on the dam.

He squinted at the distant rainmist, saw the jeep speeding along the freeboard towards them, still a couple of kilometres away.

Charlie recognized it for one of their own jeeps. Still, the sight had him worried briefly—stuck out on the limb of the dam like this.

"It's just Chrysostomo," Jorge explained sweetly. "I sent him along this morning."

"Yeah, good. But you know I ain't so jumpy as all that about the impending arrival of my killers that I can't recognize one of our own vehicles! Hell, these terrorists seem pretty much like a myth now that our friend has flown off. He's his own worst terrorist."

Jorge grinned and walked off to meet the jeep.

"What's this then, Senhor Faith?" bubbled Heinz. "Did I hear you say terrorists?"

"It's nothing—just a scare. A Security Police Captain flew in a bit ago. Why don't you two people come indoors and have a drink? And I'll see about getting your boat over the ramp then."

"So that's who it was. A helicopter flew over us. We waved. I saw them take photographs."

He took them indoors, poured a generous shot of brandy for himself, then emptied the remains into the same tumblers as Orlando and Olimpio had used.

Priests reminded him of army chaplains. A sour memory. But he wanted a drink. And he tried to keep his own rule banning solitary drinking during daylight hours.

"Somebody wants to blow up the dam," he shrugged phlegmatically. "Or kill the yanqui who built it."

"How terrible," exclaimed Heinz. "Your work is a blessing. How can people not see this? After the gloom and ignorance of the jungle savages—"

Pomar, the younger priest, did quietly recall the occasion when the Archbishop of São Paulo had ordered notices pinned to the church doors throughout his archdiocese denouncing the torturing of priests and lay workers by the security police. Maybe guerrillas, although misguided men and atheists—

But Heinz recollected something that rankled more.

"We met a Frenchman living with one of the jungle tribes. He aroused my suspicions, Mr Faith. This man was in a kind of despair. He compared the behaviour of the natives in Africa, who fight the Portuguese government with Chinese weapons, with the impotence of the savages here to do anything, as though he regretted it.

I say maybe he was a terrorist."

Charlie shook his head; he remembered the foxy-featured Frenchman passing over the dam during the latter stages of construction.

"No, he was some kinda anthropologist. He came this way. A bit of a hostile tyke. But not a terrorist for my money. Some halfcaste brought a letter of his a few weeks back addressed to England to be put on the plane—"

Charlie glanced at the empty brandy bottle.

"Would you people like another drink? I'll get a new bottle." However he made no move to fetch one.

Heinz rose to his feet.

"We must get along to the reception centre before it's dark. You've been kind, Mr Faith. But please don't ask us how many Indians we expect." The priest shook his head in a fury of frustration. "That village where the Frenchman was, was the last straw! These Indians simply cannot comprehend. I think they will just sit still and drown! We tried getting through to them with the story of the Flood. Oh, they sat and heard! Then they merely laughed."

Pomar grasped the older man's arm sympathetically.

"They will digest it their own way. Surely then they will come out of savagery to safety in their own good time, when the flood has risen some more. And remember, Father, not all the tribes were so awkward as that one."

"Which is why I didn't trust the Frenchman! I think he had been tampering with them—polluting them. Why else did they tolerate him, and mock us?"

"Sounds like a rough trip," Charlie sympathized, though he wasn't really very interested.

"Oh, it's so often this way," grumbled Heinz, pursuing the memory of failure, like a dog hunting a lost bone. "You think you're making progress. Then you're swept back to square one. You build somebody up. Then he betrays your trust. You discipline with just reward—and create only a mockery of morals. These Xemahoa Indians weren't worse than usual. They didn't use any violence against us. They were just maddeningly different. There was no real communication. This Frenchman could have helped us. But he got excited and refused. After a while he even refused to let his interpreter translate for us. When we tried to reason with him to make him see the need to move these people to the reception centre, he just stared through us, switched on his tape recorder and played some rigmarole in French. Some poetry, he said. But it was nonsense. I couldn't make head or tail of it. Maybe it was his own obsessive stupidity that appealed to these savages!"

"At least we sowed the seed, Father. God will see to its germinating. Believe me, all the Indians will be trekking this way soon, needing our help."

"The dam will see to that," laughed Charlie. "Never mind about God. Give them another couple of weeks, they'll see there's no choice. Even your oddball Indians, when they get wet enough."

In the darkness, studded by sharp stars and sailed in by scudding whale-like clouds, Charlie and Jorge walked down to the cluster of shacks and hovels that straggled away from the tin-roofed homes of Jorge's staff. Each man carried a torch, flashing it ahead down the wet dirt track. Charlie also had a revolver with him.

Paraffin lamps gleamed from the café and some of the tin homes. A few open fires burned outside the shacks and hovels.

"They oughta be hooked up to our electric supply. I mean our staff oughta be," muttered Charlie, more sensitive to the darkness since the Captain's visit.

"There's a hierarchy of light, Charlie. We see by the electric, those under us by paraffin, those under them by wood and starlight."

They headed for the café, a rambling structure with screen windows, a dozen tables inside, a kitchen out back and a staircase leading up to a bedroom perched on top of the main structure like a shoebox on top of a suitcase.

A couple of Jorge's men sat silent over beers. The mulatta woman sat at another table looking dazed, with her Indian friend. Charlie wrinkled his nose as he smelt traces of Lanca Perfume on the hot wet air—the faint reek of scented ether. Jorge and he sat at a vacant table. The slim quiet Indian boy with the squint eye brought them cool beers from the paraffin icebox in back. They smoked.

After a while, Jorge nodded to the two women, who stood up unsteadily, and walked over to their table. Jorge's workmen looked on impassively. Out in the jungle, something started to scream. Some animal or bird.

The mulatta fumbled in her bag for the small gilt perfume spray with the compressed ether in it. She offered it doubtfully to Charlie. Charlie shook his head. Jorge also refused, swallowed his beer. The woman took a crumpled handkerchief out of her bag and sprayed some ether on it, pressed it tight to her nose and inhaled deeply.

"Silly bitch will pass out," snapped Jorge, leaning forward and jerking the handkerchief away from her glazed happy features. "She's high enough already."

Her Indian friend snatched the handkerchief out of Jorge's hand before the Lanca could evaporate and pressed it to her own nose.

"Charlie, the last time you went with the mulatta—"

"Okay, Jorge."

Jorge took hold of the mulatta's hand and raised her very delicately and gentleman-like, talking to her with surprising tenderness in Portuguese, at which she giggled dazedly. Then Jorge departed with her, leaving Charlie with the dazed Indian woman who only spoke a bastard form of Portuguese worse than his own.

He smoked, and watched her across the table, while beads of moisture cut trails down the side of the misted beer bottle.

Then she was a doe-eyed dark-skinned girl with long black pigtails and a snub nose who was staring up at him fearfully as he slid his bayonet past that boy waiter's flashing knife, into his guts, where he gave it a sharp twist to the right and the left....

THREE

TOM ZWINGLER WORE a ruby tie-clip and a pair of
shiny red crystal cufflinks. Everything else about him was
in blacks and whites, including the precision of his re-
marks. Yet this triangle of red points shifted as he cocked
his head and nodded and gestured, in a dandy geometry
of camouflage and control. The psychologist Richard Jannis watched the performance with ill-concealed suspicion.
It was really an exercise in the manipulation of people's
attention—a sort of phoney traffic lights pattern—that let
Tom Zwingler through people's guard while they were
watching the dance of rubies.

Jannis himself was in his shirt sleeves. The shirt was an
optical design in green and scarlet stripes that rapidly
became offensive to the eyes, as though he was trying to
hide himself behind this visual trick.

Relations were strained. Jannis resented the American's
scrutiny. Dorothy Summers was still sniping at Sole. Sam
Bax was trying to be father figure and adept technocrat
at the same time.

The high point of Zwingler's visit was supposed to be a
viewing of the children in their basement 'worlds'. Jannis
had already protested to Sam Bax on that score, and a
compromise was reached. The American wouldn't actually
enter any of the environments—he'd just look into them
through the one-way windows.

The other two staff members at this meeting were the
Bionics specialist, Ernest Friedmann, a fussy little man
whose gently bulging eyes and rapid, anxious way of talking spoke of an overactive thyroid gland; and Lionel

Rosson who ran the computer, baby-faced with long blond hair and blue eyes—his lank frame made even more loose and unofficial-seeming by the pair of old jeans and the baggy grey sweater he wore.

Some explanations were in order before the visit downstairs and Zwingler played his cards coolly during these, appearing mainly interested in the work of the Unit, while really, Sole sensed, more interested in themselves, the staff. Sole had an uneasy sense of something else hovering in the background while they discussed the security angle, and the new drug they'd developed at Haddon; but couldn't pin it down.

"Organization-wise," the American was saying to Sam Bax, "the experimental part of Haddon is sealed off tight, but the kids out in the front wards are like in any normal hospital—you find this works out okay?"

"It has to be run this way, Tom. You see, correcting the speech defects out front, and getting the kids downstairs to speak 'defective' languages are like the left and right legs of the same body. Therapy and experiment back each other up, via the computer. We owe a lot to Lionel for the programming—quite a triumph for our computer boy, this!'

Rosson tossed his mane gracefully in acknowledgment. He alone of the staff never seemed bothered or bitchy. His presence had an aura of innocent kindliness about it.

"So you're busy making language right in the public sector, and wrong in the private? What's bad for one set of kids helps you work out what'll be okay for the other set?"

"That's about it—though words like 'bad' create the wrong impression, Tom. I'd rather put it to you that the kids downstairs are learning *special* languages."

"How about the nurses—any ethical objections?"

"No problem, Tom. They're all seconded from the Army Medical Corps."

"Hmm. Visitors? What about parents?"

"No worries there, either. Regular visiting hours for the public wards. Of course, the 'special' kids don't receive any visitors."

"Orphans of the storm, eh?"

"Couldn't put it better myself. You'll see when we go down there..."

The American glanced round the room, assessing moods and personalities. Then he said casually:

"You talked about operating on the brain-damaged kids out front, before. Cutting out injured tissue. You do the same with the kids downstairs?"

"Christ no!" Sole exploded angrily. "That's a bloody immoral suggestion. Do you think we'd damage healthy tissue?—for an experiment? The children down below never had any sort of brain damage. They're fine. They're healthy!"

"You have to realize they're his pets, Mr Zwingler," Dorothy slipped in slyly. "You'd hardly believe our Chris had his own little boy at home—"

"Hmm, this PSF drug," nodded Zwingler. "It seems a dubious distinction to me—altering the brain by surgery, and altering it by a drug, if the drug's as long-acting as Sam supposes. What's the effect exactly?"

He glanced about for another victim, fixed on Friedmann. The Bionics man's eyes bulged at the tug of his red moons, a rabbit hypnotized by a stoat. He bubbled out an eager string of explanations.

"It's a way of hastening protein manufacture. A sort of anti-Puromycin—Puromycin blocks protein synthesis, you know, and PSF facilitates it. It works on the Messenger-RNA—"

"So PSF stands for Protein Synthesis, er—Facilitator?" Friedmann nodded violently.

"A unique lever for improving brain performance!"

"You might say it's a sort of ... superintelligencer?"

"Oh, hardly that, no I don't think so. No magic increase in intelligence as such—just the learning process being speeded up—"

"Ain't learning speed the surest indicator of intelligence, though?"

"You have to appreciate the structure of nerve impulses in the brain," Friedmann rattled on. "The way the short-term electrical signals get fixed as something long-term and chemical. That's what learning is—this electricity being transformed into something solid. We can't inject information as such into the brain, like slotting in some miracle memory tape. But what we can do is hurry up the manufacture of protein while the brain is busy learning. We use PSF to help dormant areas of the damaged brain to take over language work more rapidly—"

Zwingler waved a hand, quieting Friedmann.

"But what about the special kids? Chris—you said they don't have any brain damage. Yet they're receiving this drug. They must be learning a helluva lot faster than average kids. So what's the outcome?"

The rubies sparkled sharply at Sole, amused and testing him.

"Nothing harmful, I assure you," Sole blushed.

"Oh I'm sure. I'm just curious—"

Impatiently, Richard Jannis rapped his knuckles on the table.

"Sam—I don't wish to appear inhospitable but couldn't you brief Mr Zwingler yourself? Presumably he's more interested in the Unit's work than our personalities. Do we really need to leap through the hoops one by one?"

The Director glanced at Jannis irritably. However, it was Zwingler who answered the psychologist directly, with a boyish grin of apology.

"Guess I oughta apologize to you all—I'm afraid my role over here is a delicate one. Investigatory. Yes, it does have to do with personalities. Something pretty big has

44

come up back home. We're hunting about for people to help us out."

"What kind of big thing?"

The rubies blushed more apologies—but firm as steel, with a hard cutting edge to them.

"That's just it. I'd like to get a broader view of the folks here before I go into any details—"

Sam slapped a fist on the table.

"I'll back that up. I want you to regard Tom as a kind of emissary. Emissaries are going to be quite the fashion, eh Tom?"

Zwingler flashed an appreciative look at Sam, with just a hint of a caution in it.

Sam Bax stared round the faces of his staff—pausing momentarily on Rosson, then moving on, having rejected him as in some way unsuitable (too hippy looking?)— or as too vital to the Unit's functioning...

"Chris—" said the Director firmly, "do you mind filling in Tom on the three worlds before we head down there? The language angle—"

Sole made an effort to concentrate on practical details. Zwingler's ruby chips signalled attention; their wearer waited quietly behind them, a soft predator in a dark suit.

"Well, ever since Chomsky's pioneer work, we all assume that the plan for language is programmed into the mind at birth. The basic plan of language reflects our biological awareness of the world that has evolved us, you see. So we're teaching three artificial languages as probes at the frontiers of mind. We want to find out what the raw, fresh mind of a child will accept as natural— or 'real'. Dorothy teaches one language to test whether our idea of logic is 'realistic'—"

"Or whether reality is logical!" sniffed Dorothy—as though she wouldn't be at all surprised to find reality

45

guilty of such dereliction and was ready to discipline it if she did.

Zwingler looked bored. Only when Sole got on to the subject of the next world, did his attitude change.

"Richard's interested in alternative reality states—what sort of tensions a language programmed to reflect them might set up in the raw human mind. He's built a kind of alien world down there, with its own rules—"

"You mean the sorta environment an alien being might actually grow up in, on some other planet?" The American leaned forward eagerly.

"Not exactly—" Sole glanced at Jannis; but the psychologist showed no particular desire to add anything. "It's more like another—dimension. Built out of a number of perceptual illusions. Richard's something of a connoisseur of illusions—"

"Yeah, so I notice. Okay, I get the picture. Not a realistic alien planet. More like a kinda philosophical idea of alienness? How about the third world—I guess that's yours?"

'Yes ... Ever heard of a poem by a French writer, Raymond Roussel—*New Impressions of Africa*?"

The American shook his head.

"Queer poem. Fact is, it's practically unreadable. I mean, literally. It's not that it's bad—it's bloody ingenious. But it's the most crazy example of what we call 'self-embedding' in linguistics—and that's what my children learn—"

"Self-embedding—how would you describe that?"

Having only just finished reading Zwingler's paper on the language difficulties of astronauts a few hours before, Sole found it hard to credit the American with quite such innocence of the jargon of linguistics as he made out. Nevertheless, he explained.

"Self-embedding is a special use of what we call 'recursive rules'—these are rules for doing the same thing more than once when you form a sentence, so that you can make your sentence any shape and size you like. Animals have to rely on a fixed set of signals for communication purposes—or else on varying the strength of the same signal. But we humans aren't limited like that. Every sentence we construct is a fresh creation. That's because of this recursive feature. 'The dog *and* the cat *and* the bear ate.' 'They ate the bread *and* cheese *and* fruit, lustily *and* greedily.' You've never heard these particular sentences before—they're new but you have no trouble understanding them. That's because we've got this flexible, creative programme for language in our minds. But self-embedding pushes the human mind pretty near its limits—which is why we can use it as a probe at the frontier—"

"Better give us an example of this self-embedding, Chris," interrupted Sam. "This is all getting a bit theoretical for my head."

Sole glanced at Sam curiously. Surely Sam knew perfectly well what he was talking about, too. Jannis sat back smugly, his expression implying that he was well out of this—how had he put it?—jumping through the hoops.

Still, if that was how Sam wanted it...

"Let's take a nursery rhyme then—this one's a beautiful recursive series, dead easy to follow..."

As he started reciting it, however, a memory from boyhood triggered itself in his head—and he was seven years old again, standing up in Sunday School to pipe out the same nursery rhyme as part of a Harvest Festival. He'd fluffed his lines, half-way through. Had to be prompted. The experience stuck in his nervous system, a tiny thorn of shame. Now the thorn re-emerged, producing a sudden, silly anxiety to get through the recitation safely—which made him come unstuck again, and sit there open-mouthed, waiting to be prompted...

"This is the farmer sowing his corn,
That kept the cock that crowed in the morn,
That wakened the priest all shaven and shorn,
That—"

That what? WHAT WHAT WHAT? a childish voice yammered inside his head—while another area of him watched this idiotic repetition of events and wondered to what extent all his fascination with language, particularly 'bad' language, sprang from this original public shaming...

A soft American voice came to his rescue...

"That married the man all tattered and torn—

"Come along, Chris," grinned Zwingler.

Gratefully the boy in Sole caught up the broken rhyme again.

"That kissed the maiden all forlorn—"

But the man in him halted suspiciously. Richard, Sam, Dorothy, pop-eyed Friedmann all seemed part of a grinning audience of parents watching him...

However the American hurried him on, exuberantly chanting the next couple of phrases:

"That milked the cow with the crumpled horn,
That tossed the dog—"

"That chased the cat," said Sole tentatively.

"That worried the rat!" responded Zwingler, quick as a flash.

"That ate the malt," smiled Sole.

"That lay in the house that Jack built!"

Zwingler ended in triumph. His rubies flashed a victory dance. He'd captured the rhyme. A game had been set up—and he'd won it.

Damn, thought Sole, I ought to have counted ahead. Glancing at Jannis, he caught a hint of angry disgust. A trap had been set by a smart operator, and he'd fallen into it. It was that bloody memory getting in the way. A language trap too—he should have known better.

"Any four-year-old can follow that nursery rhyme," Sole fired back, his face flushed. "It's another story when you embed the same phrases. 'This is the malt that the rat that the cat that the dog worried killed ate.' How about that? Grammatically correct—but you can hardly understand it. Take the embedding a bit further and you end up with the situation in Roussel's poem. The Surrealists tried building machines for reading Roussel. But the most sensitive, flexible device we know of for processing language—our own brain—is stymied."

"Why's that, Chris?"

Zwingler's face seemed to leer at him—but the American sounded genuinely interested. Uncomfortably Sole hurried through a brief explanation; noticing as he did so that Sam looked pleased.

"Well, speech processing depends on the volume of information the brain can store short-term—"

"This amount being limited by the time it takes short-term memory to become permanent and chemical, instead of electrical?"

"Right. But a permanent form isn't practical for every single word—we only need remember the basic meaning. So you've got one level of information—that's the actual words we use, on the surface of the mind. The other permanent level, deep down, contains highly abstract concepts—idea associations linked together network-style. In between these two levels comes the mind's plan for making sentences out of ideas. This plan contains the rules of what we call Universal Grammar—we say it's universal, as this plan is part of the basic structure of mind and the same rules can translate ideas into any human language whatever—"

"All languages being cousins beneath the skin, in other words?"

"Right again. They resemble each other like faces in a family. But each cousin's face has its own individual outlook on reality. If we could simply stack all these 'faces' one on top of another to work out the rules of universal grammar that way—well, we'd have a map of the whole possible territory of human thought—everything we can ever hope to express, as a species."

"But you couldn't just stack all these languages, could you? Some have died out and disappeared—"

"And a whole lot more might exist, but they haven't been invented."

"Which is why you're using artificial languages as frontier probes?"

"Exactly."

"But Chris. You're using this PSF chemical, to teach them. What makes you think it's a natural situation? Surely our brains would have learnt at this higher rate if they were intended to, biologically—"

"Aha—and God would have given us wings if he'd meant us to fly! Not that old argument, please. PSF is just an aid, as its name implies."

"Hmm. How long did you carry out animal tests first?"

"It isn't the same thing!" Sole said exasperatedly. "You can't teach language to a monkey or a guinea pig."

"Okay, you're the expert," shrugged Zwingler. "They're picking up this embedded speech at any rate—?"

Sole darted a brief smile at Rosson.

"I'd say it's promising, eh, Lionel?"

"More than that," nodded Rosson, with a grin of satisfaction. He too loved the children down below.

Zwingler glanced at his watch.

"May I see downstairs now, Sam? I think I get the picture."

There was a sudden minor explosion like a whip crack as Jannis slapped the side of his head with his fingers.

"Listen Sam, if he's in a hurry, he can see the kids just

as easy over the closed circuit from next door—"

"Don't be tiresome, Richard," sighed the Director. "We already agreed Tom's not going *into* any of the worlds."

"I should bloody well hope not!" snapped Jannis, his voice toughening.

The Director touched Zwingler on the arm, in embarrassment.

"If you went inside—well, it's like contaminating a cell culture with a foreign body: a word out of place could be pretty awkward, Tom."

"That sounds like the understatement of the afternoon," glowered Jannis.

But the American waved a ruby at him, blandly.

"By no means, Mr Jannis. The understatement of the afternoon, if not of the whole damn decade, was Sam's crack earlier on. About emissaries—"

The cufflink halted. Beat a hasty retreat. He's said too much, thought Sole. But too much—about what? Jannis wore a slight smile of contempt on his lips, as they rose from the table.

Vasilki had just gone into the maze—they saw her clearly through the tough thin plastic walls. Rama and Gulshen were chattering to each other outside the entry. Vidya lounged about, looking sullen.

"Why, they're Indo-Paks! War refugees? Or disaster victims? Hell, but I guess it saved their lives!"

"Precisely my sentiments, Mr Zwingler," Dorothy chirped—a Victorian well-wisher visiting the workhouse. "What else was their future but deprivation and death? As I'm always saying to Chris."

As Vasilki moved deeper through the plastic pathways, the walls increasingly discoloured her limbs. Jaundiced her body, till an alternative vision of the girl imposed itself on Sole's mind. She dragged herself through the

51

maze on skeleton legs, with the pot belly and the dead empty eyes of so many million other children cast on the refuse heap of the twentieth century. And he thought: isn't the saving of four such children a valid enough reason for this under-world's existence, whatever the outcome? How would Pierre face up to that one? The taking away of four children speaking that language, Xemahoa, to a safe place like this? Supposing the chance was offered him. He'd come round. Wouldn't he?

"Can I listen in on what they're saying, Chris?"

"What? Oh—yes, just a minute."

Sole fiddled with the audio controls on the wall panel, passed Zwingler a pair of headphones.

The American held them to one ear, pursing his lips. Meanwhile Richard Jannis stalked off along the corridor towards his own territory...

"Yeah. It is different. Boy, you have messed up the syntax!"

Vasilki had reached the maze centre. Now she was standing by the Oracle, talking to the tall cylinder.

"Kid's saying something about ... rain?"

"It does rain in there, actually. Sprinkler system washes the place out and gives them a shower. You should see them enjoy it. They have a ball."

"Nice. Say, when you go in there, how does that speech-mask gizmo you were talking about operate?"

"We go through the motions of speaking. But we only subvocalize the words. The mask picks the words up, runs them through the computer programme, then re-synthesizes the sentences out loud in an embedded form. The masks are hooked into the computer by radio."

"Neat—so long as the kids don't go in for lip reading."

"We thought of that too. That's why we call it a mask. Only place they see our lips moving is on the teaching screen—and that's mime."

Zwingler shifted the phones to his other ear.

"Wonder just how deep this embedding will reach? Will the kids try shifting your own 'corrections' back again to the norm?"

"Then," said Sole with conviction, "we really shall have found out something about the mind's idea of all possible languages."

"You mean all possible *human* languages, don't you Chris?"

Sole laughed. It seemed such a pointless objection.

"Put it another way then. All languages spoken by beings evolved on the same basis as ourselves. I can't vouch for languages that silicon salamanders elsewhere in the universe might have dreamt up!"

"Could be such beings would use a kind of printed circuit, binary set-up, more like a computer?" mused Zwingler, apparently taking the joke seriously.

Vidya trod a few paces away from the maze, to a large orange plastic doll, picked it up and set it on its feet. The doll stood as high as his shoulders.

He fiddled with its side and the doll unhinged. He lifted out a smaller doll, a red one, stood it next to the first doll, then closed the first doll's body again. This second doll came as high as the first doll's shoulders...

"Teaching aids," Sole commented as he took the phones back from Zwingler and hung them up again. "The dolls' bodies carry memory circuits imprinted with a couple of dozen fairy tales. Opening the large doll triggers one of these stories at random. But the cute wrinkle is this: they have to disassemble and reassemble the whole set in the right sequence to get the full story—and the story itself is linguistically embedded, same way as the dolls are embedded physically. There's seven in all. See, he's unpacking number three—"

However, Zwingler was still busy wondering aloud about computer-style languages.

"It's just not on, linguistically," said Rosson. "You see,

the brain has its data associated together in multi-layered networks. Language reflects this. Whereas a computer has a separate 'address tag' for each bit of data. In point of fact, Chris's embeddings may be rejected simply because the mind *isn't* a computer. It won't know where to associate the incoming data because the clues are delayed too long—and it can't afford to store so much, even if we do use PSF..."

As he spoke, Dorothy began urging the American away from Sole's world towards her own little empire by brisk rushes away from and back to his side, a hen marshalling a chick—plucking at his sleeve, finally, to shift him.

"Idea associations. Yes, that's the trouble," she clucked. "Illogical for words to have multi-value meanings. Of course, we could try teaching a form of Gruebleen, to test for logic values—"

"That sounds like some kinda rotten cheese," chuckled Zwingler.

"Oh does it! Gruebleen is a form of English. With special words like 'grue' and 'bleen'. For instance, 'grue' means something you've already examined which is green, or which you haven't examined and which is blue. But this kind of concept is much too complex for the young child, alas—"

"So it is a moon made of green cheese after all?"

"How do you mean?"

"This Gruebleen is a fantasy, like a moon made of cheese."

"We weren't foolish enough to try teaching Gruebleen, Mr Zwingler. I'm trying to indicate the lines of research we ruled out in advance—"

Dorothy shepherded Zwingler along the corridor in a series of precise, logical swoops; while Sole hung back a while, to watch Vidya. Something about the way the boy was behaving troubled him. Something jerky. Robotic.

Vidya finished setting out the seven dolls in a row.

Then his face froze into a mask, and he stared rigidly at the smallest of them.

A minute passed. Abruptly a spasm twitched across the boy's face. Like a skater coming to grief on thin ice, the tight surface of sanity cracked and he fell through into chaos. His lips parted in a scream. His face distorted. Mercifully, the sound-proofing kept the sound from the corridor. Eyes wide, Vidya stared in Sole's direction—though he couldn't see anything but his own reflection in the one-way glass. With a blow of his fist he cannoned the dolls into each other, bowling them over as if they were skittles.

Snatching up the smallest doll, he began wringing its neck. This was the only doll that didn't contain another doll inside it—yet he tore it this way and that, till tears of effort sprang to his eyes, *as though it ought to contain something more.*

Sole stared, horrified.

The fit lasted a couple of minutes at most, before Vidya ran out of energy. Slowed down like a clockwork toy. And stopped. Limply he began picking the dolls up and putting them inside each other again.

Explanations churning in his head, Sole caught up with the rest of the group.

What sort of grim Dotheboys Hall would Dorothy's logic world have turned into, but for the warmth and kindliness of Lionel Rosson? Sole hated to think. Fortunately, Sam had delegated the room to the both of them, acknowledging in so doing that while he needed Dorothy's logical intellect, he could do without her brand of logical emotions.

Still, Dorothy had put her foot down when it came to choosing names for the children. The two boys were called Aye and Bee; the two girls Owe and Zed—symbols in a logical equation.

Although there was nothing glum about the children. "They're dancers," Zwingler said, impressed.

"Did you know," remarked Rosson amiably, "that honeybees evolved their communication system away from the direction of sound to that of dance? Only primitive bees still use noises. Evolved bees developed the aerial dance to express themselves more logically. Let's hope these children dance! Would you like to see them standing still uttering formal propositions like a group of chessmen? Oh no, Tom. We teach by dance as well as words—"

On the wall screen large abstract patterns pulsed—computer feedback from the dance; and words were spoken to the kids, whose syntax reflected these patterns.

"The trouble with logical languages, Mr Zwingler," said Dorothy, "is there's no redundancy in them—"

"You mean you can't employ 'em?" grinned Zwingler.

An awkward silence fell. Schoolma'am Dorothy was peeved.

"Curiously, that is what she means," murmured Rosson, coming to the rescue. "Redundancy may be a dirty word in industrial relations—too many people to do the job. That's why the brain works so well though—plenty of back-up systems."

"Sorry, Miss Summers, just teasing. You mean normal language has to carry more than is necessary—in case we miss part of the message. So you've got some kinda noise-reducing strategy in operation here?"

Dorothy still sulked, so Rosson had to explain:

"We've built the redundancies into the design of the room itself, and into the kids' activities, particularly the dance. This way we can do without redundancies in the design of the language—"

Sole touched Rosson on the arm, strangely moved, as soon as Zwingler was heading down the corridor again.

"Beautiful scene, Lionel. You've got something good going on in there. But listen, a nasty thing happened to my Vidya. Could we talk? Not now, though. Not with this fellow here—"

"Sure, Chris."

As Zwingler approached the final room, Richard Jannis called out a warning to him, dryly.

"Don't get giddy, friend—"

But the American disregarded this piece of advice, as merely another example of Jannis's unhelpfulness.

Consequently he found himself staring into the third room, unprepared. Lost his balance. Fell forward.

Instinctively his hand darted out to save himself and slapped against the glass. The psychologist snatched him back by the shoulders, roughly, like a child.

"Don't hit the aquarium, fellow. You'll scare the fish—"

"Sorry," grunted Zwingler, as shocked by this sudden assault on his person, as by the way the room interfered with his sense of balance.

The room had its usual effect of vertigo on Sole too; however, he was prepared for it. Rooting himself to the plane of the corridor, he let his mind drop away in free fall through the twisted depths beyond the window.

It always reminded him of the illusion worlds of Maurits Escher—where towers rear up, only to turn in upon themselves like Moebius strips, and stairways lead up to platforms, located by some sleight of hand at the foot of those selfsame stairways; where figures prowl hallways which surely must rotate through a higher dimension, to enable the inhabitants thus to meet their own images heading across the ceilings towards them.

The nearest child, a girl, sat hugely picking her nose, staring at remote distances. She looked like a great smooth sexless giantess—the boy who *seemed* to be standing right next to her, was only the size of one of her legs. As they watched, a second boy walked down a stairway. Half-way down he disappeared from view, apparently into thin air...

57

"All done with mirrors, like they say?" laughed Zwingler nervously.

"Not only mirrors," retorted Jannis, keeping hold of the American while he spoke snappily about Necker Cube illusions, holographic projections, use of polarized light and variably sensitive interfaces ...

"You gotta train before you go in, like an astronaut for free fall?"

"It could be a useful stamping ground for future astronauts," Jannis granted. "The sort of concept world inhabited by the kids is perhaps more intriguing, though—"

Sole chewed on his lower lip. He could visualize Rama and Vidya emerging from their world one day all right. He could see Aye and Bee dancing out of theirs. But Richard's kids? How could they ever emerge safely into the real world? These were true prisoners of illusion.

Tom Zwingler swung away from the window as soon as Jannis released him, recovering his crisp confidence swiftly.

"I thank you for giving up your afternoon, Miss Summers, gentlemen. I realize the nuisance. Could I take up just a little more of Chris's time, upstairs, Sam?"

As they walked back towards the lift, Sole stared into the first room, annoyed and nervous, but Vidya seemed to be behaving himself.

FOUR

THOSE HOLY FATHERS did their damnedest to drag me back to their view of reality. I almost went out of my head. There are things of so much greater importance going on here in this shabby jungle village amongst these so-called 'ignorant' savages than in their bloody Bethlehem or at that miraculous dam of theirs.

Ironically, they might just have made some headway with the Xemahoa by concentrating on Bethlehem and the miracle birth. But no, they would go at it opportunistically. All that nonsense about Noah's Ark! A flood is rising, O my people. Once there was a man beloved of God who built himself a great big dugout canoe. And in this canoe he floated downstream with all his family and goats and chickens and macaws till he reached a large well-appointed reception centre on a hillside—easily recognizable by its bright tin roofs—some way beyond the Great Orange Wall.

Meddling imbeciles! I'm only just getting to the root of what is going on here, and I tell you it is delicate.

A cautious, inbred people, these Xemahoa. Had it not been for Kayapi mediating between us, I don't know how I would have got anywhere. I might have taken it for 'just' another human tragedy. 'Just' another example of human flotsam being washed away by the tide of Progress. Like any of the other flooded-out tribes.

Oh, but they have their plans about the Flood, these Xemahoa!

Those priests never dreamt that they're expecting a birth as part of their answer. Even now a woman is coming to term in the taboo hut outside the village. The Bruxo visits her every day, to chant to her and give her the drug they call 'maka-i'. I suspect it is his own child gestating in her womb—conceived in the drug trance he undertook as soon as he first divined the coming of the flood. And divine it he did, from God knows what signs. Months ago! If the Holy Fathers could have known of that pregnancy, what a field day they would have had—they would have pulled Bethlehem and Mary out of their bag of tricks then, I'll warrant.

When the Xemahoa laughed at the priests, those good men were offended by their reception. Hostility, martyrdom, poisoned arrows—that is acceptable, excellent. Straight off to the Pearly Gates. But laughter? They ought to have realized that there is laughter—and laughter. They should have had more experience of the moods of these people than myself. I only understood when Kayapi explained the distinction his people make between types of laughter.

A useful man, Kayapi—but one thing he certainly isn't is 'my faithful Kayapi' or 'my man Friday' as that priest Pomar seemed to think. The secret of his devotion is presumably the tape recorder. I guess he follows me round and answers my questions mainly because of the machine. In its own crude way it apes the drugged speech of the Bruxo that Chris Sole would have called 'embedded speech'. By leaping back and forth along the tapespool it transmutes what I call Xemahoa A into Xemahoa B— or something like it. If I didn't have longlife batteries in the machine and it was running down and wheezing to a halt, my faithful Kayapi might be off soon enough.

Yet maybe not. I guess it's also his own curious relationship to the Xemahoa tribe that keeps him here with me. The fact that he's of the tribe and also of another. He's a bastard birth. They tolerate him here, but do not allow him into any close intimacy with them. They let him circle eternally round his 'home' like a moth round a candle, which he can't burn his wings on nor escape from. And how he wishes to burn his wings!

The Bruxo has been the brightest candle drawing him here—since he was a boy old enough to travel on his own from his mother's village. I think he yearns, in his heart of hearts, to be the Bruxo's apprentice. Yet it is clearly impossible. This is one social role he can never hope to ape amongst the Xemahoa, as a half-Xemahoa himself. Anyway, the Bruxo already has an apprentice—a weedy adolescent—and Kayapi must be in his twenties now and too old to start.

Still, it's hard to tell people's ages here. They get old swiftly in the jungle. Forty-five years is quite an achievement. The Bruxo must be much older than that. His skin as wizened as a mummy's. He's tough, this old Bruxo. All the dancing and chanting he does. And, my God, the drugs. But he's an old man nevertheless—and burning himself at both ends in these desperate days. I'd give him another few months at the present rate, that's all.

Kayapi, on the other hand, has smoother sleeker skin than the apprentice boy's—milk chocolate skin like a young woman's. Good flashing teeth, too—though that isn't so odd in tribes that haven't been 'civilized' yet. Soft almond eyes with a shade of the sadness of the exile in them. The bulging well-fleshed bum of the Indian male, which looks more like our idea of a woman's. He's in his prime—but soon he will be past it. Not that this stops him from longing—or from plotting.

So much for Pomar's 'Man Friday' notion, however. A blend of obsession and self-interest is more like it.

"You know why the Xemahoa laugh at the Caraiba?"

"Tell me, Kayapi."

"There are two Laughters, Pee-áir."

"And what are they?"

61

"There is the Soul Laugh. And there is Profane Gaiety. Profane Gaiety is stupid. Profane Gaiety is children's. And old men's whose minds are rotted. And women's. Xemahoa despise that laughter."

"So that was why they laughed at the priests? Because they despised them?"

"No!"

"What then, Kayapi? Tell me—I'm a Caraiba too. I do not know."

"But there is much you do know, Pee-áir. Your box that talks words within words, tells you."

"Tell me so I may know some more, Kayapi."

"All right. That was Soul Laughter, not Profane Gaiety, we Xemahoa pointed at the Caraiba. There is much to understand about laughter, Pee-áir. When a man opens his mouth, he must take care not only what goes out, but what comes in. Something bad might creep in past Profane Gaiety. Profane Gaiety is weak. Nothing dares creep in past Soul Laughter. Soul Laughter is strong-as-strong. That's why Man does not laugh idly."

"What exactly is this Soul Laughter?"

However Kayapi lost interest. It all seemed obvious to him, I guess. So off he wandered to paddle through the floodwater. I would say splash 'like a child'. The priests certainly would. If I hadn't learnt a little of the subtlety these Indians are capable of.

A note on social relations among the Xemahoa. As far as kinship rules are concerned, there is a total lack of incest prohibition. Quite the opposite in fact. They are incestuous—in the widest cultural sense. The Xemahoa always marry within the tribe, and the husband moves into the wife's hut upon getting married. If he marries two wives, the second wife generally moves in with the first. They are really one great extended family, with most marriages being incestuous to some degree or another. Presumably they have some social machinery—raiding and capture?—for bringing outside blood into the tribe from time to time.

Unfortunately for Kayapi, he is the product of an exogamous union—a mating outside the incestuous kinship group of the Xemahoa—and, just as in some other cultures a child of incest would be a child of shame, so here the child of exogamy comes in for stigma. And this is what really buggers up his ambitions.

I wonder which of the Xemahoa was Kayapi's father, though. Must ask him.

And I wonder what relation, if any, there is between this inbred social structure—and the 'embedded' speech of Xemahoa B, the language of the drug ritual?

...Day by day I learn more about this remarkable doomed people. When I wrote that letter to England in rage and anguish, I knew so little of the true situation here!

Each day there are more clues as to the nature of this unique language, Xemahoa B. Only a drug-tranced Bruxo can fully articulate it. Only a drug-tranced people dancing through the firelight can grasp the gist of it.

Their myths are coded in this language and left in safe keeping with the Bruxo. The Deep Speech and the Drug-Dance free these myths as living realities for all the people in a great euphoric act of tribal celebration—to such a degree that they are all firmly convinced that the flood is only a detail in the fulfilment of their own myth cycle, and that the Bruxo, and the child embedded in the woman's womb in the taboo hut, will in some as yet inexplicable way be the Answer.

Kayapi is pretty well convinced that the Bruxo has the answer too.

"Why are you staying here despite the water?"

He shrugs. He spits moisture at the flooded soil with a show of bravado—or indifference.

"See, I wet it some more. I give water to the already-wet. Shall I piss on it? That is how much I care for this water."

"How can you be so sure?"

"I've heard Bruxo's words, haven't you heard them? You keep them in that box. Don't you think them in your head?"

"I haven't joined the Drug-Dance. Maybe that's why I don't think them yet. Could I join it? Could I take the drug?"

"I don't know. You have to talk Xemahoa, and be Xemahoa. Otherwise it is a flight of birds bursting out of your brain, flying to all four directions, getting lost, never finding their way back."

We are still talking Portuguese, Kayapi and me. (Alone amongst the Xemahoa—because of his bastard birth—Kayapi has been outside, has travelled and speaks a foreign language.) Nevertheless, more and more Xemahoa words and phrases are creeping into our conversation.

...So 'maka-i'—as the Bruxo's drug is called—is a kind of fungus that grows down on the jungle floor amongst the roots of a certain tree. Kayapi will not say which (or doesn't know). The Bruxo and his assistant collect it ritually once a year, dry it, pound it to dust.

The Xemahoa take it like another vegetable drug I heard about among the Indians north of Manáus, called 'abana'. 'Abana' makes the body feel like a machine, a suit of armour, but with precise long-range vision and a vivid recollection of past events that present themselves to the imagination in cartoon film clips. Like 'abana'—or like cocaine for that matter—maka-i is snorted through the nostrils. The Bruxo taps out a tiny measure of the fungus dust into a length of hollow cane, then puffs it up the nose of the recipient.

Women apparently don't take it. (But I thought the

woman in the taboo hut was taking it—I must have been wrong.)

"Why don't women take maka-i, Kayapi?"

"Because women laugh the wrong way, Pee-áir."

"What do you mean?"

"I told you there are two sorts of laughter."

He looked at me as if I was stupid, to forget. I guess social anthropologists are professional idiots, asking the questions any child should know the answer to. The trouble is, these are frequently the vital questions.

"Women do not laugh the Soul Laugh, you mean?"

"Consider, Pee-áir, what is a woman, and what is a man. When the man opens his mouth to laugh, if he fails to laugh a strong soul laugh, it may be bad for him. Something evil may rush in past his tongue while his tongue is busy laughing, not speaking words. But what does a woman open, I ask you? Besides her mouth? Her legs. That's where she keeps her soul word, so that no badness will rush in there. She does not keep it in her mouth. So she can afford to giggle."

Could it be that this maka-i fungus would cause deformed births? Or acted as some kind of contraceptive? Or maybe caused abortions? With their depleted numbers, small need they have of contraceptives or abortions!

"Do you mean that maka-i makes bad babies?"

He shook his head.

"*That* baby—the maka-i child—is not needed."

"Not needed? You mean maka-i stops babies from coming?"

"I tell you—*that* baby is not needed. What *that* is needed, it will come. Then the woman will give birth, laughing."

But I didn't understand. Kayapi wandered off, shaking his head at my stupidity, leaving me as bewildered as before. He paddled his feet. I played back some Xemahoa speech, the A and the B varieties—the daily vernacular and the knotty embeddings of the drug speech in which the myths are told—myths which they trust, as Man has always hoped throughout history, will somehow reconcile the irreconcilable realities around them.

"Where's this tree the fungus grows on, Kayapi?"

He seems to be drawing closer and closer to the Xemahoa, more remote from his mother's people and all outside concerns. He's stopping using Portuguese—speaking more and more Xemahoa to me, forcing me to pick it up.

The growing possibility of communion with the tribe—of acceptance, at last—as the water rises, is drawing him deeper into Xemahoa thoughts and ways. Increasingly he finds it unnecessary and undesirable to stay outside the circle like a jackal snatching scraps.

Fortunately I'm picking up almost enough of the ordinary brand of Xemahoa for us to conduct simple conversations in the tongue.

At times I'm afraid—scared to my marrow.

The Makonde tribespeople in Mozambique thought right along my own wavelength compared with these Xemahoa. It's a different universe of concepts here. A different dimension. A political crime is being committed against them by American capitalism and Brazilian chauvinism and the likelihood of their ever rising up with AK-47s and grenade launchers like the men of Mozambique—of their ever conceiving the political dimension—is zero, nil, less than nil. Yet my feelings of rage and impotence are almost swallowed up in the sense of intoxication about me: the sense of excited anticipation among the Xemahoa. Surely, says my rational mind, this must be an illusion. Surely!

"What is the tree, Kayapi?" I asked in halting Xemahoa.

He shrugged, turned his face away.

"Will the water kill the maka-i plant?"

"It lives in a small place. This much space."

The space between his outstretched hands.

"Here—and here—this many places."

He held up his hand in the sign for 'many' among his mother's people—five fingers spread out.

Five seems like many to some people in some cultures. Not to the Xemahoa however—which was what was frustrating about Kayapi making this sign.

Xemahoa, uniquely among Indian tribal languages, has a rich vocabulary for numbers. They are the names of things that contain these numbers in some way or other: for instance a certain macaw's wing contains so many feathers in it. A different bird has a different number of feathers. Or perhaps I should say, so many feathers that the Xemahoa themselves consider significant.

They hunt these birds for food, and feathers for decoration for the Drug Dance, so that this feather-number system strikes a special chord in their lives. Not in mine, alas. Kayapi looked at his hand making the sign for 'many' in disgust, struck it angrily against his side, pronounced the number-word in Xemahoa.

But it was a bird I didn't know. And anyway I would have had no idea how many wing or tail feathers it had, never mind which of them were significant. I tried asking him in Portuguese, got no response.

"It will die though?"

"Floods come, floods go, it sleeps."

"This flood won't go away. This flood is forever."

"Maybe."

"How about if the Bruxo took a knife and dug up maka-i and took it somewhere else and put it in the ground again?"

"Dig up a tree? Dig up the jungle? I tell you, you must treat maka-i with courtesy, politeness. You can't bully him, push him round. He goes away then. He only lives where he chooses—so many places."

He flashed his hand again. Then said the bird-number. Maybe this bird only had five feathers that counted as significant. Maybe the fungus could only colonize five peculiarly specialized places in this tangled jungle? But how was I to know!

"Show me." And I said the bird's name. "Show me that number here in the village. Show me the huts that make up so many."

I hoped that the circle of the village wasn't divided up into totem segments, and that this bird didn't also stand for one of these totem units. If that was the case, Kayapi might point out this bit of the village represented by the bird instead of the number of feather 'counters' the bird itself possessed. He gestured vaguely at the village, shook his head.

"Where the Xemahoa live, maka-i lives nearby," Kayapi said after thinking a while. "We eat the same soil that he eats. And he eats our soil too."

'And he eats our soil too.' Kayapi must be talking about two different sorts of soil—earth, and excrement.

The Xemahoa are among the tribes that eat soil. A special kind of soil, that is. A speckled clay containing some necessary dietary minerals, I suppose. I had tasted some of the clay when Kayapi showed me it. He ate a handful himself. It tasted like cold condensed Campbells corn soup—if you didn't think of it as 'dirt'. But did he mean right now that the Xemahoa not only ate the clay where the fungus grew, but also manured the fungus with their own nightsoil?—with their own shit? That seemed to be what he was saying: they were living in a symbiotic relationship with this fungus, just as it was living in a state of ecological symbiosis with its own neighbourhood —with the clay, with the tree roots.

"Kayapi, you feed maka-i your own body soil?"

He nodded, smiling. I'd been intelligent this time, not stupid.

"Bruxo or his boy feeds it. They know the rules of courtesy for offering the food. But it's the body soil of all the Xemahoa."

"Including yours too?"

It was a stupid remark. I'd touched a sore nerve there. It made him break off the discussion.

And so to another firelit dance.

The men danced but didn't actually snort any maka-i this time. Only the Bruxo was high on the fungus powder, chanting the legends. As he chanted I followed him round, recording the singsong jumble of words. Later on, I'd try and organize them into a 'sensible' form.

Kayapi was dancing round, but he paid no attention to me.

Firelight flickered on the water—they'd built platforms for the bonfires. Gleams of red and yellow snaked across the ripples their stamping feet set in motion.

After the first hour the Bruxo led them away from the village proper, out to the totem hut where the woman was hidden away making her baby.

Kayapi forgave me today. Maybe he felt closer to the tribe and less insecure after last night's dance.

"I tell you a story, Pee-áir."

"Is it the same story the Bruxo was telling last night?"

"How do I know what Bruxo said? Maka-i was in him, not in us."

"Why was that? Isn't there much of the maka-i left?"

"She needs a lot. Maybe Bruxo keeps it for her."

"She? But you said women don't take maka-i!"

Kayapi nodded.

"But she's pregnant, Kayapi!"

"You speak like a baby who has found the sun is in the sky!"

"Sorry, Kayapi. I'm a stupid Caraiba. Not a Xemahoa like you. I have to learn."

"Then I tell you a story, Pee-áir. You listen and learn."

So I listened, and recorded Kayapi's story.

"I tell you about Soul Laughter and Stupid Gaiety. Okay? Now, many creatures want to make men laugh with Stupid Gaiety so that they can get inside us, past our tongue, when it is not the master of words. The monkeys play tricks up in the trees to get us to laugh. But we do not laugh. Except for a scornful burst of Soul Laughter which sends them running away.

"Do you know how Man is made, Pee-áir? He is made of a hollow log and a hollow stone joined together. Some say a round gourd but I think a hollow stone. Now the hollow log is lying on the soil one day when along come two snakes. One is a man snake. The other is a woman snake. The woman snake wants to live inside the log, but she can see no way into it. The ends are closed up. There are no branch holes in it. She is unhappy. She asks the man snake how she can get inside. He thinks he knows the way. He runs away and brings his friend the woodpecker, asks him to tap with his beak at the log to try to make a hole. But the wood is so hard, it hurts the woodpecker's mouth. The woman snake is still unhappy. So again the man snake runs away and brings another friend. A small bird named kai-kai. Kai-kai is lighter than a feather and sings a very deep long song, although he is so small. He sings the way the Bruxo chants, round and round, deep and deep. The snake likes kai-kai because when kai-kai sings, the snake understands how to curl round and round himself. You are listening to me, Pee-áir? I am telling you."

"I'm listening Kayapi. My box is listening. I don't understand everything yet—but I will."

But Kayapi got bored with my not understanding and put the rest of the story off to another day.

*　　　*　　　*

A note on the Xemahoa language.

The form of the future tense is peculiar. I'm still not sure it is a true future tense. More like an emphatic present containing the seeds of futurity—a 'mood' peculiar to Xemahoa. They add the word 'yi', meaning literally 'now', on to the present verb, or else 'yi-yi', 'now-now'. Kayapi explained the difference to me by saying the present tense of the verb 'to eat' while holding his hand to his mouth and moving his lips. Then he held his hand further away from his mouth and pursed his lips and said the eat-verb with 'yi' added on. Finally he thrust his hand as far away as it would go and made a tight face like a man sucking a lemon and said the eat-verb followed by 'yi-yi'. I interpret these three versions of the verb as 'now', 'the immediate future', and 'the far future'—but they are all treated as aspects of the present tense by the Xemahoa.

Odd that the weight of 'now' upon the present should distance the present into the future. Yet I begin to suspect that this is an essential feature of this remarkable language. If Xemahoa B—the drug speech—is as deeply self-embedded as my recordings lead me to suspect, then an utterance 'now' is already pregnant with the future completion of the utterance. It aims to abolish the spread-out through time of a statement—which inevitably occurs since it takes time to utter a statement (by which time conditions have changed and the statement may no longer be quite so true).

Another note on the Xemahoa language.

In fact the measuring of time is more subtle than I thought. They are able to use the same bird-feather words that count numbers to measure time past and time future. However, the 'numbers' of time are not fixed units. Instead they apparently modulate according to the context of reference. The same numbers can thus measure and quantify the stages in the development of the human foetus from conception through to birth, as in another context can measure and quantify the stages of a man's whole life.

Confusing enough for a poor Caraiba like me! Yet it's an admirably sophisticated and flexible—if highly culture-specific—instrument. The qualifiers 'yi' and 'yi-yi' play an important part in this. Thus the compound word 'kai-kai-yi' signifies 'x' quanta of whatever it is (of stages of pregnancy, of the ages of Man, of sections of a ritual) forward along the time-line; while, equally useful and ingenious, the term 'yi-kai-kai' signifies 'x' quanta from the present back along the time-line towards the past—back along that embedding stream of words that bears life along.

Kayapi picked up his story at the point where he dropped it a couple of days ago.

"Are you listening, Pee-áir? Kai-kai sings a funny song. He tries to make the log laugh. Because he knows the woodpecker will never succeed in breaking a hole through the log by means of violence. His song is funny because it goes round-and-round and in-and-in. Because it sings the same shape of song as the shape of the snake when he curls himself round himself.

"Yet even this song does not make the log laugh. The log keeps his mouth shut tight. Then kai-kai has an idea. Remember, he is so light. His claws are not like the wood-pecker's heavy claws. Kai-kai's claws tickle the log..."

I didn't recognize the word for 'tickle'. Kayapi demonstrated by tickling me in the ribs.

He tickled me cleverly—the way kai-kai must have tickled the log, in the story. He was trying to make me laugh. But I remembered about Profane Gaiety and kept a straight face. He smiled approvingly.

"So kai-kai tickles the log, till the log laughs. In the moment the log opens his mouth to laugh, the woman

72

snake jumps in through the log's mouth. She coils round and round inside, before the log has time to spit her out.

"That, Pee-áir," he proclaimed, smacking his belly with the flat of his hand, "is how we men come to have entrails. But woman still has a little of the hollow of the log inside her—that's where her baby finds the space to coil up in...

"I'm hungry, Pee-áir," he grinned. "My belly has a hole in it..."

He wandered off to get some dried fish—pirarucu—which he gnawed on.

It had been raining heavily. Now, for a time, thin rays of light filtered down through the branches, creepers and parasites of the forest upon a wet world.

Away in the forest, the grunt, scuttle, splash of a wild pig, as some of the youth hunted it down cautiously—*queixada* is more vicious and violent than the jaguar. Finally, echoing across the mirror of water, a piercing squeal of death...

Today Kayapi finished the story.

"That is how entrails came to be, Pee-áir. However the man snake wants somewhere for himself also. He moves on till he comes to this stone."

"Which some say is a gourd?"

Kayapi grinned.

"Yes, Pee-áir, but I think it is a hollow stone. It keeps its mouth tight shut. It has seen what happened to the log. So the man snake wonders. Then he goes away and asks his friend the woodpecker to bite a hole in the stone. But this hurts the woodpecker's mouth more than the log hurt him. He goes right away. So the snake asks his friend kai-kai to tickle the stone, but the stone cannot feel what the log could feel. Kai-kai is too small and light. So the man snake goes and asks his friend the pigeon ('a-pai-i') to come and help him. A-pai-i treads on the stone, to tickle it, but the stone holds its mouth shut tight. So the man snake thinks again. He moves in front of the stone where the stone can see him. And there he ties himself in a knot."

Kayapi's fingers knotted themselves together, in a mime.

"When the stone sees the man snake tie himself in a knot, it forgets itself. It opens its mouth and laughs. And when it is laughing and its tongue is busy with Profane Gaiety and there are no words to guard its mouth, the man snake unties himself and leaps in quickly through the open mouth and ties himself in a big knot before the stone can spit him out. A big knot tied many times. That is how we get brains in our heads."

So this myth of the stone and the snake was their explanation for the origin of their embedded language.

Many details that had puzzled me about the Xemahoa are beginning to fall into place. Their attitude to laughter. The reason why women who laugh frivolously do not snort maka-i. (But what about the woman in the hut??) Their incestuous kinship system. Their sophisticated awareness of quanta of time, amazing among inhabitants of this great timeless monochrome jungle. Many tribes are aware of the stars—the rising of the Pleiades at a particular time of year. Yet the Xemahoa's concept of time may be unique. The way in which the object of their attention modulates the bird-feather time scale, functioning like a sort of mental rheostat, generating a variable resistance.

It's remarkable, how the Xemahoa use the concrete things of the jungle—the trees, the feathers of the birds—to code such abstract concepts! And how utterly they will be destroyed by 're-location'! How right they are to ignore it. What other choice have they? To dig up the jungle around them and move it?

It's also noteworthy how wide a scale of measurement their 'mental' rheostat permits. From the extent of a man's whole lifetime, down to the Reichian microtime of

74

orgasm. Incidentally, they are great sexual artists, I have heard from Kayapi. Unhappily for myself their incest system precludes any personal experience of this on my part—no matter how seductive these girls to my eyes and desires! (Ah, Makonde girl in the bush of Mozambique with your ebony thighs and cream of chocolate nipples, your pubic darkness, your warmth of Africa—like making love to the throbbing night itself, to the hot African night!) Yes, the stages of orgasm in their love speech would have enchanted Wilhelm Reich. They can express the whole range from this microtime of orgasm, through the stages of embedding of the foetus in the womb, to the Ages of Man—to . . . God knows what else! Could they grasp the concept of geological time in this 'rheostat' speech?

Our own Western talk of time is all wrong. All out of shape. We have no direct experience of time. No direct perception of it. But for the Xemahoa mind time exists as a direct experience. And time shifts according to the infinitely-variable resistance of the proposition. Time can be conceived directly, in terms of the things around them in the jungle. The tail feathers of a macaw. The wing feathers of the kai-kai. It is while wearing such feathers that they *dance time* to the chant of the Bruxo!

Another thing that Kayapi's story tells me—these supposed 'savages' understand that thinking takes place in the head, inside the brain—and while this may seem a pretty obvious idea to us, let's not forget that the Ancient Greeks with their Aristotles and their Platos had no such idea. The brain was just a pile of useless mush, for them.

FIVE

ZWINGLER SAT ON the edge of Sole's desk, back to the blank video screen.

"I still find this kinda embarrassing," the American said after a long silence spent staring at Sole's feet as though finding something wrong with them. "Fact is, the radio dish run by the Navy down in New Mexico has been picking up some strange traffic lately."

Sole nodded impatiently—queer enough traffic on his video screen, when his itching fingers could get to turn it on.

"This dish is big, understand—just a shade under three times the size of your own Jodrell Bank. The idea's ... well, to eavesdrop on Russian and Chinese domestic traffic as they're reflected back from the Moon. Not much signal reflects back, of course, around the order of a billion billionth of a watt if I remember right—still, that's way over the background noise, so we can use it. When the Moon isn't up above the horizon, the dish gets used for more routine radio-astronomy projects. A while ago, as it was tracking across the sky it picked up this ... well, strange traffic. Strange traffic coming from that part of the sky I should say! The Stone Scissors Paper show of a few months ago, playing backwards."

"That's the TV nude auction thing?"

The Victorian passion for naked harems and slave markets found its outlet in stagey 'masterpieces' adorning grimy municipal galleries. The Stone Scissors Paper game performed the same sublimatory role for the Media Age with far less ambiguity.

"Right! You know the game—stick out your fist, fingers, or flat of your hand—stone blunts scissors, scissors cuts paper—every lost trick loses you a garment which the studio audience gets to bid for, till the loser has nothing else left, *and then* ..."

"We don't get to see it over here," said Sam, a shade regretfully. "Government banned it after Lightpeople protests. Not that I saw much harm in it personally, psychologically speaking you need some sort of safety valve in today's society ... liberates tensions."

Sole found himself laughing—a hacking kind of sound came out of him like a bout of whooping cough ending on a high-pitched whistle.

"The Great Masturbation Show—our first cultural export!"

Zwingler jerked his hand angrily in the direction of the dark skylight.

"Damn it, Man, from space!"

"Like a used condom washed up on the celestial shore—" tears in Sole's eyes.

The rubies glared at him chastely.

"It isn't funny. The show was played over and over again, backwards. By this time of course the dish was locked on to that point in the sky—away from the galactic plane where there's less background noise or we shouldn't have picked up anything. You realize it wasn't an echo effect—the show had gone out months earlier. The thing was being deliberately retransmitted. And backwards just to rub in the point."

"Sort of electronic buggery, eh?"

"Naturally we checked there were no bugs in the circuits. The SSP Show was exchanged for some baseball game after a few hours—"

"Backwards too?" enquired Sole, for whom this whole confidential briefing was taking on the dimensions of a grotesque farce. Surely it was all a big hoax. Remember

77

the Orson Welles 'War of the Worlds' hoax broadcast and the panic that ensued—this must be something along the same lines, only designed by post-Wellesian McLuhanite man as a spoof on his own TV civilization.

"Right. Let me tell you that looked even crazier—at least you could pretend the other folks were putting their clothes on, 'stead of stripping them off. But the most important difference was this baseball match went out later than the SSP Show by exactly a week and it was followed in turn by a newsreel from a week later still. We decided it was a cute way of tipping us off when they're getting here."

"You're sure it's a 'Them'?"

"That's the problem. Them—or It—could be a robot probe presumably."

"It's nothing that you or the Russians have sent out that way? What about the Jupiter Orbiter? The Russian Saturn probe?"

"Wrong direction. Give us some credit, will you. Deep Space Instrumentation Facility monitors every bit of telemetry. Air Force radar keeps an eye on every last bit of tin trash in orbit. We know where everything is, whatever flag it's flying. This thing isn't flying any flag."

"Just flying the nude auction show? What a joke. The stars look down—as voyeurs."

"Could just be the stars," Zwingler agreed primly. "Don't see what else it could be. Frankly."

"But it's got to be a robot, Tom!" How desperately Sam sounded like he wanted to believe this version of the facts—cock of his own dunghill here at Haddon how smartly he put himself in the place of humanity, long-time cock of its. "No sane race would squander the time and resources to survey even a fraction of the stars by going there in person, on the off-chance."

"We're putting out as much radio traffic today as a fair-sized star so how long do you think it is since the signal strength became noticeable out there? Maybe they heard—and came to see?"

"No, Tom—that would put them within a couple of dozen light years of us, unless they know how to travel faster than light, which is a physical impossibility. It's just not probable, another civilization so close to us. It's got to be a robot. Maybe one out of hundreds or thousands sent out goodness knows how long ago. The thing could have been travelling for centuries before it picked up our signals. The fact that it only echoes our own broadcasts instead of sending one of its own proves it's a drone."

"Of course," Sole pointed out, "they'd have no reason to expect you to be looking out for any signals from that particular direction with the sort of sophisticated radio-dish you mention—unless you acknowledged their re-broadcasts. Have you done that—or is everyone sitting on their hands in panic?"

Zwingler nodded.

"In fact we have—we sent a 1271 bit test-panel. But no response—just our own programmes being played back at us, backwards."

Now that he'd partially absorbed it, the news exhilarated Sole rather than scared him. It seemed to absolve him from his petty worries about Pierre and Eileen and his guilt in the face of Dorothy. His experiments with the children took on a purer, clearer complexion, the sort of exhilarated mood he imagined the realization of the 'Death of God' had filled Nietzsche with. Anything was possible in the world where God was dead; likewise with a world about to be visited from the Stars. Then he realized he was using the news as an anaesthetic—and the pain returned.

"How soon is this thing getting here?" fretted Sam.

Zwingler shook his head sadly.

"At the current rate of deceleration—extrapolating

79

from the broadcasts—we reckon on it being in the vicinity of the Moon in five days' time."

Sam looked heartsick and Zwingler visibly sympathetic. The rubies circulated consolingly.

"It's been decided not to release the news."

"But that's ridiculous. How do you propose to make that stick? And for God's sake why?"

"It's too dangerous to release news of this calibre, Chris. Carl Gustav Jung predicted that the reins might be torn from our hands—metaphorically speaking. We'd be bereft of our dreams as a species—it could kick the legs right out from under us."

"Or give us a timely kick in the pants?"

"False optimism, Chris. We're going out to collect it —meet it—whatever. If it's a robot drone, humanity needn't be traumatized—not yet awhile, till we've got people prepared—maybe not for another hundred years. Naturally the Russians were bound to find out sooner or later so we took them into our confidence. They see our point about discretion, and providing there's a quid pro quo about information sharing they'll play along with us. A Russian scientist will be travelling out with our crew to intercept—"

"When?"

"They're leaving tomorrow night from the Cape. But in case it isn't a robot—"

"It's got to be, Tom! Be reasonable. The statistical chances."

"In case it isn't, like I say, is why I'm here."

Sam nodded sagely—wanting things both ways—for the safety of Mankind, and the greater glory of Haddon.

"We'd like someone from here over in the States in a consultative capacity—"

Concentrating his attention on the blank screen behind Zwingler's back, Sole thought of Vidya wrenching at the innermost embedded doll.

"Well, Chris?"

So why had Vidya done it?

"Provided you realize there might be nothing in it for you—if this thing turns out to be a robot—and let's hope to hell it is, in my humble opinion!"

"Why me?" murmured Sole. "I can't just walk out on the children on the spur of the moment..."

"Chris, my poor Chris—*think!* This is the Big Thing of all time, maybe. Whatever it is, it's helluva big. Don't you want to be involved?"

"Rather a schizophrenic attitude to this thing you've got," Sole temporized (conscious too of this aspect in himself ... damn Pierre and his untimely letter!). "You want it and you don't want it. It's the Big Thing and the Worst Thing That Can Happen—"

"Of course you can leave Haddon temporarily, Chris, you might be involved in a car smash or something. We'd have to find a stand-in then."

"Thanks a lot, Sam."

"What I mean is, Lionel can look after your kids while you're in the States. You have to go as our representative, Chris—keep the flag flying."

"May I put it this way?" Zwingler smiled. "Practical alien linguistics could be pretty essential soon."

"Unless it's a robot."

"Well, we still get our old broadcasts back—when I left the States they were sending some vampire movie..."

"Maybe our aliens have got a sense of humour—"

Zwingler shook his head.

"Doubt it. They wouldn't understand the cultural context. Baseball, striptease, vampires—it'd all be the same to them. Incidentally, how fit are you?"

"Fit?"

"It might involve you being sent into space via the Shuttle, who knows?" Ruby moons ascended, blasted off.

"Pretty big carrot, Chris—get any lazy donkey on the move."

"Equally there may be nothing in it."

Behind the American's back, the blank video screen clamoured for Sole's attention, Vidya twisting the tiniest doll on tape, inexplicably. Overhead, the neon-framed skylight black with space...

And very high overhead, way out beyond the Moon's orbit, something—a seed of the stars—returning the electromagnetic refuse of Earth back to Earth, the Coke bottles and condoms of TV culture, the Nude Auction Show, a Vampire movie screened in the wee hours when only muggers and addicts prowl the deserted streets; a sound sweep sweeping down the star lanes, decelerating as it comes...

SIX

"YOU KNOW THE snake in the log, and the snake in the stone, Pee-áir?"

"Yes I know them."

"Well, they are Man and Woman. So they want to make love. They will fuck together to give birth to the Xemahoa people. The Log and the Stone will lie together."

"The Stone will lie on top of the Log?" I hazarded, thinking of the shape of the head on top of the body.

Kayapi shook his head impatiently.

"How do the Xemahoa make love, Pee-áir? We lie side by side, so any sperm spills on the soil not on the limbs. Listen to me, Pee-áir. Do not have your own ideas, or you will not know the Xemahoa."

So much for the 'Missionary Position', I thought wryly! My mistake.

I said sorry, and he grunted a surly acknowledgment, then carried on:

"The snake in the stone and the snake in the log want to lie together. But they cannot come out of the stone or the log, or the stone and the log will close up and not let them in again. The stone and the log want to be empty. They will not be tricked a second time. So the two snakes can only half fuck. They spill a lot of sperm. From the part of their fuck that goes into the log, the tribe of Xemahoa is born. But from the part that falls on the soil —what do you think?"

I made a guess.

"Maka-i grows, Kayapi?"

He beamed a broad smile, stretched out his arm and clapped me on the shoulder many times.

I could predict that some other Xemahoa myth—taking such concrete objects of the jungle as stones and birds and plants, for its working parts—would neatly splice together the sperm that spills on the soil at night—and the *nightsoil* of the Xemahoa that they manure the maka-i fungus with. That is how intricate—and logical—this Indian culture is!

Nevertheless it was a disorderly jigsaw yet.

I didn't want to offend Kayapi so soon after showing glimmerings of intelligence, so I put off asking for the other pieces to be put into place: particularly the problem of the woman in the taboo hut, pregnant and yet receiving the embedding drug...

"Pee-áir," Kayapi said thoughtfully, "I think maybe you can take maka-i now without the birds losing their way out of your head. But it will be hard for them to find their way back if you cannot call them back in Xemahoa."

"I am learning, Kayapi. I must learn fast. The water is higher today."

He hardly glanced at the flood. Spat at it.

"That doesn't matter. I add water to it, see!"

I saw.

But I didn't really see, as yet.

Last night one of the Xemahoa girls crept to my open-mesh hammock.

"Kayapi sends me," she hissed. "To the Caraiba who is a little Xemahoa."

I started to say something in Xemahoa to her, but she stuck two fingers softly in my mouth and tapped my tongue. Just in time, I remembered the mistake that the stone and the log had made, and used my tongue to force her fingers out. She giggled as I did so. In the dark of the hut I couldn't see her face or body well, yet her giggle sounded like the giggle of a young girl.

For a moment I thought she might even be a boy. Her chest felt so smooth to my hand, the way it bulged ever so softly into nipples. But when I slid my hand lower, I knew which she was. She was wet there already. Had she been greased or ointmented? Or was she in a state of excitement already? She moaned as I touched her.

My tongue found hers, and that put an end to her giggling.

She took my penis in her hand, then chafed the knob of it gently till I was nearly coming. But I guess she was more interested in my lack of a foreskin than in exciting me just then, if the truth be told. The Xemahoa don't practice circumcision. The blunt bone of my penis was a once-in-a-lifetime curiosity to a girl embedded in this incest culture.

How do you fuck in a Xemahoa hammock?

The best way *is* side by side, I soon discovered.

If it hadn't been for the floodwater seeping into the hut, some of my sperm must surely have spilt through the loose mesh on to the soil after I pulled out of her.

The Xemahoa myths were becoming living realities to me.

Was this why Kayapi had sent the girl?

After we'd made love, the girl stuffed a couple of fingers in my mouth to stop me saying anything, and I played with her fingertips with my tongue, while she played at trying to trap it...

She slipped away before dawn, so I didn't see her face.

I slept a while.

When I woke to the daylight I noticed dry blood on my penis shaft and hairs. The first thing I thought was she must have been a virgin. But when I thought about it a little longer, and about how I'd entered her in that sideways position without any difficulty, I realized that the initial wetness of her sex hadn't been grease or excitement, but must have been menstrual flow.

She'd been having her period.

"Yes, it was her bleeding," Kayapi confirmed casually when I saw him later on.

So much for menstrual taboos, at least in this society! Unless it was a studied insult.

But this I doubted.

Maybe the fact of the girl having a period cancelled out the incest rule of the tribe. My sperm going in, was cancelled by her blood coming out, which permitted me to couple with a Xemahoa girl though myself an outsider.

I glanced casually round the girls paddling their way about the village, wondering who it had been. And whether she'd be back! But I doubted it. It had been a cultural copulation, there in the hut last night. Kayapi had sent the girl to show me myth in practice—and tie my nervous system into the Xemahoa.

I was outlining my idea to Kayapi as clearly as I could, and he was busy nodding vigorously when we heard the noise of the helicopter. The sound came chattering closer over the trees and I thought to myself, those bloody priests are coming back to try a different tack—bringing the big guns of technology to bear.

But Kayapi thought differently.

"Go hide in the jungle, Pee-áir!" he said urgently.

"What for? It's those White-Robes who spoke about the Flood. They fly a Caraiba bird." Feeling foolish, I repeated the remark in Portuguese, substituting 'helicopter' for 'bird'.

"No!"

He pushed me roughly out of the village clearing, back into the dense maze of rearing vegetation it had been hacked from.

I was wanting to stay and tell the priests to fuck off back to their miracle dam and tell them to *stop this flooding*—before they destroyed something irreplaceable. I resisted Kayapi.

Then he did a crazy thing.

He pulled a knife on me and screamed at the top of his voice.

"If you don't go hide in the jungle and stay there, I kill you, Pee-áir!"

So I retreated into the jungle. Wouldn't you? I could easily keep an eye on Kayapi's whereabouts and slip inside the helicopter to talk to the priests before he had a chance to knife me. If indeed he meant his threat—but I hadn't cared for that look in his eyes.

From cover, I watched him.

He ran to my hut and emerged a few moments later with all my equipment bundled up in the hammock and ran into the jungle with it.

I realized then that Kayapi believed enough in me to intend keeping me here forcibly with the Xemahoa—but naturally my excitement at this breakthrough was mixed with a certain irritation, not to say fear, at the means used to demonstrate it!

Already the helicopter was hovering overhead and the Xemahoa children were pointing up at it; but their parents were calling them into the huts, or into the jungle.

It wasn't priests that landed.

It was some sort of police. Soldiers. Paramilitary. I recognized the type. An elegant, viciously handsome caucasian officer in a drab olive uniform and black jackboots jumped down into the water. Then two others in boots and informal fatigues—a giant Negro with a submachine-gun, and a runtish halfcaste with an automatic rifle and fixed bayonet. The pilot sat pointing an automatic weapon out of the cabin. In the machine's guts I could see two or three other men skulking with guns.

I'd seen the same sort of thing in Mozambique.

Only there the villagers had been ready with their AK-

47s and grenades and bazookas. That particular helicopter hadn't lifted off again.

The runt and the Negro raced from hut to hut, poking their guns inside, ignoring the Xemahoa people entirely, while their officer stood masterfully in the centre of the village.

"Nothing," the Negro shouted. "There's nothing."

What kind of incredible *political* foresight was it had sent Kayapi scuttling off into the jungle with my things? I wondered too, would he have gone to so much trouble for me before I was bonded to the tribe by that ritual love-match last night?

Kayapi wandered in casually from the forest. He came from a different direction from the one where he'd taken my things.

The officer shouted at several of the Xemahoa men, asking them if they spoke Portuguese. But they all, including Kayapi, stared back at him blankly.

The runt with the bayonet finished his skirting of the main circuit of the village—and the taboo hut lay within his field of vision a hundred yards away down the forest path that was now a wet canal.

The runt hesitated, taking in the dank mass of trees between him and the hut—the menace of jungle—the distance from the helicopter. Then he pretended not to have seen it.

"There's nothing here either," he shouted.

What in hell's name were they looking for?

I couldn't believe they could be looking for the same thing those Portuguese troops had been looking for in that Makonde village when they landed their Alouette. Not in the heart of this unpolitical jungle! In the streets of Rio, yes—or in the coastal countryside. But deep in the Amazon? It seemed ridiculous.

The officer shouted into the helicopter and a miserable-looking Indian interpreter appeared, who addressed the village through a loudhailer in some Tupi dialect then in a couple of others. But there's a kind of linguistic fault-line that divides the Xemahoa from their neighbours. He couldn't communicate with them in any of the dialects he tried. And Kayapi wasn't volunteering anything.

Abruptly the officer wheeled about and snapped his fingers for the Negro and the runt who came bounding back through the flood to scramble into the helicopter. The blades turned, beating down fists of air on the water, rustling the fronds of the huts. Then they lifted off, and disappeared beyond the trees.

They could only have been in the village ten minutes.

Later I asked Kayapi what would have happened if the runt had gone as far as the taboo hut.

"We kill them maybe."

"Kayapi, you know what those guns can do?"

"I know guns, yes."

"You know carbines, rifles, pistols, Kayapi. Guns that fire once or twice or three times. You don't know those guns. They shoot *kai-kai* times in this space of time." I snapped my fingers as the officer had snapped his.

Kayapi shrugged.

"Maybe we kill them."

"Why did you hide my things in the jungle?" I demanded.

"Was it not right, Pee-áir?"

"Yes. In fact it *was* right."

"So."

"But my reason would not be the same as your reason, Kayapi."

He stared at me, shook his head, and laughed.

"Tomorrow, Pee-áir, you must meet maka-i. We all meet him together."

Preparations are going on for the dance. But it will be a dance through two feet of water. Some of the nearby

89

jungle is deep water already—six feet, or worse, where the land slopes down.

And this village is on something of a slope. God knows how deep the water will be in a few weeks. How high is that bloody dam? Thirty or forty metres?

The ants are going crazy, swarming through the branches. Iridescent blue morpho butterflies, the ones that get made into ornaments—plaques and plates of blinding blue—flutter above the waters. Red and orange macaws scatter through the trees, propelled by their own screeches. I saw a couple of alligators scuttling near the village this morning. Fish are wandering into the jungle. They'll soon be swimming through the branches.

But enough talk of nature. Description for its own sake means next to nothing. The Xemahoa know that. Nature here isn't 'pretty'. It isn't a picture, a landscape. It's a larder and a glossary. And I fancy it's more important as a glossary than as a larder, to the Xemahoa mind. Macaws are first and foremost feather-number creatures.

Kayapi came to me just now and confided what they're expecting from the pregnant woman.

Those White-Robes would have crowed with delight.

Or shrunk back in horror!

They expect their maka-i 'God' to take on flesh and blood inside her. It's the Christ thing all over again.

So that's what Kayapi meant about the maka-i baby coming 'when it was time'! That's why the woman has been high on maka-i through her pregnancy.

God knows what condition she must be in! Her nose must have half rotted off by now—if the mess that the Bruxo's own nostrils are in, is anything to go by.

And God knows what the genetic consequences may be!

SEVEN

T PLUS 3 DAYS 14 HOURS 30 MINUTES

MISSION CONTROL HOUSTON "You're closing nicely. The object maintains a steady rate of deceleration relative to Earth. I tell you, we'd be pretty scared if it wasn't. There'd be a hell of a hole someplace in Wisconsin otherwise! The size estimate is still one nautical mile diameter. You should expect visual acquisition soon."

PETR S TSERBATSKY "Surely that would depend on its mass. The hole in Wisconsin."

MIKE MCQ DALTON (NAVIGATOR) "You think it's a balloon some joker has blown up and tossed us to catch?"

TSERBATSKY "An expanded structure maybe. An interstellar ramjet scoop. I am just speculating."

PAULUS S SHERMAN (MISSION COMMANDER) "That's possible, Mike."

TSERBATSKY "Or it could be a hollowed out asteroid. Both suggestions are feasible."

MISSION CONTROL "Distance forty, that's four oh, nautical miles—it's closing at a relative velocity of two hundred and decelerating—one-ninety-nine ... one-ninety-eight—"

DALTON "So we're moving nicely backwards? Maybe we can hitch us a ride the rest of the way home. Stick out your thumb, Petr!"

TSERBATSKY "I never can appreciate this transatlantic frivolity. This is perhaps the most significant moment in human history. The first meeting with extraterrestial intelligence."

DALTON "Anybody making first contact by playing that nude auction show back at us has just got to be joking—"

MISSION CONTROL "Distance, ten nautical miles—closing at one-seventy-five ... one-seventy-four ... Cut the chatter, will you, Mike?"

T PLUS 3 DAYS 15 HOURS 5 MINUTES

SHERMAN "I can see it! There's a half moon profile out there—sidelighted by sunlight. It has to be a globe. How's the quality of the picture?"

MISSION CONTROL "There's a bit of glare. Will you move the camera over to the right?"

SHERMAN "How about this?"

MISSION CONTROL "That's better. We see it now."

DALTON "What's it transmitting right now?"

MISSION CONTROL "The movie of the Manson Musical. A New York station put it out last week. No, wait a bit. That transmission's just stopped ... They're transmitting our rendezvous diagram now—yes it's the rendezvous diagram, check. Now it's stopped. It's coming again ... no —they've changed it now. A new diagram. It shows your flightpath intersecting with theirs. Diagram's changed again. The scale's large now. There's Leapfrog and the Globe. The Globe is a perfect circle. Leapfrog's a small triangle of dots. A dotted line connects you both."

DALTON "Do we cut along the dotted line?"

MISSION CONTROL "Another change—new diagram. Showing Leapfrog sitting on the very outside of the Globe. They want you to land on them. Distance is five miles now, relative velocity fifty ... forty-nine—"

SHERMAN "Good visuals now. How do you read the pictures?"

MISSION CONTROL "Fine. Will you prepare to land on manuals?"

SHERMAN "Wilco. The Globe's shining like it's made of metal. A high albedo. No apparent irregularities. Not a rock body I'd say—so the idea of a hollowed-out asteroid is a no-no."

MISSION CONTROL "Landing plan's being rebroadcast. No fresh developments. Distance is three miles. Relative velocity thirty ... twenty-nine—"

TSERBATSKY "It makes me feel like a flea. Such size, and moving under its own power!"

SHERMAN "Houston? I'm going for a short burn to slow down the rate of closing. A point-five second burn ... now."

MISSION CONTROL "Telemetry reads your distance as two miles, Leapfrog. Relative velocity now nine—now eight point five."

T PLUS 3 DAYS 15 HOURS 28 MINUTES

SHERMAN "Landing probes making contact—now. We're down."

TSERBATSKY "It's metal—a great metal sphere. The horizon is a perfect circle round us. The surface slightly pitted—a texture like sandpaper. But no big dents or cracks. I can see great circle lines running to the horizon. It's put together like an orange."

DALTON "Smooth parking, Paulus—like in your own driveway. I guess it's a free ride home from here."

MISSION CONTROL "Not all the way home, boys. For God's sake get them persuaded into a high parking orbit. The Soviets will announce an inflatable com-sat to coincide with their arrival. That thing will be like a new star in the sky."

TSERBATSKY "And supposing it wishes to land. Gentlemen?"

DALTON "That thing, landing? It would break apart! What does it sit down on?"

TSERBATSKY "How about water?"

MISSION CONTROL "That's true, Tserbatsky. If they plan on landing that thing, we'll have to scrap the Nevada Desert plan."

TSERBATSKY "The American lakes are too public. Canada is no use in winter. How about the Aral Sea in Kazakhstan?"

DALTON "Aussieland might be better. One of those lakes in the Outback?"

TSERBATSKY "They're seasonal lakes. Empty at the moment. And too shallow anyway."

MISSION CONTROL "Don't you boys worry yourselves about the politics of it, we'll work that one out down here. You concentrate on that Globe."

T PLUS 3 DAYS 16 HOURS 00 MINUTES

MISSION CONTROL "Boys, we've reached a compromise on the landing zone—if that thing's going to land. The obvious place is the Pacific. Will you copy the co-ordinates? It's a lagoon in the Marshall Islands, southeast of Eniwetok. North seven degrees fifty-two minutes. East one-sixty-eight degrees twenty minutes. Of course, the Globe is unlikely to land—most likely it carries a scout ship on board. In which case Nevada is the prime choice."

TSERBATSKY "I request verbal confirmation of the Marshall Islands decision from Dr Stepanov."

MISSION CONTROL "Fair enough."

DIMITRI A STEPANOV (USSR CO-ORDINATOR, HOUSTON; TRANSLATED FROM RUSSIAN)

"I confirm the Pacific location, Petr Simonovich. But try to keep that thing in the sky. The Nevada Desert for any scout-ship."

DALTON "There's a hole opening up in the skin about a hundred metres off."

SHERMAN "A cylinder shape is rising out of it. It's about ten metres high by thirty across. Maybe it's an airlock?"

TSERBATSKY "A broad opening appearing in the cylinder side."

MISSION CONTROL "Leapfrog? The landing plan they were broadcasting has stopped. We're receiving a new diagram now. It shows you on the outside of the Globe—with a dotted line moving from you to the inside of it. They want you to go inside. Better get suited up, Sherman and Tserbatsky. Dalton will watch the store."

T PLUS 3 DAYS 16 HOURS 50 MINUTES

DALTON "They're getting close to the airlock now. You okay, Paulus?"

SHERMAN "We're fine. You read us, Houston?"

MISSION CONTROL "Fine—good visuals."

SHERMAN "The inside of the cylinder is empty. There's a large round chamber. Some sort of sensors and controls at the rear. We're stepping inside together."

DALTON "Two great steps for mankind? Hey Houston! The door's closing! That thing's shutting on them."

TSERBATSKY "Doors are designed to close, my friend. We're—" (LOSS OF SIGNAL)

DALTON "The door's tight shut now. The cylinder is retracting back into the skin. Can you hear me, Paulus? Paulus! Houston, the contact's been lost. Can you still hear me, Houston?"

MISSION CONTROL "We hear you loud and clear, Leapfrog."

DALTON "Something's blanketing their transmissions then."

T PLUS 4 DAYS 06 HOURS 35 MINUTES

DALTON "Houston! That cylinder's on the move again. It's coming up ... The door's opening ... There they are in the doorway. Paulus? Tserbatsky? Do you read me?"

SHERMAN "Yes Mike, we read you. But we're tired."

TSERBATSKY "Houston?"

MISSION CONTROL "Houston to Leapfrog. Sherman. Tserbatsky. Welcome back. What happened?"

SHERMAN "I guess you could say that the ball's in their court now..."

TSERBATSKY "Paulus—have you no sense of destiny! Intelligent beings have crossed the deeps of space to communicate with us. They open the door to the Universe. Let us never wittingly let it shut!"

DALTON "Great speech, Ivan, but what the hell do they look like?"

TSERBATSKY "Oh that. Appearances. They're bipeds—two arms and two legs like ourselves—only they're much taller than us, about three metres tall. They've got skinny frames, with powdery grey skins. No body hair visible on them. They have this broad single nostril in the middle of their faces—a vast flat saddle nose like you see in hereditary syphilis. And their eyes—these are set further round the sides of the head than ours. They must see through a hundred and eighty to two hundred degrees—the eyes bulge like the eyes of Pekinese dogs. Their ears look like crinkly grey paper bags—and are continually inflating and deflating. I could see small cartiliginous teeth in their mouths and the mouth itself was a bright orange colour, except for the tongue which was long and dark and red—and very supple, like a butterfly's tongue."

SHERMAN "They analysed our air and fitted out a sort of reception room for us made out of glass—for us to take our helmets off inside of. We gave them the language videotapes and microfilm. They put them through some machine—decontamination I guess—and huddled round them. They had the language tapes on a screen within ten minutes. Two of them scanning fast and listening, ignoring us. Another of them brought a communication screen we could write on."

TSERBATSKY "They treated us in a brisk brotherly way. As fellow intelligences. They were very busy. We were the tourists. They talked with a very wide range of sounds. Going up very high-pitched sometimes. I heard the top C that shatters Opera House chandeliers. And a dull low bass at other times. With a very fast shuttling between the two extremes."

SHERMAN "We negotiated with two of them by way of this blackboard screen. We drew with our fingers and images appeared. It's agreed they're going into parking orbit. They'll send a small vehicle down to the Nevada site. We asked for and got a transpolar orbit on the twenty west, one-sixty east longitude. The only land that passes over is Siberia, Antarctica, Reykjavik in Iceland, and a few bits and pieces in the Pacific. Okay?"

TSERBATSKY "Imagine, Gentlemen, we have met our brothers from the stars. And we are going to hide them away where no one sees! I am still filled with the wonder of it!"

STEPANOV (SPEAKING RUSSIAN, A PROVERB WHICH CAN LOOSELY BE TRANSLATED AS)

"Brothers is, as brothers does, Petr Simonovich!"

SHERMAN "I'm goddam tired. We're coming aboard to sleep now."

MISSION CONTROL "One thing more, Leapfrog. Did you find out *why* they've come?"

SHERMAN "Nope. Apart from the orbital and landing data, it was all one big language lesson to me. All taken up with checking out the speech tapes we brought. We didn't get down to personalities or purposes."

MISSION CONTROL "Not to worry, Paulus—I guess they got their priorities straight. How do we communicate with them if not by words?"

After he'd read the transcriptions, Sole stared at the bright red cover of the xeroxed sheets, which had been flown in direct from Houston to Fort Meade, the autofax system apparently being distrusted for the conveyance of sensitive material of this order. 'Fax Freaks' had been operating in the States for at least a year now, making it their sometimes profitable, sometimes anarchistic hobby to extract autofaxed documents from the coded signals in the public telephone system, even when scramblers were in use. There had already been one major scandal in the past twelve months, about nuclear waste disposal procedures, traceable to this particular source—amateur guerrilla technology. There were tales of industrial espionage from the pharmaceuticals industry, and rumours of phoney government memos being slipped into the system, somewhere between the State Department and the Pentagon. The personal courier had emerged from the world of autofax technology, unscathed and even with a new importance.

This cover sheet read:

SECRET

THIS IS A COVER SHEET

*Basic Security Requirements Are Contained
In AR 380-5*

THE UNAUTHORIZED DISCLOSURE OF THE INFORMATION
CONTAINED IN THE ATTACHED DOCUMENTS) COULD RESULT
IN SERIOUS DAMAGE TO THE UNITED STATES...

There was a full page of warning instructions, ending with the information that the Cover Sheet was not in itself secret, provided no secret document was attached to it. Plain to see that the National Security Agency had thought long and hard about the mad logic of secrecy.

Sole tossed the document back across the desk to Tom Zwingler.

Initially, while he cooled his heels in the National Cryptological Command, he had fretted about Vidya. Latterly, the possible impact of the arrival of these aliens had begun to preoccupy him, generating a mood of semi-euphoric pessimism.

"So you're orbiting them entirely over oceans?"

"Well—that orbit passes over a lot of shipping and right over Iceland's capital, but otherwise we're in the clear. The Soviets are announcing the launching of an expanding balloon reflector on that orbit. We'll confirm the announcement."

"Tom, you've got to be joking. How many people know already? And how many more will make educated guesses?"

"By the latest count the number in the know is pushing nine hundred fifty. That's not so huge, considering. It is an unbelievable kind of a secret, after all."

Sole glanced out of the window at the twilit woods outside. These insulated the buildings from the outside world like another Haddon Unit. Only, this place was so much vaster, so much more technologically hip, so much more secure.

Getting through the security net into the NCC was more than a matter of fitting a couple of keys in a couple of doorways. Now Sole was wearing an identity tab with coded data conveying voice and retina prints as well as his photograph.

Zwingler grinned, catching some of the comparison Sole was making, from the look in his eyes.

"The most elaborate computer system in the world, Chris. Breaking codes and ciphers and inventing 'em, is kids' play here. We've some of the finest linguists and cryptanalysts and math wizards—"

"I'm flattered," smiled Sole.

"Ah well, one thing we do lack is any little aliens running round in our basement..."

Zwingler meditated a while, then said thoughtfully:

"It's always been a way-out possibility, this. Statistically, so many solar systems have to exist out there. If only it could have put off happening for another century! Still, if we can keep it under wraps—"

"What makes you think we would be any better prepared next century? The most you could hope for by then would be a small base on the Moon. A few landings on Mars. Maybe on one of Jupiter's moons. There's no essential difference between that, and the state we're at now—compared with say a century ago. Now seems as good a time as any to sail in here playing our TV shows back at us. Letting Caliban see his features in the mirror. It's just our particular sickness that we worry about it. How would the Elizabethans have handled it? Probably written epic poems or magnificent new King Lears."

"I resent it, Chris. I feel like an atheist confronted by the Second Coming in the grand style—angels blowing silver trumpets in the sky."

"Yes, but you aren't a disbeliever in that respect. You just said yourself there must be so many other solar systems out there."

"I still resent it."

Sole listened to the noise of the building. The muted clatter of a printout. Footfalls. The flatulent bubbling of the water cooler.

"How are you going to stop them flying down to Nevada via Los Angeles, just to take a look at a city? Give all the saucer spotters a field day—"

"Oh, Sherman made it pretty plain which way we want them coming in—a DEW line approach. They'll see some of the other equipment in orbit—realize what a lot of nuclear tripwires there are in our skies..."

"So we're the big boys still," smirked Sole acidly. "Honour restored?"

"That's as may be," the other said didactically. "But we can't afford any loss of cultural confidence, can we? The world's in a pretty volatile state nowadays."

The phone burbled softly and Zwingler spoke into it briefly.

"Our plane's waiting, Chris. Orbiting should start about four hours from now. Leapfrog has just leapt off—NASA didn't want our frog in a transpolar orbit. Transfer to the Skylab Shuttle system's a bit awkward from that angle. Oh, and they tell me the Russians are flying to Nevada in their SST. The Concordski thing."

"That's bound to attract attention."

"No, it shouldn't. Nevada is mostly desert and mountains. We're not asking these aliens to land in Las Vegas you know." He smiled dubiously. "Howard Hughes wouldn't have liked it."

Sitting on the plane flying West, Sole listened in on the seat earphones to the different stations whose airspace they were passing through. WBNS, Columbus Ohio. WXCL, Peoria Illinois. KWKY, Des Moines Iowa. KMMJ, Grand Island Nebraska.

Station KMMJ was playing some oldies from West Coast acidrock bands.

The Jefferson Airplane sang:

'Hijack the Starship!
They'll be building it up in the air ever since 1980
People with a clever plan can assume the role of the
    Mighty
Hi-jack the Starship!
And our babes'll wander naked thru the Cities of the
    Universe—'

The album was called *Blows Against the Empire*.

And yet, thought Sole, the Empire still stands strong. Intercepting the first real starship. Orbiting it over oceans where none of the people, except a few frostbitten Icelanders and sailors on the high seas can see it. Flooding the Amazon. Funding through dummy foundations neuro-therapy units in other lands.

He glanced at Zwingler. The American was sleeping like a prim babe in his seat. Wasn't it a fact that all those who were in the know wanted to get this embarrassing alien business cleared out of the way as quickly and clinically as possible, so that they could get back to their own obsessions again—whether these happened to be the breaking of Chinese codes, the flooding of Brazil ... or the rearing of Indo-Pak refugee children to speak alien languages?

Zwingler was right. The visitation was as idiotic and annoying as a bout of flu—but maybe as potentially lethal as a dose of flu had been to isolated tribes in the South Pacific.

So the aliens had invited the Leapfrog crew into a cage of glass—and now this plane was heading for a man-made cage of sand hidden in Nevada. Which raised the question: who was quarantining who?

On Station KMMJ the Jefferson Airplane sang:

> 'In nineteen hundred and seventy five
> All the people rose from the countryside
> To move against you government man
> D'you understand?'

Sorry, Jefferson Airplane, murmured Sole, it's later than that already, and the Empire still stands firm.

Bored with the radio sounds, but unable to sleep, Sole hunted through his pockets till he found Pierre's letter. Idly, he recommenced reading it.

'... Their Bruxo is practising with amazing skill that deep embedding of language—that Rousselian embedding which we talked about so long ago in Africa as the most freakish of possibilities.

'To do this, he makes use of some psychedelic drug. I haven't yet pinned down the origin of it. Every night he chants the complex myths of the tribe—and the structure of these myths is reflected directly in the structure of the embedded language, which the drug enables him to understand.

'This embedded speech keeps the soul of the tribe, their myths, secret. But it also permits the Xemahoa to participate in their myth life *as a direct experience* during the dance chant. The daily vernacular (Xemahoa A) passes through an extremely sophisticated recoding process, which breaks down the linear features of normal language and returns the Xemahoa people to the space-time unity which we other human beings have blinded ourselves to. For our languages all set a barrier —a great filter—up for us between Reality and our Idea of Reality.

'In some ways Xemahoa B is the *truest* language I have ever come across. In other respects, of course—for all practical purposes of daily life—it directs crippling blows at our straightforward logical vision of the world. It is a lunatic language, like Roussel's, only worse. The unaided mind has no hope of holding on to it. But in their hallucinations these Indians have found the vital elixir of understanding!'

And now Sole sat up and really took notice. Reaching overhead, he directed the cool-air nozzle on to his face to sharpen his attention. He felt a surge of excitement—of dark doorways opening—as though it was the whole outside world he was breathing through the lungs of the plane, as he read on:

'. . . The old Bruxo snorts this drug through a cane tube into his bleeding, rotting nostrils—and he aims for no less than a total statement of Reality uttered in the eternal present of the drug trance. And by achieving a total statement of reality, to be able to control and manipulate that reality. The age-old dream of the wizard!

'But what wizard has set himself up against such dragons? The whole weight of American imperialist technology. The Brazilian military dictatorship. Imposing their will on this jungle from afar, while the Indians within it are trapped as casually as flies are trapped on a fly-strip, whilst the making of the meal goes on—the great feasting of the giants on the Amazon's wealth: the meal of spectacular consumption.

'The Bruxo is killing himself in the process. No shaman has ever dared stay high on this drug so long before—except for some myth figure, the world-creating culture hero Xemahawo, who vanished on the day of creation of the world, dissolving into the environment like a flock of birds scattering in the forest.

'For the Bruxo and for the Xemahoa, knowledge isn't an abstract thing, but something coded in terms of the birds and beasts, and rocks and plants, of the jungle—in terms of the clouds and stars above the jungle—in terms of the concrete actuality of the world. Therefore total description of this knowledge is no abstract thing—but a taking-hold of the actual reality about them. And to take hold of reality is to control it—to manipulate it. So he hopes!

'Soon, he will hold a giant embedded statement of all the coded myths of the tribe in his present consciousness. Day by day, in the drug dance, he adds more material to this statement of a totality of meaning—all the while maintaining his awareness of past days and past material as something ever-present by means of the maka-i drug—despite the terrible overload on brain and body.

'Soon, he may achieve total consciousness of Being.

Soon, the total scheme underlying symbolic thought may be clear to him.

'If this is true? That would be incredible indeed. In such a place! Such a "primitive" backwater!

'Incredible—and damnable. For just as this occurs, the genius-fly is about to be drowned, poxed out, poisoned—on that orange fly-strip of a dam! If only some of its poison might fall into the gluttonous feast of the exploiters...

'I take the opportunity of sending this cry of rage out by way of a halfcaste who is passing through. He should reach that bloody dam in about a week, and get the letter posted. He's cagey about why he's making the journey. Maybe he's found some diamonds—who knows? After all, this *mess* is supposed to contain El Dorado!

'I at least suspect I've found my own El Dorado of the human mind here—at the moment it is due to be swept away.

'They embed the Amazon in a sea you can see from the Moon—and drown the human mind in the process.

'To yourself and Eileen, my useless love.
             —Pierre Darriand.'

On the way over Utah, Station KSL announced the launch of the spectacular new Russian transpolar satellite.

"—Reports say it's brighter than the planet Venus. Only, you folks won't be able to see it unless you're an eskimo or a headhunter in the South Seas. Other news at this late-night news hour. NASA has quashed speculation that this week's launch from Cape Kennedy to Skylab Orbiting Laboratory carried a Russian scientist on board—"

Zwingler had woken up by now and was listening intently on his own seat's earphones.

"You hear that, Chris? The Globe's in the right orbit—"

Sole had been half-attending to the news, the rest of his mind still on that other amazing news contained in the letter, and the irritating suspicion that Pierre had pipped him at the post again—first his wife, now his work ...

"Apparently folks are 'speculating'," he sneered.

Zwingler laughed.

"Phooey. That's no sweat, Chris. A little bit of speculating? I tell you, the thing's going okay."

EIGHT

THE DAY AFTER he snorted the fungus powder and finally met maka-i, Pierre left the Xemahoa village, filled with a consciousness of what he must do that was as urgent as it was ill-defined.

Kayapi went along with him—he flourished no knives this time, made no threats. All the Indian said was:

"Pee-áir, we got to be back before maka-i is born, okay?"

Pierre nodded absently. He was still caught up in the experience. It was like the first sex experience, but a first sex experience of the whole consciousness. Overwhelmingly so—to the point of ecstasy and terror. He could concentrate on little else.

He had to rely on Kayapi to locate the dugout they'd arrived in. To empty out the rain slops. Clean the outboard. Pile Pierre's things under some plastic sheeting.

Kayapi assisted without any complaints. He seemed to appreciate this irrational purpose that was urging Pierre to make the journey north to the dam.

He navigated the dugout, while Pierre stared out through the rain into the flooded maze of trees.

The bunches of epiphytic and parasitic plants crowding the terraces of the branches triggered a memory of a city far away—and highrise flats that he vaguely remembered being crowded with people all facing north during some disaster—a planecrash or a fire. Where had it been? Paris? London? Or was it just an image from a movie, that had suddenly woken to life? Saüba ants, driven off the forest floor, made tracks along low branches with leaf segments held over their bodies like columns of refugees protecting themselves with parasols. Macaws fired tracer messages of feather-numbers through the high leaves—numbers that he couldn't count.

When the pium flies descended on them in bloodsucking, stinging clouds, Kayapi rummaged through Pierre's things till he found a tube of insect repellent to smear on the Frenchman's skin, so that his flesh wouldn't swell up with the dropsy these flies left as their calling card.

At midday, it was Kayapi who pressed dried fish into Pierre's hand and urged him to eat.

Pierre stared for hours into the dull green chaos of the forest that periodically came aflame with birds and butterflies and blooms.

There was chaos there, to a foreigner's eyes—but there was no chaos in his mind.

There was a dawn of understanding.

Or rather, it was a *memory* of the dawn of understanding—which he struggled to hold on to.

His nostrils itched with the memory of maka-i, as though they'd been bitten raw by pium flies.

The day seemed endlessly, timelessly, long, like a long track rising over bleak, lonely mountains from the valley of the previous night, which a mist drifted up from now, to veil—yet without there being any clear line of demarcation between the two zones. He must have emerged from the experience at some particular time, he reasoned. Yet the boundary wasn't definable. The greater could not be bounded by the lesser. The perception of last night could not be imprisoned in terms of today's perception, when it was a vaster, more devastating mode of perception. Thus its bounds could not be set. How could a two-dimensional being who had been able to experience three dimensions set up a frontier post anywhere in his flat territory—and say beyond this point lies the Other? For the Other would be everywhere—and nowhere, to him. And as for clock-time, Pierre had let his watch run down and wore it only as a bracelet now. Time seemed like a useless ornament—a distraction. The sense of time he'd possessed the night before hadn't been time by the calendar or time by the clock. It hadn't been historic time, but a sense of the spatio-temporal unity out of which space and time are normally separated into an illusory contrast with one another.

In this three-dimensional flatland of ours, words flow forward and only hang fire of their meaning so pitiably short a time, while memories flow hindwards with such a pitiably feeble capacity to hold themselves in full present awareness. Our illusion of the present is like a single dot on a graph we can never get to see the whole of. It is a pingpong ball dancing on a jet of water, unaware of the jet. The jagged inkdrip of a thought recorded by the electroencephalograph pen.

Last night he had understood Roussel's poem easily, effortlessly, and entirely. He held its embeddings in the forefront of his head. Held and held and continued to hold, while subprogramme after subprogramme started in, deferred to the next subprogramme, and sub-deferred again—and everything fitted together. Visual images of the embedded poem flowed within one another, all held together in a wheeling zodiac that spun round the deepest self-embedded axis in his mind.

Yet there had been terrible danger. He still sweated at the thought of it.

He had tamed the poem—and therefore the experience—only because he knew it so well already in its separate parts. Just as the Xemahoa already knew the separate elements of their coded myths, from childhood.

Throughout the Xemahoa chant-song, that many-part fugue of the Xemahoa B language, he felt his mind was splitting, flying apart, fluttering to pieces. He had feared the birds were all flying out of his head and near to losing their way in endless jungle.

It was Kayapi who netted his birds and herded them together. Kayapi saw what was happening to him and dragged him by the hand to the tape recorder, switched the poem on.

Kayapi knew the track of his lost flock of words.

Now—with the same competence—he piloted Pierre through the drowning jungle where ants fled like refugees, and wild pigs splashed and grunted, where butterflies made clouds of colour, and pium flies descended in searing fogs, while the snouts of caymans nuzzled the waves of their wake.

All these creatures were the tools of Xemahoa thinking. Today, the jungle seemed to be one vast beating brain.

Destroy these tools, and you would destroy the Xemahoa. For then they could not think anymore. They would become Caraiba, foreigners, to themselves.

Through the afternoon the fugue of thoughts faded in Pierre's head, as he stared at the wet trees. By nightfall, the rainclouds had moved away from moon and stars. The dugout continued on its way through broader and broader channels by moonlight. It passed over flooded acres, through lagoons bristling with drowning vegetation. Pierre knew he would have got the outboard propeller tangled before many miles were up. But Kayapi piloted them through effortlessly and untiringly, sensing the right channels with a dexterity that shamed the Frenchman. Yet, for Kayapi, wasn't it his own drowning mind that he was navigating?

Finally, hours after nightfall, the Indian did get tired. Abruptly he beached the dugout on an isle of rotten logs, stretched himself out and slept.

Pierre also fell asleep eventually; yet slept more fitfully, haunted by dying images of the embedding dance. In his dream birdfeathers formed into a giant roulette wheel. He rolled round this, his body bunched up into a ball, until the circle of numbered feathers flew apart, took wing in all directions, and lost themselves in the greater wheel of the zodiac of stars—shocked out of interstellar darkness into sunlight only by the dawn booming of a band of howler monkeys migrating through trees across the lagoon.

Kayapi immediately sat up, grinned, and set the boat on course again before producing some more dry piraracu and some pulp cakes.

"Kayapi—"

"Pee-áir?"

"When we get there—"

"Yes, Pee-áir?"

"When we reach the dam—"

But what? *What!* He didn't know!

"Kayapi, how soon is maka-i to be born?"

"When we get back."

"Tell me what tree maka-i lives with in the jungle?"

"The tree called xe-wo-i."

"What's that in Portuguese?"

"The Caraiba have no word."

"Can you point one out to me?"

"Here? No. I said, Pee-áir, there are *kai-kai* places only." He flourished the fingers of one hand.

"Can't you describe the tree?"

He shrugged.

"It's small. Has a rough skin like the cayman. You remember eating some soil? The tree was just beside there."

"What? But I didn't see any fungus there."

"Maka-i was asleep. When the waters come and go, he wakes."

"Oh, I see—the fungus only grows after the ground's been covered with water. Is that right?"

Kayapi nodded.

Why hadn't he thought of taking a sample of the soil that day to run a chemical analysis on, instead of just eating it! Why hadn't Kayapi told him then that that's where maka-i grew! Instead of just asking him to eat some earth without explaining. But of course the Indian couldn't have conceived of taking a soil sample to a laboratory. His body was his own laboratory.

Now that Pierre saw the soil-eating incident in perspective, it all seemed like part of a carefully scripted initiation course. Maybe eating the soil had been some sort of necessary biochemical preparation, before the fungus drug could act on him?

The intricacy of the links that held the mental and social life of these people together! Links between tree and soil and fungus; shit and sperm and laughter. Between floodwater and language, myth and incest. Where was the boundary between reality and myth? Between ecology and metaphor? Which elements could safely be left out of the picture? The eating of a handful of soil? The spilling of sperm on the soil? The counting by significant feathers (in whatever way these were 'significant')? The tree that the maka-i grew on?

The scientific answer was to take soil samples and specimens of the fungus, and blood samples from the Xemahoa. To analyse, to synthesize, ultimately to market the results in a neat round pill. Twenty-five milligrams of 'X'. What would they call the drug? 'Embedol' or some such name! First the scientific journals, then the dope market.

Undoubtedly some measurable biochemical change took place within the brain—in its ability to process information, to hold vastly greater amounts before the attention than usual. Might it not even be possible that maka-i actually did convey power over Nature—power to intervene and change the world? For what was nature, what was the whole physical world, except information chemically and physically coded—and he who held access to the information symbols in their totality held direct access to reality, held the magician's legendary powers in his grasp. Even this did not seem totally impossible to Pierre, in the aftermath of his experience—though Logic and Reason fought against this fantastic dream.

At the very least the Xemahoa had a marketable 'high' to set beside mescaline and psilocybin and LSD. Their high was more specific in its function than those other psychedelic drugs. Still, it could be made into another commodity for purchase by the freaked-out pissed-off playboys of the Western World!

Twenty-five milligrams of maka-i. Of embedol. With all its messy appurtenances lopped off. The eating of soil. The rotting of the nostrils. It would be one hell of a commodity.

Yet for the Indians it was that very complex of physical and metaphorical events—the soil and sperm and shit and bloody nostrils—that made up life and meaning and existence.

In the tin refugee camp beyond the orange fly-paper set up to trap them they would be shadows, not substances. Shadows whispering bastard Caraiba words as they faded. The birds would have flown out of their heads over a featureless waste of water with no way home . . .

When Kayapi and he got to the dam, he must—
What? *What!*

The sun shone again for a while. They passed through clouds of butterflies. Through swarms of flies.

At midday they chewed more of the dry fish and pulp cake. More rain clouds started massing overhead and soon began trailing a grey curtain of water through the drowning forest.

The problem of what he would *do* when he got to the dam was snatched from his hands in late afternoon.

Their dugout was passing through rainmists between steelwoods, mahoganies and rubber trees—grist to the future timber dredges—when a flat-bottom boat with a powerful outboard came abreast of the dugout. Two men and one woman were sitting in it. Pierre found himself staring at the muzzle of a submachinegun . . .

"Put your boat over there under cover," the woman ordered. Her eyes burned into them distrustfully and feverishly. Beneath the smeared dirt and fly bites puffing her flesh she was maybe young and beautiful. Her companions looked tired and on edge, in their dirty grey slacks and shirts. They had a fervent hunted look about them.

So, perhaps, did Pierre.

Both boats were soon guided under the foliage.

The woman tossed her head fretfully.

"Who are you? What are you doing here? Looking for wealth? Prospector?"

"No, senhora. But I'm in a hurry. I've something to do."

"You're American?" Her eyes hardened. "Your accent sounds strange. You have something to do with the dam?"

Pierre laughed bitterly.

"Something to do with the dam? Oh that's a joke! Yes, I should indeed like to do something with the dam. Blow it sky-high, to begin with!"

The thin feverish woman watched him contemptuously.

"I suppose you mean to do that with your bare hands."

"He's some crazy priest, Iza," one of her companions said.

"I'm no bloody parasite priest—nor prospector—nor a policeman either!"

These people didn't look anything like those in the Amazon area who might predictably be armed the way they were. Nothing like the private thugs or prospectors or adventurers. Nor anything like the paramilitary types whom the helicopter had brought to the village. Suddenly, Pierre realized who they might be—and who the men in that helicopter had been searching for. Yet it seemed incredible, so deep in this wet chaos of the Amazon.

"Why do you say policeman? You think we are police?"
Pierre laughed.

"No, my friends. It's clear what you are. A helicopter landed in the village I was in some days ago. Armed men searched it. They were looking for you. You're guerrillas. That's obvious to me. You look like the hunted, not the hunters! They had an easy insolence about them. Particularly their officer. Though they were cowards, too."

"Paixao..." muttered one of the men, nervously.

"And what did you tell this officer?"

"I told him nothing. I hid in the jungle. Or rather this Indian here pushed me into the jungle to hide me. I thought it was the priests coming back with their nonsense about saving the Indians. Maybe they thought a helicopter would make an impressive Noah's Ark! You realize the dam is responsible for all this flooding?"

Pierre got a sarcastic look in reply.

"Joam, search him and the boat."

As the man called Joam made a move to step into their dugout Pierre noticed Kayapi furtively sliding a hand for his knife; and caught his wrist.

"All right Kayapi—they're friends."

He told Joam:

"You'll find I'm a Frenchman. A social anthropologist. I'm studying the Indians they are about to destroy so blindly with their dam."

Joam pulled the plastic sheeting aside and rummaged through the dried food, medicines, clothing, pulling out the bag containing Pierre's carbine and tape recorder and his papers.

The dance-chant of the Xemahoa rang out abruptly among the branches, as he touched the playback switch. The other man and the woman hadn't seen what he was going to do. They brought their guns up.

"Good machine," Joam grunted, flipping it off.

From the bag he took Pierre's passport, field notes, and diary.

He handed the passport over to Iza. She read through it carefully.

"So you only entered Brazil a few months ago—but you speak excellent Portuguese. Where did you learn it, Portugal?"

"No, Mozambique."

"There's no visa for Mozambique."

"There's a visa for Tanzania. I went over the border into the free zone with your comrades in arms, the Frelimo guerrillas."

"So you say," muttered the woman, doubtfully. "It may be true. We'll find out."

Meanwhile Joam flipped through the pages of Pierre's notes and diary, reading random passages.

Pierre leaned towards him, urgently.

"These notes are written about a people who are going to be destroyed. Who know it. Who fight back in the only way they can. In terms of their own culture."

"There are other ways of fighting," snapped Iza.

"Precisely!" sighed Pierre. "There is the way that you and I can fight. There is the political fight. But for these Indians to adopt a political stance would be meaningless. Ah, it was so different in Africa with the Makonde people!"

"Come along then, Monsieur—tell us about Mozambique and Frelimo. In detail."

Pierre smiled wryly.

"To establish an alibi for myself?"

"You have nothing to fear if you're a man of good will."

So Pierre told about the Makonde people who straddle the frontier of Tanzania and Mozambique—of the independent African republic, and the colony which the government in Lisbon insisted year after year was an integral part of metropolitan Portugal, using, as powerful

116

arguments in their favour, Huey Cobra gunships, Fiat jet bombers, Agent Orange crop defoliants, and napalm raids. In the towns and cities posters of particoloured white soldiers holding particoloured black babies in their arms proclaimed 'WE ARE ALL PORTUGUESE'. Yet three-fifths of the land had been out of effective Portuguese control for a decade and more. Pierre told how he crossed the river Ruvuma by dugout into Cabo Delgado province on what was by now a guerrilla milkrun, so far from Portuguese control was this free zone of villages and dispensaries and schools. It was guarded by Chinese ground-to-air missiles that made low-level helicopter sorties or jet attacks virtually impossible. The main danger came from high-level bombing raids—spasmodic, meaningless raids that blasted holes in the wild bush and occasionally filled the dispensaries up with broken bodies and the bomas with gutted bellowing cattle. Pierre told them, joyfully, of attacks on the Cabora Bassa dam on the Zambezi which had delayed that project of exploitation for so many years, upping the ante intolerably for that tiny peasant empire Portugal. Told them how he had gone on one such raid.

Finally, they believed Pierre and relaxed and handed his papers and even his carbine back to him.

"Your Indian friend did you a good turn, Monsieur," Iza said. "That Captain you saw may have been Flores Paixao. That one is a vicious swine—well-trained by the Americans in counter-insurgency techniques. A torturer. A professional sadistic beast. Keep out of his way."

"Does the fact that you're here mean you are strong enough to carry the struggle into the whole of Brazil?" Pierre asked her eagerly.

"The whole of Brazil!" Iza echoed his words, sounding sick and sad. "Who can deal with the whole of Brazil? Don't be foolish. All that our puppet government can do to govern this Amazon is to flood the whole area, so that the problem disappears! We are here to destroy such an illusion. Our government has mortgaged the whole Amazon basin to America. Built roads for Bethlehem Steel and King Ranch of Texas. These 'Great Lakes' will split our country in two parts. One part, an American colony looted of its minerals to maintain U.S. technology. The other, a Vichy-style régime for us Brazilians—the passive consumer market."

Pierre thought sadly: these people are as near to the end of their tether as I am myself. Yet their enemy is my enemy.

"We shall let the world know what real Brazilians think of this 'civilizing' venture!" Iza cried passionately. "The tricks are endless. To impoverish us. Drain our resources. Stop us from using our own wealth ourselves. North America needs it desperately. Such are the ironies of so-called aid that in fact Latin America is aiding North America to the tune of hundreds of millions of dollars annually! The cash flow is always one way. North! These Amazon dams are the greatest conspiracy and perversion yet. So we strike at them."

She fell silent, sick and tired. Her energy supply snapped abruptly. Her eyes burnt with fever—not the fever of a sickness, but a terrible exhaustion, mixed up with a fervent despair.

"I know," said Pierre gently. "The dam has to be destroyed. It is destroying ... wonders, in the jungle here. Wonderful people. Washing them away into the concentration camps of priests. Their language is ... a wonderful cultural discovery for me. I'm sorry, this might seem like a minor problem to you people. But I assure you it isn't. And yet—I'm torn two different ways, meeting you."

"Why were you going North?"

Pierre shivered.

"I don't know rightly. I had no fixed idea. It frightens me, now I've met you, my aimlessness. My instinctiveness. This obsessed journey. Talking to you reminds me of such a different world—one that means nothing here among the Indians. I feel with you, I think with you. But what can be done? Can the dam be destroyed so easily? Surely it must take lorry loads of explosive to destroy such a thing?"

"There'll be explosives there," Iza promised. "And the flood pressure will assist us. We shall also kill the American engineers and their lackeys."

"Other dams will be under attack too," the second man —Raimundo—added hotly. "Even at Santarém itself. Whatever happens, the lie of this Amazon development will be shown up before the whole world."

"What sort of weapons have you got?"

Iza hesitated.

"You think of this as suicide in your hearts, don't you?" Pierre asked flatly.

Joam shrugged.

"The terrain is not so favourable."

"These attacks are tactically vital!" Iza burned with an end of the tether passion that broke through the crust of her weariness every time that the obsessive pressures built up in her afresh. "We have to make our presence known, in a shocking and symbolic way. Back in the early days of our struggle Carlos Marighella wrote that there was no timetable for us and no deadlines to meet. But the situation has changed. This yanqui scheme for the Amazon is a monstrous distraction from reality. A fire extinguisher that may quench the realities of revolution for years! The Amazon is the pressure point of imperialism, today. It is our job to panic the Americans. Here where they believe themselves safely protected by their flood. Hidden away from the violence of the cities and the coast."

Kayapi had been sitting idly all this time. Now Pierre turned to him.

"Kayapi?"

"Yes, Pee-áir."

"These people are going to attack the dam. Shall we go along with them?" he asked in Portuguese.

"If *they* go, no need for you to go yourself," replied Kayapi in Xemahoa. "They are your shadows. You, the substance. Maka-i is being born soon. You must be present. These men will work for you."

"Why is the opinion of this Indian so important?" demanded Joam angrily. "Is this savage to decide what you do, for you?"

Pierre stared at Joam in revulsion. 'This savage!' Pierre could have wept—to swell the flood.

"I'm sorry," Joam apologized. "Naturally Socialism is for all. What I mean is, the Indian isn't yet qualified to decide."

You pay your money and you take your choice. Of Marx or Christ. What did the choice matter to the Xemahoa! Whichever gained control over them, they would be destroyed. The birds of their thoughts scattered. Trapped with birdlime in tin huts.

"I'll wish you luck," said Pierre, making up his mind abruptly, arriving at the impossible choice. "I love you as comrades, as deeply as I hate the dam. I want you to destroy it. So much. I want you to empty out that yanqui fire extinguisher."

"Besides," interrupted Kayapi, "you never hit anything with your gun, Pee-áir. You are the listener and learner, not the warrior. Bruxo knows. Why do you think he let you meet maka-i the other night? Why do you think the girl comes to your hammock? Why do you think I show you how to eat the earth? Your box-that-speaks is your weapon, Pee-áir, not the gun. I do not say you lack courage. You met maka-i. But you are a different man. Your life has a different shape. Consider wisely. Do not let the birds of your thought fly the wrong way."

'You let me come this far towards the dam, Kayapi!'

"Your birds had to fly this way. Now they need to return. These people will do your work."

"Why do you talk two different languages to each other?" demanded Iza. "He understands your Portuguese perfectly well. Can't he reply in Portuguese?"

"It's important that he speaks in his native language. A great thing is happening in the minds of the tribe. He wishes to belong."

Kayapi looked sullen.

"Maka-i will be born, Pee-áir. Hurry up."

"You said there was time!"

"I was wrong. There's no time. It happens soon."

"He says we have to go back," Pierre told the guerrillas. The woman gazed disbelievingly at Pierre.

"Why?"

Pierre chose his words carefully.

"What is happening in his village is very important, as a human event. If I'm not present to see what happens, something amazing might be lost. I can't risk it. Not just on my own account. But, well—for Man."

"How can you say so, when you have been with Frelimo and seen what they do for Mankind?"

"This tears me apart. Half of me wants to go on with you. Half has to return. I need to be two people at once."

"An amoeba," Raimundo sneered. "A shapeless amoeba wants to split in half."

"When you meet maka-i," Kayapi whispered, "you are two men, three men, many men. Your mind is great with words. You speak the full language of man." But was Kayapi his evil genius or true guide?

"Dear people. Comrades. Iza, Joam, Raimundo. I'm going back with him to the village."

"What made your mind up?" Raimundo jibed. "The sight of guns? The reality of a point-four-five INA submachinegun? The thought of it going bang bang? You despicable bourgeois intellectual. No doubt Ford or Rockefeller is paying you to visit this jungle to dredge up this mystification. Who knows who is paying?"

"Shadow and substance, Pee-áir," hissed Kayapi. "Is it not strange to meet your shadows in the jungle? They meet you to show you how they will go on for you. Do you imagine it is an accident we meet them?"

"I'll do what you say, Kayapi. You've been right before. In my own terms, it's wrong. But they can't be my terms if I'm to understand Xemahoa. If I'm wrong then I shall let everyone know it. I promise."

"Fair promises," snapped the woman. "We've wasted time and energy on you. I suppose we should shoot you both, for security. But we're not going to. You can have the opportunity to feel like a worm. Perhaps then you may keep your promise! Such as it is. I guess that is public relations if not exactly revolution. Fuck off then, French-man."

Pierre and Kayapi set off southwards again through the flooded creeks and lagoons. To Pierre's eyes the water already seemed centimetres higher than on their journey north, and it still rained.

As evening fell, Pierre finally asked the Indian.

"Which of the Xemahoa was your father, Kayapi? Is he still alive?"

"Can't you guess that, Pee-áir?"

"The Bruxo?"

Kayapi nodded.

"He visited my mother's village. They said they wanted to honour him because of his power and his knowledge. Wanted to steal some of it maybe. But my father was cunning. He insisted on a bleeding girl. The same as for you, Pee-áir. So that there will be no baby from him, and the Xemahoa can stay together. But something happened anyway, he was so powerful a man. The girl made a baby. I am his halfson. It is my grief—and my glory.

You know about being half, Pee-áir. Half of you went north with those men."

"True, Kayapi."

Kayapi abruptly swung the dugout towards the bank, drove it deep into the branches, killed the engine . . .

"You hear?"

Pierre strained against the rainfall of water on leaves. At last he caught the deepening beat of a motor. Kayapi was pointing upwards through the branches at the sky.

Some minutes later, a helicopter passed through the rainmist, following the line of the watercourse—a dark ugly whale lumbering through the wet air.

It shone a spotlight on the waters below. Kayapi pressed Pierre down into the bottom of the dugout, so that his white face and arms wouldn't show.

NINE

THE JET BEGAN its landing approach over mountains which moonlight cut out harsh and rutted with shadows. These rapidly dipped into foothills as the plane fell keeping pace with the falling ground. Hard to be sure they were descending except for the gut sense of changing inertia. Then the jet touched and was rolling along a level barren valley between landing lights towards a bright-lit cluster of buildings. A droop-nosed SST with cyrillic letters on its side dwarfed the other jets parked there.

Despite the presence of these brightly lit buildings and jets, the whole area struck Sole as empty and meaningless. These artefacts existed in a limbo like a flat concrete zone hidden away in the subconscious of a catatonic. They represented wealth, surely. Investment. Expertise. But investment in nothing; expertise for no apparent motive; a bankrupt wealth. This meeting place between Man and Alien might have been set down prepacked in this desert valley, clipped off the back of a cereal carton.

An armed military policeman in a white helmet met them outside the terminal, checked their names off a clipboard and waved them upstairs.

Here they found forty or fifty people gathered in a long room, one wall of which was glass, giving a view of the airstrip illuminated by its landing lights and the dark moon-silhouetted hills.

The crowd formed local eddies of three or four people each. Zwingler acknowledged a few nods, but made no move to join any of the sub-groups. He stood with Sole looking out at the night while the last few arrivals filtered into the room. Sole heard Russian voices as well as American. After ten minutes the soldier stepped inside and flashed a brief, subdued salute at a man in his late forties with short-cropped wiry black hair highlighted by a few grey strands, lending him a certain maestro-like presence.

"They're all here now, Dr Sciavoni—"

Sciavoni looked as though he could be holding a conductor's baton—he had something of the poise and personal electricity. But maybe not for a symphony orchestra, maybe for a night club band. Sciavoni wasn't quite impressive enough for the occasion he was now called upon to supervise.

He had a habit of opening his eyes imperceptibly while he was speaking to someone. The extra white made the eyes seem to gleam from his sallow face with an inner light. But it was a mechanical trick rather than real charisma.

Sciavoni cleared his throat and made a speech of welcome.

"Gentlemen. Ladies too, I'm pleased to see. First off, let me say how delighted I am to welcome you to the State of Nevada. And to the USA, for those of you whose first visit this is—" He smiled engagingly at the Russians in their heavy tweed suits.

Tomaso Sciavoni, who'd been put in charge of the reception team, worked for NASA. Sole's attention wandered as 'the conductor' talked on about the communication and data-processing facilities available at the airstrip —facilities of no-place they seemed, servomechanisms of the void in Man. He found Sciavoni's slightly theatrical gestures and occasional gleams of the eyes as meaningless, after a while, as this whole house of cards erected in the desert. Apparently the place had something to do with the Atomic Energy Commission—but all trace of alternative function had been carefully erased. A quiet fantasy developed in his mind of white-helmeted soldiers walking round the desert with giant gum erasers, rubbing out a face here, and a building there, and a jet plane somewhere else—and pencilling in alibi men and alibi machinery. When the alien spacecraft landed, did they hope a giant eraser would descend from the sky and remove it conveniently too?

Sciavoni broke off talking about protocol and personalities and cocked his head, as news came through the plug in his ear.

"Tracking reports a separation," he announced. "Right now the Globe is heading up over the East Siberian Sea. A smaller vehicle is veering away, swinging sharply towards North America. Altitude is falling rapidly. It's at eight hundred nautical miles now. Velocity is down from an initial ten thousand to nine thousand five and falling—"

Sciavoni carried on a running commentary as the smaller vehicle dropped swiftly across the roof of the world. Above the Arctic ice. Over the Beaufort Sea. Mackenzie Bay. The Yukon. Then along the chain of the Rocky Mountains, till over Western Montana it began sharply decelerating and losing height.

"We've got visual acquisition now. The vehicle's a blunt cylinder shape about a hundred metres long by thirty. There's no indication of the means of propulsion. It's crossing the Idaho stateline now at an altitude of eighty nautical miles. Velocity down to three thousand—"

"I'll tell you one thing, Chris," hissed Zwingler. "We'd give our eyeteeth to be able to handle re-entry the way they're doing now. I hate to think of the energy wastage—"

"They're across the Nevada stateline now. Altitude ten nautical miles. Velocity one thousand. Commencing rapid descent—"

"What are we all standing about inside for anyway?"

Sole turned away from the throng that were now pressing closer to the window, hesitated only briefly before heading downstairs.

The soldier stepped in his way to scrutinize his identity tab, then pushed the glass door open and followed him outside.

Sole gazed north.

Already a shape was visible. A rushing blob of darkness against the stars.

"Can't hear a sound. How's that thing keepin' in the air?" The soldier shivered.

"I hate to think. Antigravity? That's only a word. It doesn't mean anything."

"If there's a word, Mister, must mean somethin'—"

"No, there are a lot of words for things that don't exist. Imaginary things."

"Such as what?"

"Oh I dunno. God, maybe. Telepathy. The soul."

"I don't much care for that notion, Doctor What's-your-name. Place I come from, words *mean* things."

The squat dark cigar shape, without portholes or fins, hung briefly over the airstrip. No lights or jetglow visible. No engine noise audible.

Slowly and silently it slid down on to the concrete, a couple of hundred yards from where they stood. At the last moment before it grounded, Sole glanced up at the mass of faces pressed to the long window upstairs. They looked like kids staring into a sweetshop.

Then came the sound of people fighting their way downstairs, pushing and elbowing.

"How about some traffic duty, soldier?" said a familiar voice.

Zwingler darted a curious glance at Sole, while he dusted off his own suit and smoothed the creases out of it.

"Gentlemen! Ladies!" cried Sciavoni. "Let's not trip each other up. May I suggest we stick to protocol? The alien vehicle will be met by the agreed delegation of five, consisting of Dr Stepanov, Major Zaitsev, Mr Zwingler, myself and Dr Sole—"

Sole reacted with surprise.

"I didn't know about that, Tom, honest. When was that arranged? I can't have been concentrating."

Zwingler laughed eerily.

"Your subconscious must have propelled you down-stairs, in that case. You know, there was a time when I wondered why you, with your dubious attitudes, were in-volved in that speech project at Haddon. Not any more. You must have a helluva inbuilt pragmatism. Things just arrange themselves for you, without you paying attention."

"Bullshit, Tom."

Zwingler dealt him a mock blow in the back, pushing him forward.

"Do the Dr Livingstone bit for us. We didn't perform any too well in the opinion of the Russians. What was that Paulus Sherman said? Balls in their court? Balls to you, Doctor Sole—"

As the five men approached the dark cylinder, a circu-lar doorway opened up in the side and a ramp slid down to ground level. A cone of yellow light flooded the con-crete.

"Will you go up first, Dr Sole," requested Stepanov, the burly Russian scientist whose name Sole remembered reading in the Leapfrog Transcripts. "Both great powers need somebody to hate cordially—"

Yet, in the event, precedence was decided for them.

An eerily tall figure moved into the shining cone of light and came down casually to meet them.

It was half as tall again as a six foot man. Skinny and flat-nosed with great sad eyes set far apart and with ears like crinkly paper bags and a dark orange slash of a mouth—as the Leapfrog astronauts had reported. A simple transparent mask covered its mouth and nose. Thin scarlet wires ran from ears and mouth to a pack strapped on to its long thin chest. The figure wore a grey silky coverall and grey forked boots, like a Japanese workman's.

No air tanks. The face-mask would have to be a permeable filter membrane...

The being drifted down the ramp towards them, casual and faintly sad, looking a little like an El Greco saint, and a little like a starved Giacometti sculpture.

Sole couldn't think of anything momentous—or even unmomentous—to say.

So their visitor said it for them. He spoke neutral east coast American—a perfect copy of the accent of the speech tapes flown up by Leapfrog.

"Nice planet you have here. How many languages are spoken?"

Zwingler jabbed Sole in the back a second time, more viciously, near his kidneys.

"Why, thousands I suppose," stammered Sole. "If you count all of them. Dozens of major languages at least! We sent you tapes of English, that's the main international language. You've learnt remarkably fast! How did you do it?"

"By recording your television transmissions on the way in. But we needed a key. Which your astronauts gave us. So we saved time."

"Well ... shall we come on board your ship? Or go inside the building?"

(And the incredible thought drummed through Sole's skull, as insufficient as it was all-embracing: that this nine-foot-tall being is from the stars!—that those specks of white and blue and yellow up there have swollen up huge and filled the sky with alien light for it...)

"I prefer the building."

If this visitor could learn perfect English in three days from recorded TV and a hastily cobbled together teaching programme, what techniques they must have. And—

the more devastating thought—what minds.

"You can imprint a language directly into the brain, then?" Sole hazarded.

"Good guess—provided it conforms to..."

"...the rules of Universal Grammar! That's it, isn't it?"

"A very good guess. You are saving yourself information repayment. We shall not waste much time here—"

"You worry about wasting time?"

"True."

"Let's get on trading information then. We're all geared up."

"Trade it, yes—you have the correct formula."

"Good man," whispered Stepanov gruffly. "You have my confidence."

The people outside the terminal broke into a spontaneous round of applause as Sole led the tall visitor through them—almost as though it was some grand sporting achievement to be nine feet tall. Sole wondered whether the alien would recognize this banging together of hands for the primitive courtesy it was—look, our hands are otherwise occupied, no weapons in them.

"Careful of your head—"

The alien stooped to negotiate the door.

"Upstairs?" he enquired. And people gasped to hear him speak.

"Upstairs," Sole confirmed.

People seemed like a flock of tiny bridesmaids flooding upstairs behind them, tripping over the alien bride's train. But if Sole was a bridegroom, with all the anxieties of a virgin on the first night, how many marriages of species had this being already been involved in across the light years—and how many divorces, as quickly over and done with as the State of Nevada's own quickie divorces? That was the disconcerting question.

"He learnt English in the time since Leapfrog delivered

the speech tapes," Sole warned Sciavoni as they re-entered the momentarily deserted reception room. "Direct neural programming."

"Christ. I guess that's to our advantage though, communication-wise."

"Seems he's anxious not to waste time. Wants to trade information—"

"Fine. Stick with this thing, Chris." Sciavoni smelt strongly of some pine-scented shave lotion or deodorant, Sole noticed—and this smell got mixed up with the alien being in his mind for a while, creating a picture of a chemical forest of hydroponic tanks in that Globe in the sky.

Sciavoni turned to address the tall grey visitor, but hadn't a chance to say anything before the being spoke himself.

"I shall make a statement—for brevity's sake?"

"Why surely," smiled Sciavoni lavishly, staring up at that face a yard above him with its broad orange mouth —hunting for definable expressions.

Blunt teeth with no incisors, noted Sole. No meat tearing or ripping in their recent past—long evolved past their animal origins? Or eating a different kind of diet in any case the long butterfly tongue? In some respects they were primitive teeth, simply modified cartilage. Or else, devolved teeth—which suggested ages of evolution.

And the blunt flat nose—it was said that Man's nose would have flattened back into his features in another hundred thousand or million years, as the animal urgency of scent messages receded further and further . . .

Those flexible, sac-like ears, that might pick up far slighter signals than the human ear, yet adjust faster than a cat's eye to sudden alterations—a wide acoustic spectrum and considerable sophistication in processing sounds, evident there.

As the alien talked, the maroon butterfly tongue flickered over the blunt teeth.

"We call ourselves collectively the Sp'thra. You do not hear the ultra and infrasonic components of the word so I drop them. It means Signal Traders. Which is what we are—a people of linguists, sound mimics and communicators. We have individual names too—mine is Ph'theri. How did I learn your language so quickly? Besides being expert communicators in many modes, we use language machines. You use these here?" He addressed Sole.

"No ... though we're developing concepts—"

"Information may be traded about language machines, then. You wish to know where we come from? Two planets of an orange sun a little larger than your own, further along this same spiral arm inward towards the galaxy heart, but below the main mass of suns—"

"But you didn't come from that direction," a heavy Russian voice like dumplings in a greasy soup protested.

"True, we have been further out—we return inwards now. But our home star is in the direction I say—One One Zero Three away, using your light year units—"

Eleven hundred and three light years.

A moment of disbelief; then shock waves rippled through the room.

"Tell us how you travel so far!—how is it possible?" demanded the same oil and suet voice.

The reply flicked back across their heads like a full stop on a typesheet, a tight blackball.

"No—"

Sole scrutinized those alien features. What expressions did another of the Sp'thra read in them? What did those soundless flickerings of the tongue signify? The narrowing and subsequent bulging of the eyes? The faint colour shifts of the otherwise grey skin? Ph'theri's eyes possessed a double nictitating membrane that flickered across the bulge of the eyes from either side. Every time he blinked, the twin membranes met each other—a brief, transparent window that lagged an instant behind the reopening of

132

the eyelids, giving the eyes a kind of cloudy afterglow. Ph'theri blinked maybe once a minute to begin with, later more rapidly.

Sole also wondered how easy the visitor found it to read the ape signals of Homo Sapiens.

The refusal had triggered a spate of minor arguments in the room—about faster than light particles, and hibernation travel, holes in the fabric of space, and relativity—that grew noisier and more chaotic till abruptly Ph'theri held up his hands.

Bright orange patches the size of a large coin spotted each of his palms. The long thumb sprouting from the centre of his wrist bone and normally resting on the middle finger of three, was now twisted aside to display this orange patch.

A Russian woman physiologist fiddled with her own hand, manipulating it, trying to work out what sort of dexterity that isosceles arrangement of the hand might make possible.

The central thumb seemed exceptionally mobile. It arced across the orange blush on the palm and back again, in a pendulum or metronome action. Demonstrating impatience? Giving warning? As Ph'theri swung his thumbs to and fro, covering and uncovering the orange patches, Sole heard Zwingler gasp and saw him swing his own twin ruby moons into action, defensively.

Ph'theri's abrupt, absurd gestures had their effect: people stopped chattering and gaped at him.

"I must make one thing clear," the alien said loftily. "There are answerable questions, and non-answerable questions, at this stage. The formula for discussion is *trading* information. We owe you some free data, for the trading language you supplied us. Since we took the trouble to come to this planet, naturally we shall assess the trade value. Is this acceptable? If not, we mean to leave—"

Another babble, of astonished protests, began to grow.

But Sciavoni quickly nailed it dead.

"Careful," he cried. "What if he means it?"

"I quite agree," Stepanov thundered at his team. "We have to accept, of necessity—

"—at least, as a tactic," he growled sidelong at Sciavoni.

"Go ahead, Ph'theri," begged Sciavoni, signalling his orchestra to soft-pedal it. "Tell us any way you want to—"

"We Sp'thra are in a hurry," said the alien. "Because of our mode of travel. The technique is non-negotiable, understand. But I may say as courtesy information that, in general terms, it involves sailing the tides of space. There is a balance of energies as the spiral arms of the galaxy rub against one another. As their energy fields tense, slip and leap. Let me make a comparison. A planet has a hard surface over a soft core. The surface slides this way and that in sections. Consequently it has earthquakes. Likewise the arms of the galaxy rub against each other till they bleed energy. Till stars must explode. Or till they are forced to swallow themselves—to disappear to a point—"

"Collapsars," an American voice murmured, enthralled.

"We Sp'thra sail near the fault lines where the tension is greatest—the cracks in the dish of curved space. Space is a bowl that perpetually cracks and remakes itself like the planetary crust. We can measure the course of the tides that flow underneath space and beneath light—through the sub-core of the universe, on which matter floats and light flies—and sail these—"

"So you can travel faster than light!" boomed a golden crew-cut astronomer from California.

"*No!* We sail *below* light—using the points where the tide is about to change, to throw us quickly on our way. But only some tides are fast and powerful, others are slow and weak. And tides periodically reverse. The fastest tide to the Sp'thra twin worlds is available at present. Soon it will switch and flow back out again, diminishing. Either we hurry—or go the long way round, sailing slowly on lesser tides to reach a major tide-race. We came slowly into your solar system for the reason that tides are too 'choppy' to sail where much large matter is irregularly dispersed. We have to revert to orthodox planetary drive. The tide effect only becomes feasible beyond your outermost gasgiant's orbit in deep space—"

A remark that would have produced some consternation up till the year before, when the trans-Plutonian planet Janus had been found at last and named after the two-faced Roman god of doorways—doorway to the Solar System and doorway to the Stars.

As it was, the Californian grinned at a colleague and said:

"Like surfboard riders! Seems there's truth in my kids' comics—these guys'd be Silver Surfers, I guess, only they're a bit tarnished lookin', and ride a beachball 'stead of a surfboard—!"

"This tide business could explain the whole damn set-up of collapsars, quasars, gravity waves—right down to the organization of stellar populations!" his older, grizzled colleague flung back excitedly.

"What is this orthodox planetary drive, please?" interrupted the Russian, who had earlier asked about the star drive.

Ph'theri raised one hand, set that thumb of his to playing tick-tack across the orange mark on his palm. Caution, Stop, thought Sole. A universal traffic signal?

"That question is technical, in the 'trading' category—"

"Go on, Ph'theri," Sciavoni said hastily. "We're just excited."

Ph'theri lowered his hand.

"Let me give you an example of trading. Who can read the tides to best advantage? Obviously a swimmer whose mind is evolved by tidal rhythms on his planet. We Signal

135

Traders found after much searching of stars by slow means, a world of Tide Readers. These beings trade us their services. It is a highly assessed trade, and still essential to us—"

"Are they fishes, birds, or what, these 'Tide Readers'?" enquired a ruddy-faced Navy man, whom Sciavoni recollected was involved in a project down in Miami to train whales and dolphins to service subsea stations and defuse mines—one of the leading hunters for the key to the so-called Cetacean Languages.

Ph'theri fluttered a hand impatiently.

"They read atmosphere tides, but theirs is a gasgiant world, and they are methane swimmers—"

"Fair question, you'll admit, Sciavoni," the sailor apologized in a blustery way. "Maybe we've got ourselves a tradeable commodity in our whales. Whales as starship pilots, imagine—"

"We saw your whales on television," Ph'theri retorted dismissively. "You have no concept of the tide forces operating in a gasgiant. There is no analogy on this planet. Only the gasgiant is as vast and complex as the star tides. Even so, the Tide Readers need our machines to stand between their minds and the reality—"

"You can't build machines to read these tides yourself?" the sailor grunted, disappointed.

"Let me explain. We did not evolve in that way. But the Tide Readers did. Tide-reading is an inherited part of their reality, coded into their nervous systems. We Sp'thra cannot instinctively read the tides, no matter what machine-assist is used. Yet the steersman has to be a living being, to react flexibly enough. We buy this ability of theirs—"

Yet hereabouts the alien's cool detachment evaporated. A queer change seemed to be coming over him. Like a medium going into a spirit trance, he began to elaborate, almost lyrically:

" 'Their-Reality', 'Our-Reality', 'Your-Reality'—the mind's concepts of reality based on the environment it has evolved in—all are slightly different. Yet all are a part of 'This-Reality'—the overall totality of the present universe—"

His voice rose shrill with emphasis.

"Yet Other-Reality outside of this totality assuredly exists! We mean to grasp it!"

His eyes blinked rapidly. He licked his lips in a lizardy way.

"There are so many ways of seeing This-Reality, from so many viewpoints. It is these viewpoints that we trade for. You might say we trade in realities—"

Like a patent medicine salesman launching into his spiel—or was it more like an obsessed visionary? The latter was perhaps nearer the truth, Sole decided, as the alien talked on raptly:

"We mean to put all these different viewpoints together, to deduce the entire signature of This-Reality. From this knowledge we shall deduce the reality modes external to It—grasp the Other-Reality, communicate with it, control it!"

"So then," broke in Sole, getting excited himself, "what you people are doing is exploring the syntax of reality? Literally, the way a whole range of different beings 'put together' their picture of reality? You're charting the languages their different brains have evolved, in order to get beyond this reality in some way? That's the idea?"

"Nice," conceded Ph'theri. "You read our intention well. Our destiny is to signal-trade at right angles to This-Reality. That is the tide of our philosophy. We have to journey out at right angles to this universe. By superimposing all languages. And our language inventory for This-Reality is nearly done—"

Sole was not interrupting now—as the others had been with their clamour about technology—but clearly touch-

137

ing upon an obsessive chord deep in the alien, harmonizing with his people's search among the stars.

Sciavoni was nervous at first; then accepted Sole's lead as the only visible thread in the labyrinth.

Ph'theri regarded him sadly.

"The length of time already elapsed is agony to us—"

"Agony? Why is that?"

"Perhaps the answer will mean nothing to you. It is our quest, not yours, to go at right angles to This-Reality. Maybe a quest specific to our species?"

Sole recalled the stringy, bitch face of Dorothy Summers as she raised a logical quibble some time ago at Haddon during one of their bull sessions there.

He shook his head in bewilderment.

"This idea of getting outside of the reality you're already part of—it's illogical," he protested. "Reality determines how you view things. There's no such thing as a perfect external observer. Nobody can move outside themselves or conceive of something outside of the scope of the concepts they're using. We're all embedded in what you call 'This-Reality'—"

"It may be illogical in This-Reality. But in *para*-Reality, other systems of logic apply..."

Harking back, as an anchor, to Dorothy's preoccupation with Ludwig Wittgenstein, Sole felt tempted to quote the Austrian philosopher's bleak summing up of how much, and how little, human beings could ever hope to know.

"Whereof we cannot speak, thereof we must keep silent—" he murmured.

"If that's your philosophy," the alien said haughtily, "it is not ours."

"In fact it isn't our philosophy at all," Sole rejoined more briskly. "We humans are constantly searching for ways to voice the unvoicable. The sheer desire to discover boundaries already implies the desire to pass beyond them, I suppose."

The alien shrugged. (His own native gesture? Or was he picking up the gesture speech of human beings already?)

"You cannot hope to explore all the boundaries to reality on one single world, with only one intelligent species working on the problem. That isn't science. That is ... solipsism. I think that's the word."

"Yes, that's the word—defining the universe in terms of one individual."

As the alien spoke, Sole marvelled at the extent of Ph'theri's stock of words—wondered exactly how the trick was done. Neural implant of *so much* information?

"One planet is solipsism. The Sp'thra duty is to avoid solipsism to the nth degree."

"But we're all embedded in one universe ultimately, Ph'theri. That's a sort of solipsism nobody can escape. Or by 'one reality' do you mean one *galaxy*? Are other galaxies other modes of reality? Do you people plan on intergalactic travel?"

An overwhelming impression of a huge wild sorrow came from the alien's gently-bulging, widespaced eyes. A wise calf waiting outside the slaughterhouse kind of look.

"No. All the galaxies of This-Reality obey the same general laws. We are searching for another reality. We have to achieve it. We are so late."

Again, this time factor.

"The problem," Ph'theri said dismally, "is what a two-dimensional being would face, trying to behave three-dimensionally: to the mocking laughter and love-taunts of superior three-dimensional beings—"

It sounded like nonsense or some kind of schizophrenia. Whose mocking laughter? Whose love? Whose taunts?

Sole decided to get back on a more solid footing.

139

"It all comes down to the laws of physics and chemistry that govern this reality, doesn't it, Ph'theri? Those decide how much we can ever know—or communicate. How much the brain of Man or Alien can think."

"True."

"We ourselves are experimenting with chemical techniques to improve the brain's capacity. We want to seek out the exact boundaries of universal grammar."

Several Americans and Russians stared at Sole. He was aware he was giving something confidential away, but didn't care right then.

"That approach is worthless," Ph'theri said impatiently. "Chemical techniques? Trial and error? Don't you realize there are a myriad conceivable ways in which proteins can be combined to code information? More than the sum total of atoms in this planet of yours! The rules of reality can only be understood by superimposing the widest range of languages from different worlds upon one another. *There* is the one and only key to This-Reality—and the way out."

Sole nodded.

"Ph'theri, another question I must ask—what you're saying now, is it being monitored and aided in some way? Your fluency has me worried."

Ph'theri pointed a finger at the scarlet wires leading from his lips and paper-bag ears into his chest pack.

"True. This is sending signals through the ship outside into the language machines in our larger ship in the sky. It is also a witness to our trade negotiations. With machine-assist, I save time. Vocabulary fast-scan. Heuristic parameters for new words—"

"Yet even without this machine link-up you speak English—by direct programming into the brain, you said?"

"Yes, though not so easily. The technique is . . ."

"...I know, tradeable. Was I wasting time just now, asking about grammar and reality?"

"No. We are understanding each other at the optimum rate. We thank you. And assess it highly."

"That's good. But I suppose you want to get on to what we're going to trade each other. You talked about buying realities—"

There were instant protests in the room. Voices cutting Sole down to size. Insisting that he didn't have any mandate to negotiate.

Ph'theri raised both arms high in a histrionic gesture.

"There is low likelihood we find any trade worth losing the tide for, on this world. In too many ways you are predictable. So, is this your representative, or not?"

"Let's hear Dr Sole bargain on our behalf," growled Stepanov, "since that is apparently unavoidable. We're not at the United Nations now. I'm sorry to say we're in an auction room—and the bidding has already commenced."

Zwingler nodded sarcastically in Sole's direction; and Sciavoni squeezed the Englishman's elbow surreptitiously, like an embarrassed godfather.

"Touchy impatient bastard! Do your best, Chris."

Yet Sole felt suspicious of loopholes in this alien's logic and integrity. For bargaining is a competition, not a free exchange of gifts.

"Presumably you want information about human languages?" he said, gently detaching himself from Sciavoni's grasp.

"Yes. So long as we select the format—"

Sole tried another tack. Laid down a challenge.

"I think you're being dishonest, Ph'theri. All this business about you people being the right ones to assess values, on account of you came here first—and pushing off if we don't behave ourselves. In fact, we came out to you to start the trading, when we gave you a language to trade in, out by the Moon. That cost us some effort—as much effort for a culture at our stage, maybe, as it costs you to hop from star to star. We have a right to assess the value too. What you've told us—it's interesting, but it's pretty thin and mystical-sounding, a lot of it. Not like what we gave you—a complete working language. Which, by the way, tells you a hell of a lot about us human beings and our outlook on reality. I'd say you're already in our debt—you're just trying to browbeat us with these threats about leaving, to get something on the cheap!"

For the first time since his arrival, Ph'theri seemed nonplussed—stood there wasting time, while the seconds drew out visibly. Sole noticed how the Nevada skyline was lightening with premonitions of dawn.

Finally Ph'theri clasped his hands together.

"Some credit is owing to you, true. But in some situations no-information is valuable. Who knows, the fact that we have not flown over your cities may be highly assessed by you?"

Sole ignored this, despite venomous looks darted at him, and argued strenuously:

"You can't possibly trade without an agreed system of communication, Ph'theri. Right? We gave you that when we gave you the key to English. Right? But by giving you it, we gave you the outline idea of all human language as such—since all human languages are related deep down. You want to buy an exact description of human language, to get at our basic set of concepts? I'd say you're already some way there for free, thanks to us!"

Ph'theri waved an orange palm cursorily.

"May we appear over your cities? Interest ourselves in recording architectural and urban data?"

"We would prefer," intervened Sciavoni nervously, "to arrange tours for you. There's such a lot of air traffic over our cities, you see. The system's really very complicated—"

"So you accept the pay-off?"

Ph'theri's question produced an awkward hush. Nobody was willing to commit themselves. During the silence that followed, the alien's paper-bag ears inflated to pick up tiny sounds, brought him by the scarlet wires.

Ph'theri was the first to speak.

"The Sp'thra make the following offer for what we want to buy," he said to Sole. "We will tell you the location of the closest unused world known to us, habitable by you. The location of the nearest intelligent species known to us ready to engage in interstellar communication, together with an effective means of communication using modulated tachyon beams. Finally, we offer you an improvement on your current technology for spaceflight within your solar system—"

"In return for which you want more tapes and grammar books on microfilm?"

"*No.* That has been your mistake all along. Tapes and books cannot provide a full model of language in action. We need six units programmed with separate languages as far removed from each other as possible."

"Units?"

"We need working brains competent in six linguistically diverse languages. Six is an adequate statistical sample—"

"You mean human volunteers, to go back home to your planet with you?"

"Leave Earth for the stars?" cried an American whose face—younger then, grinning toothily from the cover of *Newsweek*—Sole remembered from one of the Apollo missions. "I'd sure say yes to that, even if it did mean never coming home again. That's the human spirit." The astronaut stared defiantly round the room, as though he'd staked a claim to something.

"No," Ph'theri retorted sharply. "That isn't reasonable. To have our ship crowded with a zoo of beings on the loose. We have been trading with many worlds. If

143

we took beings on board from every one—"

"That globe of yours is one helluva big!"

"And I say it is full—it carries the space tide drive, which is not small. The planetary drive. And the ecology for the methane Tide Readers, who are huge beings."

"But, methane breathers! We humans can fit in with you, surely," the astronaut begged. "You're just wearing a simple air filter."

"Atmospherically compatible you may be. Whether culturally compatible, is very doubtful."

"Then what do you mean if not live human beings!"

"What we say—language-programmed brains. In working order. Separated from the body. Machine-maintained compactly."

"You want to cut a human brain out of its body and keep it alive in a machine for you to experiment on?"

"The requirement is for six brains, programmed with different languages. And instruction tapes."

"Jesus Christ," murmured Sciavoni.

"Naturally we consult on which units are most suitable," said Ph'theri.

TEN

LIONEL ROSSON TOSSED his hair fitfully as he came into Haddon Unit out of the crisp January air, unshouldering his sheepskin coat hastily as he encountered the wall of heat.

And how about the hothouse growths within?

Damn Sole for a bastard, ducking out of sight at this first sign of trouble on his mysterious errand to America. Leaving Rosson, like some little Dutch boy, to stick his thumb in the leaking dyke. Then watch helplessly as the cracks got wider and wider.

Sole's alibi was really as thin as ice. If Sam Bax didn't keep up the illusion of its solidity by skating over it.

Who had that man Zwingler been?

And what was this instant-mash 'Verbal Behaviour Seminar' the American had invited Sole to attend? Rosson's private theory was that some space tragedy had happened that no one had been told about. Some radical breakdown in communication with the long-flight astronauts as they swung round the world for months on end in Skylab. They'd been expelled from the womb of Earth, with its comforting tug of gravity and its well-spaced sunrises and half a hundred other natural and necessary signals, longer than any other men had been. Had they altered their patterns of thinking to fit some new celestial norm? Or fallen in between two stools—bastards of Earth and of the Stars? And now they needed rescue—conceptual rescue, before they could be rescued physically. Was that it?

A memory nagged at him—something he'd read years

ago, that the initiate to the Orphic Rites in ancient Greece had to learn by heart for recitation after death. 'I am a child of Earth and Starry Heaven. Give me to drink of...' Of what? The waters of forgetfulness—or the waters of memory? One of the two; but he couldn't remember which it had been. Yet the distinction was critical. Perhaps it was critical too, for the Skylab astronauts.

That man Zwingler's paper had been about 'Disorientation in longflight astronauts', 'Disorder of conceptual sets'. What if astronauts did lose their wits in that place of exile between Earth and the Stars? In that mind limbo up there. Who knew what experiments Skylab really carried as a payload? How it fitted the nowadays mood that avenging angels should always be floating overhead. Prometheans who had mastered the secrets of nuclear fire, only to become mankind's own liver-eating eagles, soaring in perpetual orbit.

Rosson wondered too, what link, if any, there was between this hastily-convened conference on verbal behaviour, and the new Russian moon visible only over Reykjavik, Siberia and the Solomon Islands. A grandiose and meaningless gesture, to inflate such a vast balloon and hang it like a lantern in the sky—where nobody would be seeing it. So unlike the Russians. They always aimed for the maximum propaganda appeal.

Whatever the truth was (and presumably Sole knew it) damn him for a bastard ducking out of the Unit right now. At the very time when his precious Vidya was about to go crazy—and his embedded world was coming apart at the seams...

He passed the fir tree, still standing there at the foot of the Great Staircase. Though Christmas was past, it still lacked a few days till Twelfth Night—and the full ritual was being observed. The tree looked more like a skeleton than ever. An X-ray of a tree skirted about by thick green dandruff.

They should take it away sooner. It had become depressing.

Should he trace a message in the scurf for the nursing staff to read? 'Bury me, I'm dead'. No point. They had military minds, and stuck to regulations. Regulation 217 subsection (a)—'Christmas trees shall remain in situ till the Twelfth Day of Christmas'. Something like that.

He passed through the security airlock into the rear wing, knocked on Sam Bax's door and walked in.

"What is it, Lionel?"

Sam Bax didn't seem overjoyed to see him. He hadn't, lately.

"Sam, I must know when Chris is coming back. The situation's getting more touchy every day. There could be some real damage done before long."

"Why can't you hold the fort yourself, Lionel? I'll ask Richard to take turns with you if you want. But you were Chris's choice."

"You haven't told me when Chris is coming back. Or what he's doing."

"Lionel, I frankly don't know when he'll be back. Tom Zwingler telephoned from America yesterday. It seems Chris has some significant contribution to make."

"What to?"

Sam Bax spread his hands on the desk top. The gesture was one of showing all his cards, but the cards were all face down.

"Ah—there you have me. But I promise you, so far as this Unit is concerned, Chris's visit to the States can only bring profitable feedback."

"Great, Sam! Just great. And what the hell's the virtue in finance if there's nothing left worth financing!"

"It can't be as sticky as that. Surely you're exaggerating. Everything went perfectly smoothly up till now. I wouldn't have let Chris go otherwise."

"Have you monitored the embedding world lately?"

The Director glanced down at his hands, then shiftily at the telephone.

"Well you know, Lionel, there was this seminar in Bruges. Then the business about the army wanting to withdraw their nurses for active service. And all the boring financial nonsense—which I must admit Chris's trip might alleviate indirectly, if not directly. Frankly, I'd like to hire a few more high-calibre staff. But the way things are—" His vague excuses tapered off.

Rosson tossed his mane fretfully.

" 'More high-calibre'? And how do you intend that diplomatic phrase to be punctuated? Ah, never mind! Sam—I asked you, have you monitored Chris's world lately?"

Sam shook his head—preoccupied with other thoughts. With Chris? With America? But why? Presumably that Zwingler man had told Sam the real reason. Whatever mental disaster it was that had happened up there in Skylab. This talk about finance was all eyewash. A put-off.

"Give me half an hour, Sam. I'll play the relevant bits of tape for you. You'll see why I want Chris back here— whatever's going on over there. And I don't need Richard to back me up, as you know very well. Hell, Sam—it's Chris that the kids know best, and need. Same as Aye and Bee and the others know me and need me. I'm talking about contact. Touch. Play! I'm not bragging, Sam. Nor am I bloody well defending my own status. I'm stating psychological facts that you could probably even get Richard to agree to. These kids have established rapport with Chris just as mine have with me. Dorothy or Richard won't do as substitutes—if I can't handle it myself—and you know damn well why!"

"Calm down will you, Lionel? Now listen to me. I'm not calling Chris back from the States whatever goes wrong here. Not if the whole Unit burns down. And I mean that. You'll have to handle it by yourself. Naturally I'm willing to see the tapes."

"You seem to have forgotten about the Project, Sam! Six months ago and you'd have rushed to the screen to see those tapes. Now it's all this finance and organization caper—and what Chris is doing in the States. Why? Sam, what the hell is going on over there? Has there been some mental breakdown up in space? That's what it looks like to me. What's so interesting that it makes you unconcerned about a mental disaster on your own doorstep?"

"A mental disaster—among Chris's kids? You'd go so far as that?" For the first time Sam looked concerned, briefly.

"That's what I've been trying to tell you!"

The screen lit and snowed with static, cleared to show Vidya opening up the largest of the talking dolls, taking the smaller doll from inside it, and shutting the larger doll neatly before moving on to the opening of the smaller.

"This is incident number one. The same day as that man Zwingler visited us."

"No connection, I trust," grunted Sam.

"Of course there's no connection!" snapped Rosson. "I'm just telling you when it happened."

"All right, Lionel. You just seemed to have it in for Tom Zwingler—"

Rosson gestured at the screen.

"It was the story of the Princess and the Pea, Sam. I checked. How the real princess with the fairest skin in all the land—the least blunted nerve endings to you, Sam!—is the only girl that can feel the pea hidden under a pile of feather mattresses."

"Yes yes," said Sam impatiently.

They reviewed the first 'fit', the one to which Sole had drawn Rosson's attention before leaving.

"I wondered whether it might have had anything to

do with the story itself—that business of mattress upon mattress upon mattress. Then the hard pea—the nub of the matter—at the very bottom of the pile. It's a sort of mocking comment on the embedded speech, isn't it Sam?"

Rosson blanked the screen and punched a new set of figures from memory.

The screen snowed once more and cleared.

"This is the second episode, Sam—this happened about forty-eight hours later, after Chris had left."

Three children surrounded the Oracle in the centre of the maze. But Vidya was resisting the room's whisperings and hypnotic programming of events.

He was shouting and screaming, raging round the outside of the maze walls, whipping them with a piece of plastic pipe—and howling at the children inside.

Rosson switched the loudspeaker on and incoherent cries rang out.

"I couldn't make head or tail of it, Sam. The computer claimed it was a genuinely random string of syllables. But I'm beginning to suspect it represents a reversion to babbling, only on a much higher level."

"Or a childish tantrum."

"Yes, it expresses itself as a tantrum—I can see that. But is that all there is to it, for Christ's sake! What sort of situation does this kind of reversion to babbling normally occur in? Only when a much younger child has suffered a brain injury then goes right back to the beginning of the language learning process again. Vidya's far too old."

"Unless the PSF has changed things?"

"Precisely, Sam! That's what I'm thinking. The brain's programme for acquiring speech must have been disrupted somehow."

"Or speeded up?"

"One of the two. Wish I knew which. If you want my candid opinion, what we're seeing here is some kind of clash between the brain's own programme for generating language, and the programme we've imposed on it—the embedding programme. But the embedding programme isn't simply being tossed out by the brain. The PSF allows a much greater tolerance of data. So his brain must be trying to weave the embedding into the brain's 'natural' design for language. And the two designs just won't and can't match. The boy's brain has *jammed*—on account of its sheer versatility. And that jamming has thrown him right back to a random babbling stage. The set of rules has failed him—so he's reverting to Trial and Error methods. God knows what'll come out of this present babble, though!"

Sam Bax saw Vidya race round the maze. He whipped the walls. He howled. He babbled incomprehensibly.

"The lad looks well enough co-ordinated," he remarked. "Nothing much wrong there. Agile lad."

"*Watch*, Sam."

After several more circuits of the maze, Vidya cried out like an epileptic and collapsed beside the maze entrance. His slim body writhed about. His fingers flexed. He clawed at the floor as if to tug it up in strips. Finally he lay still.

"Dizzy! I'm not surprised. Running round and round like that."

"Dizzy my arse! The boy had a fit. He was working himself up to it. He's giving himself his own shock therapy. Discharging the contradictions in his mind."

Rosson tapped out a fresh code on the console.

The screen cleared to the scene of Vidya's recovery. The boy got up calmly and trotted into the maze.

"Now the next episode—"

"Lionel, I hate to break this off. But I'm expecting another call from the States."

"Will that be Chris calling?"

"Sorry, Lionel. I simply won't have Chris distracted."

"I can imagine what he'll have to say about *that* when

he gets back here to find Vidya babbling his brains out and throwing fits!"

"Which is precisely why I won't have Chris told now. But I'll tell you what we'll do. We'll set a nurse on permanent stand-by. He can go in there and trank the child if there are any more incidents. We'll keep him that way till Chris gets back. Keep him on ice. Will that suit you?"

Far from it.

However Sam Bax was already heading out of Sole's room, leaving Rosson staring at a blank screen.

ELEVEN

"WOULD YOU PEOPLE do the same, Ph'theri?" Sole asked. "Would you trade us a living brain from one of the Sp'thra?"

"That depends on how we assessed the trade gain. Yes, if it was adequate."

"So you wouldn't personally refuse to trade your own brain, even? If you were chosen?"

"The Sp'thra are Signal Traders. Surely the trading of a live brain is the ultimate form of signal trading. The brain contains all the signals of a species."

"How long will these brains be kept alive?" Sole was asking; but the astronaut who had earlier staked his claim so vociferously cried out:

"I'd want a ticket to the goddam stars in exchange for six human brains put in a tin box. Star travel, no less, sir!"

Ph'theri raised a hand, exposing the orange palm flash.

"You cannot hope to trade starship technology for six brains from a world such as this. You reject the trade deal, then?"

"We're not necessarily rejecting anything," Sciavoni protested quickly. "But you know exactly what you want. What are we getting out of it? It's too vague. How far is this habitable world? We could probably detect it ourselves long before we had the means to go there. How far's this intelligent race? Maybe so far communicating would be a waste of time! And these technological improvements—"

Sole's query about how long the brains would stay alive

was shelved for the moment, by tacit consent. The prospect, after all, was no more terrible—far less terrible indeed—than X or Y or Z happening elsewhere in the world, in Asia, Africa, or South America.

"To give the other side all the information," argued Ph'theri in a finicky way, "is the whole content of the trade—"

"To be sure! But you really must let us know less approximately. We can't buy a pig in a poke—"

Sciavoni mopped his brow, though the sun had barely risen on the building and the air within was merely warm. Sole realized how rigid his own stance had been for so many minutes past and made an effort to relax. The incoming sunlight woke other people up too, physically. A nose blew honkingly. Glasses were taken off and polished. Feet shuffled. Hands plunged into pockets. One man lit a cigarette, with a tiny stab of flame.

Ph'theri stared at the smoke and the smoker.

"You meet the sun with burning? Is that customary here?"

"More like habitual," grunted Sciavoni sardonically.

Outside the window the ship Ph'theri had come in lay with the ramp jutting out of its side like the tongue of a man hanged at dawn.

"The technology we offer will enable you to reach the inner gasgiant of your system in twenty of your days. With good energy conservation. Or else reach the outermost gasgiant in one hundred days, retaining fifty per cent energy. You want other destinations listed?"

Sciavoni shook his head.

"We can work it out from that. How about the method?"

"The method will be adequate, you have the word of the Sp'thra for that. Signal Trading demands truth, otherwise there is only disorder and entropy, and reality will never be articulated—"

154

"Okay, damn it. How about those stars then? How far?"

Ph'theri's ears crinkled, cubed and inflated, as he concentrated on the whispering of the wires.

"In your light years, the closest habitable planet known to the Sp'thra is approximately Two One units away—"

A Russian scientist calculated swiftly and looked crestfallen.

"Which means 82 Eridani, Beta Hydri, or HR 8832. Nothing closer. So Alpha Centauri and Tau Ceti and all those other promising stars are useless."

"Not at all," the younger of the Californian astronomers contradicted him. "The operative concept is 'known to the Sp'thra'. Don't forget that. We've no guarantee they know all the local stars."

"The message distance is Nine Eight light years," Ph'theri said flatly.

"One way?"

"True."

"But that means—let's see, ninety eight times two ... one hundred and ninety six years to send a message and get an answer! Did I hear someone mention a pig in a poke, Sciavoni?"

"You did indeed."

The astronomers began to squabble about tachyons—particles supposed to travel faster than light implied a shorter transit time—but Sole felt impatient.

"We need to find out some more about these peoples' *motives*," he snapped. "Ph'theri—why are you so anxious to escape from 'This-Reality'?"

"To solve the Sp'thra problem," Ph'theri replied shortly.

"Maybe we can trade some help in solving it?"

"Very unlikely," said Ph'theri coldly. "I would say it is species-specific to the Sp'thra."

The Englishman shook his head.

"No. The problem has to involve all the species in the universe—if you're approaching it by comparing all their

155

languages. That stands to reason. Unless … is it a sexual problem? I suppose that would be intimately specific to the species. Obsessional, too, into the bargain!"

"A breeding problem? The Sp'thra have no breeding problem on the twin worlds."

"An emotional problem—a problem of feeling?"

Ph'theri hesitated, though his ears did not modify themselves to listen to any words whispered into them. He considered the question, himself, for what seemed minutes on end.

"There is an emotional area beyond sex, true. You have a word 'Love'. Perhaps that is the name of the problem. But it is not a problem of love for the Sp'thra mate—that sort of love is a form of solipsism, which we detest. 'He' loves himself in the mirror of 'Herself'. 'She' loves herself in the mirror of 'Himself'. That is to love the signal of the Self. The transmission of the genetic code, the ritual greetings, the embrace gestures are part of this same solipsism. But there is an area of emotion we feel, which involves Bereft Love—that is our problem." The alien faltered. "The Bereft Love we feel for the Change Speakers—"

Sole waited patiently, but nothing more was forthcoming. The alien had clammed up.

Sciavoni was whispering angrily to the astronomers, "We've got to know what makes these creatures tick, before we can judge their honesty. If that involves defining their concepts of Love and Morals, that's okay by me!"

"Who are these Change Speakers, Ph'theri?" Sole demanded. "Is that another species?"

The alien stared down at the man, disparagingly. Nothing of the missionary about this bastard, thought Sole, wincing under that aged, grey gaze. Slowly—spelling it out to a child—the alien explained his faith … or science … or delusion: a queer fusion of the three that Man would maybe need to hypnotize himself with the like of, if he was ever to drive himself to the Stars.

"They are variable entities. They manipulate what we know as reality by means of their shifting-value signals. Using signals that lack constants—which have variable referents. This universe-here embeds us in it. But not them. They escape. They are free. They shift across realities. Yet when we have successfully superimposed the reality-programmes of all languages, in the moon between the twin worlds, we too shall be free. It has to be soon. The time span to date is One Two Nine Zero Nine, your years—"

"Sweet Christ, this all started thirteen thousand years ago?"

"True. The primitive startlings. The first quarrying of the Language Moon. That happened soon after the first dawn of Bereft Love for the Change Speakers. At first exploration went slowly, jumping from star to star. The subsequent discovery of gasgiant Wave Readers approximately Seven Zero Zero Zero years later, saved much time—"

Sole felt horrified at this span of time. What was Homo Sapiens doing then? Painting the cave walls at Lascaux?

"A physical search for the Change Speakers in this Three-Space would be useless," said the alien meditatively —in a measured, weary way, as though he'd explained all this before across the universe till he was sick of it. "A speech-changing search is the only hope. Only at the places where the languages of different species grate together, presenting an interface of paradox, do we guess the nature of true reality and draw strength to escape. Our language moon will finally reveal reality as a direct experience. Then we shall state the Totality. We shall stand outside of This-Reality and pursue our Bereft Love—"

"Is it Beings you're searching for, Ph'theri? Or a Being? Or the nature of Being? What?"

"There are races that have many more inflections of

157

the concept 'Being' than yourselves," Ph'theri replied witheringly. "The Change Speakers are *para*-beings. We Sp'thra feel a deep bereft 'love' for them, since they phased with the twin worlds so many years ago. And went away. They change-spoke away from Sp'thra—by modulating their embedding in reality—and left us...

"LEFT US," he howled terrifyingly, though he did not move or wring his hands or show any sign of tears, as a human being giving vent to such an expression of loss would—he stood, bound up in an alien agony, Cross and Crucified united in the same tall dry form. Raised arms and orange palms would be too feeble a protest to express this pent-up inner grief.

"I don't get it," Sole shouted in frustration—though nobody else was making a noise now. Many had moved back from the alien, as if scared. "How do you communicate with creatures that are changing meanings all the time? What sort of permanence is that? But—thirteen thousand years! And you've kept this crazy love alive for all that span of time? How—and why?"

Ph'theri's cry had been like the howl of an untuned radio set—when he got to tune himself in again, his message came through clearly enough, for an alien answer to a human question.

"The Change Speakers desired something when they phased with the Sp'thra—what it was we did not understand. They themselves were hurting with love. Our signal trading quest is to cancel the great sense of their sadness, so that we Sp'thra can be left alone again—without that vibration in our minds, imprinted so many centuries ago by their passage. Yes, they branded us! They left a long echo in their wake. It is the eddy in water left standing in a bowl. A retinal image of a blinding light. We are haunted by the Change Speakers. By this ghost of love, which is pain."

"Did they 'phase' with no other races you've met on

your travels?" asked Sole. "Has no one else got this echo in their minds?"

"Surely we humans have, in the person of Our Saviour!" an evangelical Southern voice cried out. "I swear it's God he means, in his alien way—"

Sciavoni made an angry *pianissimo* gesture.

"No, it's a collective psychosis," a Jewish specialist in Abnormal Psychiatry from New York offered as his diagnosis—though he sounded hysterical himself. "These aliens are collectively insane. Their obsessive activity is simply a way of hiding the truth from themselves—by turning their delusory system upside down and externalizing it. All that time ago some collective madness took hold of them. Maybe a genetic mutation. Or some bug they caught on their travels. Maybe they're breathing their mind poison out into our air and minds right now?" His voice rose giddily. "What have we done to quarantine ourselves and this creature? What's fifty miles of wild country—to a star virus?"

"Not so," howled Ph'theri, raising both arms and ticktacking his thumbs in the utmost anger or agitation. "We Sp'thra are not sick. We are *aware*. Change Speakers exist —in another reality plane! When they phased with This-Reality, the event set up a resonance which is this Bereft Love and this Anguish and this Grim Haunting all at once. You have not known this. No other race has. The Change Speakers modulate all the reality tangents to the plane of our embedding here. But where they brushed, they set that point in this universe resonating—like a sounded bell in ancient Sp'thra. With the reality-pictures of so many species in our moon, we shall transcend This-Reality as they do, pursue the Change Speakers and—"

Ph'theri hesitated.

"What then?" pressed Sole. The alien's arms collapsed. A mute, eroded witness to the inexplicable, he admitted:

"We disagree what to do. Signal them? Love them? DESTROY them for the anguish they inflicted on us? Some heretics even suggest that the Change Speakers are ourselves, from some far future or alternative reality. A pre-echo of our own Evolved Selves resonating back in time —to force us to assassinate them in a future that has grown intolerable to them, but which they cannot escape from of their own will. These future Sp'thra, caught up in the incredible anguish of some unknown situation—perhaps it is Immortality?—can only commit suicide through the agency of their earlier selves; so the story goes—"

"Is this a popular explanation among your people?"

"No! This heresy has appeared several times since the language moon was hollowed out, been discounted and destroyed—"

"And those who believed in it?"

"Destroyed too! It is against the signal-trading destiny and duty of the Sp'thra."

"For God's sake, the creature is paranoid! Isn't it obvious his whole race is? Assassinate the future? Assassinate schmassinate!"

"Who would say that your own species is mentally pure," accused Ph'theri, "when you send out repetitive pictures of dying, killing, maiming and torture?"

"But that isn't the idea of being a human being," the psychiatrist protested angrily. "That is a misreading. Those things are all accidents, mistakes, disasters."

"Really? You seem to dote on them. As we see it, your signals are you. These things are your sport, your art, your religion. Why do you bilk at trading six brains of Earth, whom a great destiny awaits—to escape from the Embedding with the Sp'thra. To master the tangents. To enjoy the freedom of love sated and satisfied!"

The Embedding.

It was a concept that seemed to haunt the aliens as

fiercely as it had, in another context, haunted Sole. Was there any real comparison—or was it just a chance similarity of words?

It didn't seem like a chance similarity to Sole, right then. More like a miraculous discovery.

Sole felt himself filled with wonder, as he saw his way through to a fusion of Ph'theri's obsession with his own.

"Ph'theri—I've tried to achieve a kind of 'embedding', to test out the frontiers of reality, using young human brains. Maybe it's a coincidence of words? No, I don't think so. You think it's impossible to test out reality with one species on one planet. Tell me this, Ph'theri, would you be willing to miss the tide if it was worth your while? If it brought your search to an end? If it saved *all* time for the Sp'thra?"

Sole fished Pierre's letter out of his pocket.

And began to tell the tall alien all that he knew of the Xemahoa tribe of Brazil . . .

Outside, it was full daylight now. The sun shone on to Ph'theri's ship, on the desert scrub, the peaked mountains beyond. The sky hadn't a single contrail in it. The area must have been cleared of air traffic.

When Sole had finished explaining—and while people stared at Sole, bemused—Ph'theri considered for a long time. His paper-bag ears crinkled through rapid shape changes as he communicated like a silent ventriloquist with the other Sp'thra.

The alien finally addressed the crowd.

"If this is true, we Sp'thra shall miss the tide. And for the Xemahoa brain unit, we assess the value thus: the transfer to you of interstellar travel techniques, together with the lending of one gasgiant Tide Reader. This 'package' will enable your race to reach the Tide Reader star within five of your years and make your own trading arrangements."

161

A hush of awe filled the room. The bright sunlight made it a moment of eternity.

Then a groundswell of naked greed took hold of the crowd, and Sole felt himself being clapped and pounded on the back.

"You damn clever bastard," Sciavoni hissed in his ear. "Was any of that true?"

"But it has to be," muttered Sole. "Doesn't it?"

"Sure as hell it does!" Sciavoni laughed.

"Hey, Dr Sole," another voice insinuated, "we'd better be turning the taps off down Brazil way, hadn't we?"

"Before we lose our baby in the bathwater, eh?"

An almost hysterical gaiety. Amid it all the tall Sp'thra stood like a gloomy lighthouse in a storm.

As the babble grew deafening, Ph'theri's ears scaled down to flat cardboard packets.

A sub-committee of the Washington Special Action Group met in a walnut-panelled room with false windows. Views of New England in the Fall surrounded them—a blaze of russet trees, that could change at the touch of a switch to the Everglades, Hawaiian beaches, or the Rocky Mountains.

The President's Chief Scientific Adviser, a German emigré with a leonine head of white wiry hair, said:

"There's a hell of a lot more to it than just snatching a couple of Indians. We've got to safeguard our assets— and if these Indians have stumbled on to something so unique that it's worth the secret of star flight to our friends, then we need it too—"

"We're going on pretty slender evidence. A letter from a crazy frog full of propaganda," said a quiet man from the CIA, who'd been doodling on his notepad, producing a series of awkward drawings of a winged dragon like an advertisement for a correspondence course in art in a comic book.

"But we know the thing's possible. What did that man Zwingler say they'd discovered at that Hospital in England? Some kind of chemical to enhance the intelligence—"

"He said they weren't sure of that, sir."

"Yes, but they said lasers were impossible a few years ago then they were in commercial production not long afterwards. The more we find out about the mind, the more likely it seems we can make it do tricks we never dreamed of. The Russians can make a person feel bravery or fear just by injecting a chemical into the brain. Any emotion they like. We can prevent senility to a certain extent. It's no big deal to predict we'll be able to make people think *better* in the near future—"

The President had a visionary—some would say, romantic—taste in scientific advisers. The current adviser's rise to power took him out of an obscure professorship in social psychiatry at a Mid-Western university, through the Hudson Institute's Committee on the Year 2000, to his present position, with a speed that alarmed some of his former colleagues. Not that he was a young man. On the contrary. He'd stayed a suspect maverick for too long, pursuing research into dubious topics such as genetic intelligence and conditioning techniques. However, the President had a firm faith in the possibility of managing people and events according to well-defined scripts drawn up by 'responsible' psychologists and sociologists. Or, as he put it in a State of the World message, of 'orchestrating domestic and international events to make harmonious music'.

"Take that Russian who was smashed up in a car crash in Moscow. Bokharov. They reversed his death okay but they couldn't do anything about the damage to his brain during the time he was dead. His value as a scientist was quartered. But look what we accomplished with that nuclear fusion man at Caltech—"

163

"Hammond?"

"Sure. His IQ rating was going off by a few fractions of a percentage point. Not enough to make any difference to the average guy. But in a top scientist like him, that's the difference between excellent routine work—and what for want of a better word we got to call genius. We managed to buck him up for those vital months till we caught up with the Russians—"

"That was using DNA extract?" a sharp-faced Italian-American—the Treasury Department's head of drug intelligence—asked the Adviser, who nodded.

"Imagine if we could inject some drug that makes the difference of whole percentage points of intelligence at the peak of a man's career. Give him the power to integrate everything he knows. We got to save the whole environment of these Indians—we need that drug, and at this stage that means the whole natural system it comes from."

"It ain't so awkward as it sounds," said the CIA man, looking up from his dragons. "We can repair the dam afterwards—make it smaller. Then the area those Indians live in can be made into a sorta reserve—big enough so they don't cotton on and act unnatural, like stop cultivating the drug..."

TWELVE

CHARLIE HUMMED, TO cheer himself, as he rode back through the rain from the other side of the dam.

How soon before he would be 'Ridin' home to Albuquerque' like the song said.

He needed cheering. Images of the Nam haunted this landscape more and more these days.

The heat. The waiting. The sense of being trapped.

The café tarts stinking of ether. Girls who really knocked a man out! Anaesthetize was the name of the game...

Jorge was standing waiting at the end of the dam in the wet, waving the jeep down frantically...

"Charlie!" A cry of fear.

The noose round Charlie's neck tightened a stage further.

"That Captain Paixao is here. With two prisoners. They're questioning them in the store shed. A man and a woman."

"Were they coming to kill me?"

"You selfish sonofabitch! Paixao and his thugs are torturing them for information—a woman too!"

Charlie bit his lip.

"Shit ... that's bad. I guess we'd better—"

"What had we better? Put a stop to it? How do you do that—you tell me!"

"Shit, Jorge, I dunno. But one thing I'll do right now is see what's goin' on."

Jorge climbed on board the jeep, clothes dripping wet from the rain.

Charlie revved the jeep towards the most distant of the tin sheds.

Graders and bulldozers were parked on the concrete there—and so was Paixao's helicopter. The pilot sat smoking a cigarette, pointing an automatic rifle idly at the approaching jeep.

The door to the shed was guarded by another of Paixao's men, with the face of a boxer dog and black bushy sideburns.

He shouted at the jeep as they pulled up.

"What's he sayin'?"

"To piss off—it's none of our business."

"Say I insist on seeing Paixao."

Jorge translated, then gave Charlie a despairing look.

"Captain will come see you in his own good time, he says."

"Well that ain't no good. Say I need some equipment outa that shed. Urgent—for the dam. Oh fuck it—make something up. How did they get in there anyways—smash the lock?"

"They took the key off me," flushed Jorge.

"You mean you gave them it—knowing this would happen?"

"What the hell could I do? They're the police. They want to do it here, not in the village—too many witnesses there."

"You're sure that's what they are doing? Maybe it's not so bad."

"Oh Charlie, Charlie—I heard such screams before I ran off to meet you."

"See anything through the window?"

"That man said he'd put a bullet through my foot for me if I went anywhere near."

"Dammit, he won't dare shoot me! Jorge, you stay with the jeep. If anything happens drive off and raise Santarém on the radio. Don't try to help."

Charlie tugged Jorge over into the driver's seat as he was getting out. The guard shouted something at him as he walked towards the window.

"You speak English?" Charlie shouted back, still walking.

Inside his head a question lit up in bright red lights: Charlie, what the hell are you taking this risk for? To stand up straight and true in Jorge's eyes? Or to make up in some way for that girl's suffering eyes and that boy spitted on your bayonet and that blazing hut long ago?

Events spun round him faster and faster like a malicious wheel of fortune. The Huey Slick, the wet heat, these interrogations of prisoners—hide as deep in the Amazon as you can, these things will hunt you down like Furies.

Charlie peered through the dripping bars.

Only one of the two lights in the shed was working. It cast giant shadows into the gloom beyond the crated equipment and fuel drums, where a group of figures were. Charlie wondered why they were standing in darkness. Whether the second light bulb had just packed up. Then he made out the cable dangling from the light socket down to the floor.

Charlie ran at the door and tried to push his way past Sideburns.

The guard shoved him back roughly into the rain.

"You bastard, it's my goddam hut! I got to see Paixao. Understand, Paixao?"

The man nodded and made him a sign to keep his distance. He banged his gun butt a few times on the door behind him. The gun was pointing approximately at Charlie's groin.

"You stupid shit," Charlie swore under his breath.

They had to wait a time till the door opened and Orlando's ratty features thrust out.

The halfcaste heard Charlie's inept attempts at framing

sentences in Portuguese for a while, impassively, then walked away. Charlie couldn't be sure that he had been understood at all, until the Captain himself came to the door.

Paixao had that antiseptic band-aid smile stuck on his lips.

"Mr Faith. You'll be glad to hear we have trapped two terrorists on their way here to kill you. They admit as much. Unfortunately we lost one of their group in the jungle. But he will probably die there, without any supplies or transport. We shall not borrow your shed much longer. Another hour then we shall be on our way. You can wait that long?"

"Excuse me, Captain, but I want to know what you're doing to those people in there!"

Charlie thrust himself past Paixao and stared down the shed.

One figure lay huddled on the floor.

The other figure somehow seemed to be standing on its head. Then Charlie made out the rope round its ankles. The rope looped over the roofbeam, suspending the body. The legs were bare. Maybe the whole body was naked— but Paixao's men stood in the way.

"What you doing, man!"

"You did your duty in Southeast Asia, Senhor Faith, so you must understand about doing one's duty. A rat has been caught in a trap. It's necessary to squeeze the rat. No need to involve yourself. We just need your electric supply for our—recording gear. And a roof over our heads."

"Is it true one of those people is a woman?"

"*Both* are guerrillas, Mr Faith. Both are saboteurs and murderers. Enemies of civilization. And your potential assassins. The question of sex is immaterial."

Ah, girl with your doe eyes, what did it matter, what happened between us, when anyway you had to die? Was that the thing called rape—that explosion of my own anguish?

To tell the truth, Charlie wasn't even certain that rape had occurred. He wasn't certain *what* had occurred after he felt the sinking home of the bayonet. Charlie reconstructed a probability of rape, that was all. It was an identikit picture of what might have taken place. And he was an identikit soldier performing identikit deeds as per boot camp training.

Then the hanging body swung round and Charlie saw her breasts. And the wires.

He ran down the room.

The Negro Olimpio caught hold of him roughly and pinioned him till the Captain caught up.

Charlie couldn't believe the scene—a human being hung up like a slaughterhouse animal. Maybe that was why he stood so limply in Olimpio's grasp. The identikit had taken over once again. As it had taken over for the woman hanging upside down, turning her into a laboratory animal. Only Paixao seemed wholly alert and aware.

The Identikit Charlie Faith could think of nothing particular to do or say. Olimpio propelled him easily back along the room and thrust him out into the rain.

"Mr Faith!" Paixao called after him. "Do remember that it's *your* life."

A scream of animal misery overtook him outside. This —combined with the slap of rain—shocked him back to awareness from his mental haven.

Charlie ran to the jeep.

"Jorge, you idiot, we got to get the key to the generator shed! We got to switch the current off. I hope you didn't give them that key too?"

Almeida slammed the jeep into gear viciously and trod on the accelerator.

"You think I wanted to give them the other key, you bastard?"

When it was done, and the generator shed relocked, Charlie climbed back into the jeep to find Jorge playing with the .38 he kept under the driver's seat.

"Pass that over, Jorge, huh?"

"So you can give it to the Captain—like I gave him the key?"

But he handed it over to Charlie and Charlie made a display of checking it was still loaded, while Jorge drove the jeep back towards the store shed. He hadn't told Jorge to drive there. Now they were heading that way, he found he didn't dare tell Jorge not to.

Paixao greeted Charlie at the doorway.

"An unexpected failure of energy, Mr Faith. You wouldn't be so kind as to switch the electricity back on? No? Well—I would use the helicopter batteries except for the rain, and it's tactically stupid to tie the craft down with such poor visibility. If you value your life so lightly, at least we value our dam more highly! Luckily I have a whip in the helicopter. Of tapir hide. Did you know that in ancient Chinese legends the tapir was said to be an animal that feeds on dreams? I wonder what secret revolutionary dreams my tapir whip can discover? What a shame for her you turned the electricity off. Electricity leaves no scars—except maybe in the soul. But the tapir whip, in the hands of an expert like Olimpio—to put it bluntly, Mr Faith, it flays a person alive."

His voice hardened to ice and steel.

"So will you kindly switch the electricity back on!"

Charlie hesitated.

This was the crossroads he'd tried to avoid for years.

Something hard in his trouser pocket was pressing against his thigh.

"Captain Paixao, if you don't get outa here with your

prisoners and take them to jail in the proper way—"

"Yes? What will you do, Mr Faith? Do tell me—I'm curious. Being myself the proper authority in the matter."

"I'll kick up one *helluva* stink in Santarém and with our embassy and with the news media in the States. I'll name names and everything. I'll take it up with the Church here in Brazil! How d'you fancy being excommunicated? That's what the church thinks of torturers these days!"

"Instead of employing them, eh? What threats! You'd think you were the Papal Nuncio himself. Mr Faith, you are naïve. In the most unlikely event of my exclusion, let me assure you without a doubt that I would be received back into the bosom of mother church *like a shot* once civilization had been successfully preserved. This clerical liberalism is no more than a kite flown in the wind. When the wind falls, the kite will be hauled down soon enough by Rome. Now, you hear me. I wish to speak to this bitch! What shall it be? You choose. The Electricity—or the Whip?"

Charlie chose.

He pulled out the .38 and pointed it at Paixao's belly.

THIRTEEN

ZWINGLER SAT A while with Sole as the Air Force jet hurried them down through Mexico and Central America and on over Colombia. He asked questions about Pierre and read the Frenchman's letter through a couple of times carefully.

"I guess this is one piece of protest writing that might pay off," was his acid comment as he handed it back.

He left Sole feeling as though he was harbouring some leper or criminal who happened—purely by coincidence —to have some useful contribution to make to society. He held long hushed conversations with the three other passengers.

These three men were introduced to Sole as Chester, Chase and Billy. Chester was a tall Negro with a kind of ebony beauty about him that was just a bit too slick and superficial—like a tourist carving at an African airport. Billy and Chase were clean-cut out of cemetery marble, two Mormon evangelists. Sole imagined the two large steel suitcases they'd hauled on board and blocked the aisle with as packed with thousands of Sunday School texts.

At a Brazilian airstrip on the edge of the Great Lakes scheme they transferred to a light survey plane and flew on over the devastation of the great flood. In some places all except the tallest trees had drowned. Soon they entered rainmists, where the boundaries of earth and sky and water had dissolved. The blur of a dirty aquarium tank hung about them for one hour, for two.

* * *

The helicopter pilot who was going to fly them on the last leg of their journey climbed on board out of the rain at the southernmost of the subsidiary dams—a tall easygoing Texan wearing a holstered pistol. Gil Rossignol was his name—a name to set you thinking of the French quarter of New Orleans and showboats, of cabaret and gamblers with concealed derringers—except that Rossignol's raw T-bone bulk contradicted this image flatly.

"Hi! You Tom Zwingler?"

"Didn't they give you a recognition phrase to say?"

"Why sure they did—it slipped my mind. Pardon me. Quote, Why is the sky dark at night?"

Zwingler nodded.

"The answer is—because the universe is expanding." He flashed his ruby moons apologetically. "I just want to do this thing properly."

"Professionally," agreed Chester.

The Texan grinned.

"So long as you don't ask me what it's supposed to mean, sky being dark at night, and the universe and all!"

Sole found a sentence from Shakespeare in his head, and quoted it on impulse.

"The stars above, they govern our condition."

Chester stared at him curiously.

"Just a bit of Shakespeare," shrugged Sole. "We wouldn't be here right now if it weren't for the stars."

Zwingler waved a ruby at him, disapprovingly.

"I seem to recall how the guy in King Lear who said that got his eyes put out for his trouble. Stars aren't going to govern our damn conditions. The whole point of the exercise is how we're gonna set conditions for the stars!"

To Gil Rossignol, he said:

"We want to have a word with the engineer in charge here. After that we'll hop over to the reception centre for the Indians—we ought to doublecheck on the whereabouts of the village before we head down there."

The Texan shuffled his bulk about awkwardly.

"Trouble is, Mr Zwingler, there's been some real mayhem here. Charlie Faith—he's the engineer—he got himself a crack on the skull and he's concussed. He's been flown out to hospital in Santarém. Far as I can make out from his Brazilian assistant—who's in a frankly unstable state of mind right now—to tell the truth he's pretty drunk and been sniffing ether—Charlie pulled a gun on some policeman who was interviewing political suspects in a pretty brutal style in one of the sheds here. And he got a rifle butt in his head."

"Did you say political suspects? Here—in this middle of nowhere?"

"We've had the word passed down that there's goin' to be some kind of attack on Amazon Project personnel. The communists are getting anxious. Seems like they need to make a big scene in the world press. They've sent combat units up here. One of these units was bein' questioned when Charlie got in the way—though far as I can make out they'd come to kill him, not make friends with him."

"How 'brutal' was 'pretty brutal'?" Sole demanded.

The Texan gazed out of the plane window.

"Wasn't pretty at all, I guess. They had this girl hanging upside down nude with electrodes on her tits and eyeballs and I dunno what. Charlie switched the current off so they fetched a whip and sorta ... flayed her I guess you'd say. She wasn't worth lookin' at when they'd done, the Brazilian said, just a carcass of raw meat. Personally I don't blame him gettin' drunk after that—but he ain't worth speakin' to right now—"

Zwingler looked horrified—his moons fluttered out of control.

"Disgusting. Perverted—yeah, filthy. Doesn't bear contemplating. Some of these governments we support, I dunno—"

"We got a job to do, Mr Zwingler," Chester sighed. "Never get anything done if your eyes are full of tears."

A job, cried Sole silently—such as kidnapping? And scooping out somebody's brains to sell? Is the whole world in Hell, and the Galaxy too—where a whole race of beings roam in a mental torment they call 'Love' to buy brains for a language computer? One thing to fix the mind on: one beautiful thought—Vidya and Vasilki safe in their refuge...

"These guerrillas," the Negro enquired, "are they just planning on killing people—or sabotaging as well?"

"I guess they'll try sabotage if they can manage it— there've bin minor cases from time to time—but hell, ain't much they can do to a ten mile earth wall like this one—"

"Not much those commie guerrillas can do, maybe." Chester's teeth flashed a dazzling toothpaste smile, sharp as a knife cutting butter. "How convenient these guerrilla attacks could be, consid'rin'—"

Chase and Billy stayed behind at the dam with their two steel suitcases and the survey plane. Tom Zwingler had to change his clothes for something lighter and left his ruby tiepin and cufflinks with Billy for safe-keeping.

Gil Rossignol piloted the others southward after a visit to the Indian Reception Centre.

Zwingler pored over thermographic pictures of the area radioed down by an Earth Resources Inventory satellite a few hours before they left the States, pinpointing the few remaining heat sources in that monotony of cool water. Father Pomar had scribbled notes on to a map they brought. The map was hopelessly outdated by the flood. Nevertheless the Texan flew on through a fog of rain, fast and unconcerned, relying on instruments and dead reckoning.

"Ain't nothin' to bump into, friends," he yawned. "Nothin' stickin' up."

Pomar had circled two heat sources in particular, bemused by this means of locating the remaining Indians. Privately he disbelieved that a few cooking fires could be filmed through rain from a height of a hundred miles. But he kept this opinion to himself and begged to come along for another assault on the Xemahoa conscience. Zwingler, naturally, refused.

Maybe he was more anxious to miss Pierre, than to meet him?

Sole asked himself this, but couldn't decide—sensing his own relief when the first heat source proved abortive. A village several feet deep in water—deserted, with the sodden embers of a fire propped upon a rough platform. It reminded Sole of pictures of the Inca Hitching Place of the Sun—the Solar Altar at Machu Picchu—oddly out of place in this jungle far from the Andes. Maybe these Indians were some degenerate descendants of the Incas —futilely calling on the Sun from a platform of fire? And only succeeding in calling down a helicopter, directed from space by infra-red spy eyes, wanting to sell their brains to the stars.

No one was about.

They hovered over the clearing for a few minutes, their downdraught winnowing the flood, before soaring up again and resuming their southward course.

Yet there was no need to feel ashamed of meeting Pierre, in the event. The Frenchman and all the Xemahoa men were high on the fungus drug—and oblivious.

The score of large straw huts that made up the main village enclosed a lake like a coral atoll. Rossignol landed the helicopter here on its floats and tossed an anchor into the water. The other three men let their bodies down gingerly into the brown water, then waded thigh-deep towards the small clearing where the dance was going on.

The Indians were naked, apart from their penis sheaths ornamented with dazzling feathers, like clumps of surrealistic pubic hair. They waded with glazed eyes around a small hut, led by a man so patterned with bodypaint it was hard to say what age he was—whether he was human, even. The loops and whorls on his body made him into a moving collage of giant fingerprints. Were the red blotches on his lips pigment—or blood? They looked horribly like gobs of blood spilling from his nose. He chanted a wailing singsong which the fat-bummed men took up in turns, chanted for a time then let drop into the water with glazed giggles. Nobody paid much attention to the new arrivals—whether white or black.

"They're stoned outa their minds!" laughed Chester. "That's one way to greet the end of the world."

Then Sole saw Pierre Darriand himself wade from the further side of the hut—naked as the rest of them, with his own penis sheath and grotesque clump of blue feathers sprouting out above it. His chalk-white limbs stood out among the Indians' like a leper's.

He hesitated briefly when he saw the three of them, but stumbled onwards with the dancers, shaking his head with a puzzled frown.

"Pierre!"

Sole waded towards him. With a shock of disgust he saw the black leeches clinging to Pierre's thighs and suppurating flybites pocking his white frame.

"I got your letter, Pierre. We've come to do something about it."

(But don't say what!)

Pierre cried out some words in the same singsong way as the Indians.

Chester caught hold of his arm and shook him roughly.

"Hey Man, we got to talk to you. Snap out of it."

Pierre stared down at the hand restraining him, flicked at the black fingers with his free hand and said something that sounded more lucid but was still Xemahoa.

"For heaven's sake speak English or French. We can't understand you."

Pierre began to talk in French; but the syntax was hopelessly mixed up.

"I can't make head or tail of it," Tom Zwingler sighed. "It's like he's free-associating."

"The sentence structure is all broken up, that's true, but maybe he's trying to translate what the Indians are chanting—"

Pierre fixed Sole with a curious stare.

"Chris?" he asked cautiously. Then abruptly he pulled his arm free of Chester's grasp and stumbled off. He took up the chant of the Painted Man. Grinned at the naked Indians about him. Fluffed up his blue bush of feathers with a gesture of childish pride.

"Did you see the bloodflecks in his nose?"

"The man's mindblown," sneered Chester. "We're wasting our time on him."

"He must have kept some records, Tom. He was the methodical type. A bit romantic—but methodical. Probably we're interrupting him at an impossible time right now. Let's go look in the huts for some notes or something."

"Okay—we'll leave these guys to their games. Wonder why they're dancing out here, 'stead of the village."

"Water's not so deep here—that's why maybe."

Chester found Pierre's tape recorder and diaries in one of the huts, slung in a hammock above the water.

Sitting inside the helicopter, Sole translated Pierre's diary aloud. With a growing thrill of conviction he read from entry to entry. At the beginning of the New Year, the diary lapsed for a while and there were several blank pages before it resumed—as though Pierre had lost track

178

of time and the blank was all he could put down to express this.

"So he met the guerrillas?"

"Seems that way."

"And now this drug-dosed baby is on the way. So that's what's happening. It's amazing. He's found out so much—he's been at the hub of things all along."

"I agree with you, Chris, it's highly plausible. But remember, Nevada is the real hub of events. Like the man said, it's the stars above govern our condition."

"Yes," agreed Sole dubiously—so glad that Pierre was stoned out of his mind. How long would he stay in that condition?

Zwingler nodded to Chester.

"Okay. I approve. We'll go ahead with Niagara Falls."

"You reckon?"

"I damn well hope so! Everything in the Frenchman's papers suggests it's okay. Gil, would you call up Chase and Billy?"

"That's good," the Negro smiled. "I like things to go with a bang."

"Chase," Zwingler said carefully into the microphone, "why is the sky dark at night?"

"On account of the universe expanding," crackled the reply.

"That's right, Chase. Now listen to this. The word is Niagara. Niagara, confirm?"

"Niagara—that's all?"

"For the moment. The Falls part to be delayed till the helicopter gets to you. I'm sending Gil to pick you up and bring you down here. Start Niagara Falls as soon as you pull out. We'll evacuate onward to Franklin. Tell Manáus to send the jet down to Franklin to pull us out, will you? And pass the news to Stateside that the situation here is positive. We're sending documents and tapes for analysis. Get them to Manáus by way of the spotter plane as soon as you can—have the documents telexed from the consulate there."

Zwingler had the instructions read back to him before signing off.

"What, you're sending Pierre's records back to the States?"

"Sure. They're our only instruction manual for Xemahoa."

The three men climbed back into the muddy water, Chester carrying a long canvas bag and Zwingler a TWA airline bag. They waded into Pierre's hut as the helicopter took off. Zwingler dumped the airline bag beside him on the hammock.

"How about some explanations, Tom? I'm all at sea."

"Okay, Chris."

"What's this Franklin place then?"

"It's a jungle airstrip used for surveys for the Amazon Project, south side. It can also handle jets, incidentally. The other Roosevelt, Teddy, has a river named after him hereabouts so we called it Franklin—"

"And Niagara Falls?"

"Maybe it's a bad choice of a codename. Says too much about the operation."

"A waterfall? Pouring water?"

"Uh-huh. Billy and Chase are gonna pull the plug on the dam. What those guerrillas couldn't manage in a month of sundays we can do in two minutes flat. The Lord giveth, and the Lord taketh away—"

"How do you pull the plug on all this, Tom? I thought the idea was just to fly a couple of the Indians out."

Zwingler shook his head briskly.

"If there's anything in this drug business, we got to save the whole ecology, Chris. That's the thinking at the top, back home. Your friend Pierre ought to be pleased.

Billy will be using two mines. One kiloton apiece. Water action will finish the job. Strip the dam away like sealing tape."

"Christ, you're not thinking of using nuclear explosives?"

"Nuclear's just a word, Chris—don't get all worked up about a word. They're only one kiloton apiece. Together that's only a tenth of the Hiroshima bomb."

"But what about fallout—and the flooding?"

"There'll be very little fallout. Barely detectable. Billy will mine the dam over on the far side. Flooding? Well, I guess a guy could as easily get killed crossing the street in New York or London or Rio. Let's call it the automobile casualty factor—that's all it is."

"They'll say the guerrillas did it," grinned Chester. "We'll let that word get out, even if it does mean a prestige buck for them. Nobody'll know it was nuclear, small blast like that."

"But downstream?"

"That reception camp's on fairly high land, ain't it?"

Sole felt a sense of neutrality. Yet this neutral cool was invaded from within by sparks of hot excitement and restlessness. Not anger, but excitement. It was as though Pierre had all along been a political superego. And Pierre was switched off now. Yes, it was like Nietzsche said about God being dead—anything was possible. Sole's mind pursued this idea obsessively, while Zwingler talked on.

"This automobile casualty factor is a good concept to keep in your head through all this. We're handling the future of man among the stars—not to mention on earth. An explosion might hurt some people. I'm not saying it will, just might. Likewise it could upset these Indians when we take their Bruxo away. But they'll easy get over that. With their Messiah born. The flood vanishing. The fungus sprouting again. This man Kayapi in the saddle, who knows? Later on we'll be able to synthesize the drug.

It could be dynamite to your PSF, Chris."

How marvellous for the Xemahoa, this turn of fortune —which happened to fulfil their prophecies. How amazed Pierre would be when he came to his senses.

Sole's fingers had located a loose end of fibre sticking out of the hut wall, and been tugging it this way and that restlessly. He realized he'd cut one of his fingers on the sharp edge and it was bleeding; popped the finger in his mouth and sucked it gaily like a child.

Now what was that concept he had to keep in his mind?

The automobile casualty factor. A nice bland phrase.

Only one thing was wrong with it. There weren't any cars driving round in the jungle.

Don't split hairs.

Split dams.

Split them like you split the seal on a pack of cigarettes. Whatever is sealed shall be unsealed, when the embedded child is born. He felt exhilarated and euphoric. Yet cool, at the same time. A well-tempered shiver of excitement filled his body and spirit.

He felt sure Pierre would understand. To understand all, is to forgive all—isn't that an old French proverb?

And to know all, is all that really counts. That was why the Bruxo had snorted maka-i, till his nose ran red. That was why the Xemahoa men danced in a trance, sucked by leeches.

To know the whole truth of life, as a direct experience.

From his canvas bag Chester was taking the components of an oddly-shaped gun which he now began fitting together.

"What's that, Chester?"

"You know those Indian blowguns, fire curare darts. This baby fires anaesthetic needles. Bring down a rhino before it reached you. That fast, man."

Why of course. How merciful. How sensible.

How well thought out.

Pierre's closeness elated Sole now rather than anything. His worries had gone. Had there ever been any real worries?

FOURTEEN

THE VIEW ON the screen looked calm. But Rosson was well aware it was a deceptive calm. There was violence in the children's minds now. Mostly it kept below the surface. But every day some time it erupted.

They'd accomplished what it had taken hundreds of generations of Stone Age children to accomplish—and done it in a flash of days. They had invented language. But what language was it they had invented?

Vidya, followed by the other children, had passed through the babbling phase. It was now clear to Rosson that it hadn't been just a babbling of sounds—but a babbling of ideas and concepts. They had resumed whole speech. However it was a whole speech that bore little relation to the whole speech they had been learning before the crisis. And it was interrupted by storms of violent, destructive activity that left the children lying about the room exhausted, hunted nearly to death by the pack of zombie words.

The computer programme to analyse their new language lay barely started on Rosson's desk. He had no time. Things were going too fast. He felt like a blind man staring at Madame Curie's blob of radium—seeing nothing, but getting his blind eyes burnt in the process.

As he watched, Vidya rose with a savage snarl twisting his face. He began to stalk an invisible prey. Picking up speed, he trotted off in a long ellipse around the room.

Every time a crisis occurred, a fresh variable seemed to be thrown into the equation. Fresh neural pathways fused open. The brain was blowing fuses—but the fuse wires sprouted across the gaps spontaneously, and rapidly—almost as a function of the fusing itself.

The experiment was out of control now, and only Rosson was interested.

What to do about it? Withdraw PSF from their diet? When the drug was so obviously producing results?

Vasilki got up next and set off on her own course round the room, helter-skelter.

Then Rama. Then Gulshen.

Soon the four children were running round the room, faces warped with concentration.

Briefly Rosson switched the monitor to the two other environments, hunting for a nurse. But there was nobody on duty in the logic world. Nobody seemed to be on duty in Richard Jannis's world.

He telephoned the nurses' standby room upstairs.

"That's Martinson? Rosson here. Get down to the Embedding World will you? You may have to use the Trankkit. But stay in the airlock till I tell you. I want to watch the crisis develop—"

Then he cut back to Sole's children. Zoomed in on their snarling, obsessed expressions.

The ellipses they were running wound tighter and more furiously as he looked. He understood the relation between movement and speech in his own logic world. There, the dance of the children was a redundancy strategy—letting language be purified of excess. But here something else was going on. Some different, new relationship between motion and thought. Between the movement areas of the brain and the symbol areas. Were the tensions in the children's minds discharging themselves out of the symbol world of thought and language, into the world of movement? Or were new symbolic relationships being formed by these mad bursts of activity themselves?

Rosson chewed his fingernail as he thought about the

effect of new cross-modal connections forming in the
brain . . .

"Martinson here. I'm in the airlock. They've got some
pretty vicious expressions on their faces, that lot, Mr
Rosson—"

"Yes, well don't go in yet."

Suppose PSF speeded up the manufacture of 'information molecules' to such an extent that the mind got over-
saturated, would the mind be forced to create fresh
symbols to carry on functioning? And would these symbols be formed in the action centres of the brain, if the
normal symbol areas were already overloaded? Then these
would be 'action-symbols'—symbols that sensed it as their
duty to manipulate the outside world directly. The way
that magicians used to believe they could, through their
spells and magic shapes—their 'reality symbols'.

The children raced closer to a fearful density of symbolic experience.

Abruptly, they collided. Limbs were mixed up together
as madly as a Hindu god's. Then the four bodies were
hurled apart as if by an electric shock.

They fell apart so violently that Gulshen was left lying
up against the maze wall with her left leg crumpled
under her body at an impossible angle.

"Martinson—get in there! The girl's smashed her bloody
leg!"

FIFTEEN

PH'THERI EMERGED FROM the scout ship towards midnight and waited under the sharp desert stars till Sciavoni went out to greet him.

Military police hurried round the building complex alerting Americans and Russians.

The alien stood there looking sad and haunted. But when he spoke, he sounded more impatient and irritable than sad.

"Concerning the trade exchange—"

"Won't you come inside the building, Ph'theri?"

"It is larger here. I see quite well in the dark."

"As you like. We have a human corpse on ice—shall we bring it on board your ship?"

"To the ramp will do. Other Sp'thra will take it inside."

"Can't we look in your ship then? We're very curious."

"Technology is trade-assessable—"

These monotonous economics were beginning to get on Sciavoni's nerves. He was supposed to believe these creatures were haunted by some kind of thwarted love—like Abelards of outer space, mutilated philosophers hunting for their Heloise in another dimension. Yet they carried on their love affair like spooks or machines.

"The corpse, Ph'theri! How about that? Isn't that worth a peek inside your ship?"

The alien exaggeratedly shook his head, a consciously reconstructed gesture creakily at odds with his anatomy.

"No. Because the corpse is a necessary sub-item of the main trade deal. We have to know in advance the right way to separate brain from body. Are you capable of performing this operation?"

187

"I guess not. Give us five years—"

"Wait five years? Ridiculous!"

"No, you've got me wrong. I don't mean you've got to wait. I mean in five years our doctors oughta be able to maintain the brain in isolation. The psychological problems might be the hardest nut to crack. Tell me this, Ph'theri, what will you do to stop these brains going crazy when they're cut off? They're humans—we've a right to know."

"We do not intend to let our property be hurt. The brains will have sensory links with the outside world. The primary difference is, they will no longer be mobiles. But they will not be idle. They have work to do, preparing them for their place in the Language Moon. You worry about their rest and dreaming function? Whatever is necessary for the human brain will be provided. The Sp'thra are used to minds from a thousand cultures of space, water, air and earth, remember. Entertainments? We have many hours of your TV output that can be screened before their eyes—"

"They'll still have eyes?"

"Eyes usually are an integral part of the brain in the case of hominids. Isn't that so with you? We shall examine the dead one. Bring it over to the ramp now—"

"Surely, Ph'theri. But I still think a corpse rates a look round your ship."

"Why can you people not trade-assess correctly? If your culture revered the corpse, as the Xorghil dust-whales do, things would be different. These dust whales are the sentient patterns imposed on the densest dust of a bright nebula, who tow their dying individuals towards a stellar contraction pool where their dead bodies may finally be compacted into a star and reborn as light. They care. But your culture cares nothing for corpses. Witness your entertainments! What is not valued by you, is not trade-assessable. Surely that is obvious?"

Sciavoni called through the crowd of people who had gathered.

"Somebody bring the body out. Up to the foot of the ramp. They'll take it from there."

"What's so obvious about it?" growled a Russian scientist. "So now we are the ones to suffer the fobbing-off with a few shiny beads—like your feathered Indians here in America were traded beads for their precious pelts and skins? As though we are the primitives! Quite a neat dialectical irony. Yet how naturally the spirit of man rebels against such an exploitation, when our dream is of the stars and mastery of nature!"

"It seems other beings have already mastered nature pretty effectively for themselves," sighed an American voice. "Maybe we oughta be thankful they think enough of us to want our brains. Even if they buy them like apples off a stall."

"I'll remind you people," Sciavoni snapped, "that the price tag for a human brain may still turn out to be a ticket to the stars—"

"S'posing anything materializes out of the Amazon," grunted the elder astronomer from California.

Ph'theri's paper-bag ears swelled up to capture the exchange of words.

"How soon till the Brain that Self-Embeds is here?" he demanded.

"Soon, soon," soothed Sciavoni.

Ph'theri threw up a hand peremptorily. Was it only an illusion—a reflex of their minds—or did the palm actually glow in the dark?

"Now who is being vague?" asked the alien icily.

"For Pete's sake!"

Sciavoni's eyes ranged frantically through the crowd for the discreet man from the NSA who was handling liaison with Brazil.

"Mr Silverson, what's the latest situation report, please?"

Silverson was a slice of low-calorie crispbread beside the doughy crusts of the Russians. Faintly scandalized at the number of people present, ambiguous in the darkness, he reported:

"Niagara hasn't fallen yet, Mr Sciavoni. We reckon it'll be at least twelve hours after that event before our team evacuate from Franklin. Big Bird and seismographs are on the look-out." He hesitated. "Perhaps I should add there's been some guerrilla activity reported throughout the Project area. We don't know what effect this might have—"

"We're proceeding as fast as we can, you see, Ph'theri," Sciavoni said defiantly.

Ph'theri's ears shifted shape again as he paid attention to the scarlet wires.

"The Sp'thra suggest this time bonus: you may come inside our ship with your recording equipment, if the Brain that Self-Embeds arrives within forty-eight hours. Now what about the normal language brains?"

"That's being taken care of, right now. You'll be given English, Russian, Japanese, Eskimo, Vietnamese and Persian language samples—they ought to fit the bill, linguistically."

Merchant Seaman Noboru Izanami's first journey outside of the home islands of Japan led him straight to San Francisco. He passed through the Golden Gate, where suicides stand and face the city to die, and it seemed to him like a great *torii* gateway to the shrine of the American dream.

Noboru took the elevator up Colt Tower, and shot off half a reel of film from the top. Then he turned his steps towards the Japanese residential area off Post and Buchanon, to wander nostalgically along the shopping streets, delighted to find an American city so like a Japanese one. He ate a bowl of fried soba noodles in a restaurant called Teriko's—with a display of plastic replicas of the Japanese food in its window. Outside Teriko's he met two native San Franciscans. One of them was a second or third generation Japanese immigrant, who still miraculously spoke Japanese.

"*Eego sukosi mo wakaranai?* No, Lloyd, he don't speak a word of English. *Ano né, kizuke no tame ni ippai yaro, yoshi?* I'm askin' if he'd care for a pick-me-up, just along the street a little way. *Tyotto sokorahen made—*"

Noboru worried in case he'd be a nuisance.

"Don't give it a thought. *Do-itashimashite. Anata no keiken no ohanasi ga kikitai no desu.* I'm makin' out we'd love to hear 'bout his travels. Such as those are, Lloyd, such as those are!"

Noboru introduced himself with a tight little bow.

"*Watakusi wa Izanami Noboru desu. Doozo yoroshiku!*"

They set off eastward along Post Street, wreathed in smiles.

"*Gaikokungo wa dame desu kara né!*" Noboru wrinkled his nose apologetically.

"Seems like he's no damn good at foreign languages, Lloyd. Just our boy."

A low-slung ambulance slid through the snowploughed streets of Valdez, Alaska, towards the airfield. Its windscreen wipers scooped out arcs of glass from the feathery snow.

A flat-faced, blubbery woman lay on a stretcher breathing noisily through her mouth.

"Why does she have to be transferred in this kinda weather?" whined the nurse. "Who's gonna explain to her? She can't speak a word of English. You know that?"

"I know," the driver called over his shoulder. "They got some Eskimo interpreter woman in Anchorage."

"What I'm thinking about is her husband. How do we

tell him she's been spirited away a hundred miles, maybe die on her own, nobody talking to her she knows?"

"A kidney machine has come available. She needs it. Simple."

"I don't get how an illiterate Eskimo woman has all this care lavished on her so sudden. Kidney machine treatments come expensive."

"Maybe it's her lucky day. Make sure you tell her man it's all for his woman's good, huh? Fisherman, ain't he?"

"Ordinary fisherman. I don't get it."

The ambulance slid softly through the snow.

SIXTEEN

AT NIGHT, THE women of the village replenished the wood on the bonfire platforms in the small clearing and set light to them.

Fire flared across the flood. Danced on the waves the stamping feet set up.

Pierre was still wading round the hut and moaning—his blanched body ghostly in the flickering light.

With nightfall insects also descended. The three undrugged spectators felt the needle-pricking and the fierce flushing itch. Tom Zwingler located a tube of insect repellent in his bag.

"I'll swear things are crawling on my legs," shivered Sole as he smeared some cream on. "You saw all those damned leeches on Pierre. Can't you feel something?"

"Won't get through your clothes," hoped Chester, who did not like the idea of being fed on by leeches. "Water's moving about your legs, is all."

"Why is it?"

"All the dancing."

"Flies don't seem to bother the Indians much. Maybe it's the fires. Women and kids have moved near them."

"Let's move nearer. The men are all stoned anyhow. They couldn't care less."

"Queer, isn't it—not caring about strangers watching this? A foreigner even taking part in it. I got the idea they were secretive from what Pierre wrote."

"We don't exist, man," sniggered Chester. "Just let them wait." He brandished his dart gun in the air.

However, wait was all they had to do. No helicopter showed up.

They stared at the ecstatic faces in the firelight. Waited, while the Bruxo with bloody nostrils led the men endlessly round the hut.

Listened, without comprehension, to the myths being chanted.

"There's an undertow, Tom—"

"Shut up about them fuckin' leeches will you? Sure I feel something—but just shut up about it!"

"You think it's the dam, Chris?"

"Maybe."

"Shit, man, this place'll take days to drain!"

Tom Zwingler thought about it.

"We're near one of the main river channels. But it must be emptying at one hell of a lick if we feel effects already—"

"Didn't you say the dam would strip away like sealing tape?"

"I guess I did, Chris."

"If we're feeling it here, what the hell's it like downstream!"

"Maybe a bit more than we anticipated? If that's the case, where the hell are Chase and Billy?"

"Could be the water is pulling," grunted the Negro. "Better than leeches I s'pose."

"What was the time fuse on those mines, Chester?"

"Fifteen minutes, Mr Sole. They just had to dump the mines down the side of the dam from the helicopter—"

"Isn't that cutting it a bit fine?"

"Christ, no—they fly straight on after dumping them. No sweat—they'd be miles out of the blast zone."

When the second steel suitcase had slid underwater, Gil flew the machine on along the line of the dam for four kilometres to the trees.

As they rose up over the first wall of forest, a line of half a dozen coin-size holes suddenly punched themselves in the plexiglass.

Gil's jaw shattered.

Flew away in a spray of blood and bone splinters.

He fell across the altitude control stick, his heavy body thrashing about on top of it. From the remnants of his mouth gurgled a sheeplike bleat.

Like water spilled from a jug, the machine began to fly at the ground.

Billy caught hold of Gil's body; but they were too close to the trees already. The helicopter struck. Turning over twice, its blades scythed leaves and branches before they crumpled up and snapped.

The wrecked machine settled into a nest of branches and hung there, dripping fuel. It didn't burn. But the broken bodies inside burned with pain enough.

Billy fought back the nausea of his broken bones and got the hatch open. He peered down upon tier on tier of interlocking branches. Red macaws spattered through the foliage, visions of his own heartblood, as Billy fainted.

Burning with fever, flybites and hunger, Raimundo stumbled out from the cover of the trees on to the freeboard of the dam. He tried to see where the helicopter had fallen. But couldn't.

Yet he heard the noise from the treetops, then the sudden silence, and a sullen grin spread across his face. The automatic rifle trembled in his hand as he turned away from the forest to face the causeway stretching endlessly towards the east.

How bitterly he hated this dam. How purely too. For days as he waded through the jungle the dam had been burning into his mind's eye like a red-hot bar. Even the agony of worms hatching out in his wounds meant nothing.

It stretched into the distance—on one side it drowned

the world, on the other side it strangled it.

Then, absurdly, as he stared, the dam bloomed into a sunburst. Before his eyes flowered an incandescent point of sunlight, that bored painfully into his vision.

Instinctively he jerked his head away.

The sunburst moved with his head, though already the actual light had disappeared in a boiling cloud of mud and foam.

The ground snatched itself away from his feet, a fist of air slapped him down.

Raimundo picked himself up and fled back into the trees, terrified and confused. He collapsed inside the forest, exhausted. He still saw that heatflower—it glowed with the power of his hatred, and only faded as his strength ebbed.

SEVENTEEN

Now, at long last, a climax seemed imminent.

As the first bodies began to brush directly up against the wet straw wall, the Bruxo emitted a series of snorts from his bloody nostrils like a bull with asthma, slowing the dance to a halt. Then the painted figure shouted out at the top of his voice what even Sole, ignorant of the Xemahoa language, could recognize for the grand finale of the myth cycle.

In the silence that followed, with a final wag of his orange bush of pubic feathers, the old man disappeared into the hut.

The rest of the men drifted together before the doorway, with the Frenchman near the back of the group—tight albino buttocks among all the rotund tan-brown bums.

"I'm going to have another shot at talking to him—"

The play of light and shadows on the men's sweaty bodies made their decorated genitals seem grotesquely deformed. Already he was surrounded by alien beings as alien as any of the Sp'thra, as he slipped through the Indians to his friend's side.

"Pierre—"

The Frenchman stared in his face and nodded in recognition. His eyes were widely dilated by the drug—the pupils all black filling up the whole space of the iris. Sole glanced down. That ridiculous penis sheath of his with its blue bush! Eileen would— But what would Eileen think? Sole dismissed the thought, half-formed, and it easily disappeared.

"Do you realize the water's going down, Pierre? The dam's gone, you know. Finished. Kaput."

"Quoi?"

"The dam's been blown up, Pierre. Can't you feel the water pulling your feet?"

Pierre stared at the water then bent down to touch it. He thrust his hands under the surface and groped about.

"The Xemahoa are safe. So is the fungus."

A scream of pain cut through the night from the inside of the hut, followed by a howl of words in the Bruxo's voice that set the crowd shuffling about nervously.

Sole seized hold of Pierre's arm and dragged him upright.

"What the hell was that?"

"C'est une césarienne, vous savez—"

"A caesarian? You mean the old man's operating on that poor woman?"

Pierre nodded enthusiastically.

"But he'll kill her—he's stoned out of his mind. He won't know what he's doing!"

"Oui, mais la pierre est coupée—"

"What stone is split?"

The Bruxo must be opening the pregnant woman like you'd crack a nut to get the kernel out, thought Sole in horror—as another scream set the crowd rustling.

"What stone?" repeated Sole.

But he already had the answer—it was in the Xemahoa story about how the brain came into existence. He tried to remember what happened, according to Pierre's diary. A stone had been tricked into opening itself up—and a man snake had slipped in and tied himself in knots. The origin of the brain that invented the embedded speech, Xemahoa B.

The rest of the story was about the origin of entrails. By the sound of it, the woman's entrails were being ripped open brutally now to bring that brain-child out into the open!

A last scream. Then the Bruxo shouted, and his shout rapidly became a howl that drove the Xemahoa back in an agitated pack—as though something evil was writhing out of the hut, some invisible snake coiling across the water. They knocked into Sole and Pierre, nearly sweeping them off their feet.

From the corner of his eye, Sole noticed Chester hoisting the dart gun behind the crowd, hoped he wouldn't be stupid and bloody-minded enough to use it.

The Bruxo rushed out of the hut, his eyes wild and hysterical. He waved bloody fingers at the crowd, took a couple of steps forward then fell into the water. He crouched there like a beast and howled a single word.

"MAKA-I!"

"Bugger taboos!" snarled Sole. He dragged Pierre with him towards the hut, skirting the roaring creature in the water.

Nobody tried to stop them.

Inside, he shone a torch on to the rough pallet bed.

The woman lay in a semi-conscious state with her baby tucked against her breast. Her belly gaped open, roughly cut by the sharp flint lying beside it. The chopped-off birth cord hung out of it.

But the baby—

Sole stared at it, too shocked to feel sick.

Three brain hernias spilled from great vents in its skull —grey matter slung in tight membrane bags about its head, like codroe at the fishmonger's. The top part of its face, beneath those bags of brain, had no eyes—two smooth dents where they ought to have been.

From several places in its torso spilled ruptures. They jutted out of a body that only approximately contrived to contain itself within itself.

Pierre bent over the tiny being pulsing by the woman's side. The question whether it was male or female seemed immaterial now.

"Living!" he cried in a kind of raptured disgust.

"Yes, Pierre—alive. But for how long!"

The head squirmed towards the sound of their voices. The eyeless forehead tracked them. The mouth opened red and empty as a baby bird's and a shrill squeal came out of it.

"Ah," sighed Pierre, as though he understood something in that primal squeal of sound.

From outside, incredibly, came cries of joy—unmistakable shouts of victory.

Sole whirled away from Pierre to the door to see what was going on.

Kayapi stood by the Bruxo, gesturing at the waters—he'd realized at long last that the flood was going down.

Solemnly, the young Indian put his arm round the Bruxo's shoulder and helped him up. Coughing, and bleeding from the nose, the old man clung to his natural son, to stop himself from stumbling.

The Bruxo's apprentice splashed towards them but Kayapi made an angry, spiteful gesture at him to get back, and the youth shrank away through the other men, unnoticed and unwanted.

Sole returned to the bed and plucked Pierre away from the woman and her freak. He came away reluctantly, rubbing his eyes.

"What's Kayapi saying now, Pierre? Translate, damn you."

"Maka-i himself drinks the flood," Pierre stammered.

"Yes?"

"Feel him drink the waters—they pour down his throat—"

"Go on."

"The great plan has worked, thanks to Father Bruxo.

But the baby—ah, the cunning devil, Kayapi—!"

"Go on!"

"The baby isn't Maka-i himself. It's his message to the Xemahoa. Maka-i cannot come in person. But it's a true message he's sent—he drinks the flood to prove it. Now his message has to be explained to the Xemahoa by the right man—"

"I've got it!" Sole cried.

"Eh?"

"Listen to me, Pierre, you go to Kayapi and tell him he's right about the baby being a message and having to explain it. But remind him that he can't do that while the old Bruxo's still here. He'll have to go away—and we'll take him away! Say that. And the woman in the hut too, we'll take her. Go on, promise him. You don't know how important it is."

(Christ, though, the woman—would none of the Xemahoa women enter the hut to help her? She had to be kept alive, her mind was saturated in the drug awareness!)

Sole dragged Pierre across the clearing to face Kayapi.

"Go on, tell him," he shouted. "We'll take the old man and the woman. Then Kayapi will have a free hand—"

Leaving him standing there, he hurried on to Chester and Zwingler, praying Pierre had the wit to do what he was told. Chester was still waving the dart gun about, but with less confidence now. Tom Zwingler started asking questions, but Sole interrupted:

"Either of you know any first aid? The mother is lying all torn up by the clumsiest caesarian operation in history and we need her—she's saturated in the drug. She'll satisfy the Sp'thra, same as the old Bruxo will. And if Pierre tells Kayapi what I said to tell him, we'll be able to take mother and Bruxo out of here without having to fire a single dart into anyone."

"Is the baby alive?"

"Christ, that's a disaster. It's alive—but with multiple

hernias, brain and body. Kayapi's trying to explain it away right now. But we've got to save that woman, she's hurt bad—"

"Can you handle it, Chester?"

"Gimme the bag." The Negro thrust his dart gun at Zwingler to hold and rummaged through the airline bag.

"Some sulfa powder here, and penicillin tablets. A few other things. See what I can do."

He grinned broadly.

"Hope she doesn't think the Devil's come for her."

"She's in no shape to think anything. Here, take the torch—you'll need it."

Chester pushed his way brusquely through the Indians. Their whole attention was centred on Kayapi now. Sole still felt surprised at how suddenly the 'taboo' on the hut had evaporated now that the child was born. Now it didn't seem to matter who went in there.

"Where the hell's the bloody helicopter, Tom?"

Zwingler tucked the gun under his arm and shrugged.

"How far's this Franklin place?"

"Eighty, ninety miles. We shan't have to walk. They'll have a helicopter. They'll send it, if anything's happened to Chase and Billy."

"They just might send it too bloody late."

Zwingler swung away from Sole abruptly, to end the conversation.

Overhead, a skyful of stars and scudding rainclouds. He stared up at them, pursing his lips—whistling soundlessly.

After a time, the clouds gathered into larger masses that masked the stars, and rain began to fall again.

Now that the Xemahoa knew the flood was receding, no one bothered to heap any more dry wood on to the bonfire platforms. In another half-hour the fires guttered out.

EIGHTEEN

Memo to: CHIEF OF STAFF, US ARMY
CHIEF OF STAFF, US AIR FORCE
CHIEF OF NAVAL OPERATIONS
COMMANDANT OF THE MARINE CORPS
CONSULTANT MEMBERS, US INTELLIGENCE BOARD
DIRECTOR, NATIONAL AERONAUTICS & SPACE
ADMINISTRATION
Subject: WASHINGTON SPECIAL ACTION GROUP MEETING # 1
ON PROJECT "LEAPFROG"

13. ...But beyond the technological and political desirability of acquiring this knowledge lies a whole psychological domain, which we might go so far as to characterize as a crisis in this planet's Nöosphere (to borrow the theologian Teilhard de Chardin's word for the zone of operation of the human mind).

This crisis has been looming over Mankind ever since the Neolithic Revolution first ushered in the germs of a technology that would transform the natural environment.

In a very meaningful sense, the crisis that we have reached in the late 20th Century is the logical outcome of technological civilization itself. Once the technological path is chosen, Man must elect to expand outwards by means of his technology—or else collapse. No steady-state is conceivable or desirable once expansion has begun. The steady-state may be dreamt of or fantasized about—but it is merely a pipe-dream which will not work in practice, and which would have disastrous cultural and psychological repercussions, if any sustained effort was made to make it work.

Technological and cultural de-escalation is no more possible than Devolution is biologically acceptable for a species. In the same way as biological evolution is an anti-entropic process, leading towards ever more complex states of physical organization, so technological culture (the culmination of a million years of evolution) involves an ongoing process of complexification and expansion.

Nevertheless a critical point does occur in this growth process. This is the stage where there appear to be 'no further worlds to conquer'—and where the side-effects of conquering the one world that is available appear to be producing an increasingly negative pay-off. At this stage a take-off to Stage Two technological culture has to occur —the stage of planetary and stellar exploration and expansion. Otherwise a disastrous and traumatic collapse must surely ensue.

The disillusionment with Project Apollo must be viewed in this light. Man has reached the Moon. Where is there to go now? The answer seems to be 'nowhere that we can realistically hope for'.

The assault that has been gaining momentum for a decade now, of ecopolitical protest groups, implies a profoundly damaging psychological withdrawal from these delimited boundaries. It would terminate Stage One without ushering in Stage Two. The result could only be apathy and decay on a planet-wide scale—besides being politically contrary to what we conceive of, fundamentally, as our identity as a nation. (See Hudson Institute Papers HI-3812-P, 'The Perils of the Steady-State'; HI-3014-P, 'The End of the Neolithic Nöosphere: Implications for US Policy'.)

The alien visit is bound to hasten this process of disintegration and withdrawal disastrously, as the full implications of the haste, and indifference of the beings known as the Sp'thra to the finest ambitions of the human race, come to be more widely realized.

14. The exchange of six live brains, competent in six human languages, should thus seem to go ahead, with the overt aim of obtaining an improved form of planetary travel technology (together with some other data of primarily academic interest).

15. However, it must be strongly emphasized that although the donkey allows himself to be lured by a carrot, yet the human being is painfully aware (however tasty the carrot may be) that there is a field full of such carrots, elsewhere, in the control of a farmer. Were the human being in the place of the donkey, he would be well advised to remember how hard his kick is, and how unexpected, and to what good effect it can be delivered; and how essential to his psyche this act might be.

16. Attached are detailed action recommendations codenamed 'MULEKICK'; together with a summary of the key psychological features thought to underpin the Unidentified Flying Object phenomenon, codenamed 'WELLES FARRAGO'.

'WELLES FARRAGO' also includes a summary of ways to manipulate religious and social hysteria as (a) Diversion from Undesirable Goals; (b) Shoring-up of Fragmenting Societies; together with a tie-in to the action recommendations detailed in 'MULEKICK'. Adjustments have been graphed for a wide spread of cultural norms ranging from the Post-Industrial, late sensate culture of the United States, through the various Chaos, Crisis and Charisma cultures of underdeveloped nations (with special emphasis on Brazil and its neighbours).

17. In view of the exceptional sensitivity of both 'MULEKICK' and 'WELLES FARRAGO', access *must* be limited on a strict need-to-know basis.

NINETEEN

Roused from sleep, Sciavoni gulped down a benzedrine tablet and a glass of milk then pulled on his clothes and stumbled from the room with the military policeman who wakened him.

Silverson was waiting for him on the ground floor.

"Before you talk to the alien, Mr Sciavoni—Franklin has had to send out a search and rescue mission to look for Zwingler and his Indians."

Sciavoni, who had been dreaming an Italian spaghetti Western till just a couple of minutes before, found this information faintly confusing and shook his head sleepily, hoping the pill would hurry up and take effect.

"The thing is," Silverson whispered, as they headed for the door to outside, "guerrilla activity's getting worse down there. We just heard the bastards dynamited Project Headquarters in Santarém. Apparently the whole situation has been much worse than the Brazilian authorities realized. In a sense, this exonerates us for blowing that dam. Let's say it confuses the issue nicely. But we still don't know where Zwingler and that man Sole are, even if they're still alive—"

"So I have to stall Ph'theri?"

"Yes, that's no joke," sympathized Silverson. "But that ain't all. I fear our friends made too good a job of blowing the dam. The really worrying thing is reports of the sheer volume of water emptying down that river. We're afraid the lower dam is going to be overtopped. If that happens and the weight of both lakes gets down to the primary dam upstream of Santarém—well, that's that. I wouldn't like to be in Santarém."

Sciavoni passed a hand over his tousled wiry hair agitatedly. NASA spent billions of dollars to safeguard the lives of a trio of human beings a quarter million miles from home—the idea of protecting life sank in after a while.

"Still," Silverson consoled, "I hear the guerrillas blew up a barge-load of gelignite inside one of the locks at Santarém. So when the structure fails, it can always be blamed on them. It'll make it seem more plausible they sabotaged the upper dam too."

"Bad. It's bad. Look Silverson, I can't concentrate on that aspect right now. All I want to know about is Sole and Zwingler and those blessed Indians."

"Well, like I said. Franklin has a search mounted now. They know roughly where to look."

However, Ph'theri wasn't to be stalled, out there under the stars which were his stars.

"Forty-eight hours," the alien said sharply, raising his hand. "The time bonus lapses—"

"It's the terrain, Ph'theri. Dense jungle, it's terribly difficult . . ."

"Is there any real evidence for the existence of this Self-Embedding Brain? We have traded with species who thought themselves wily, before."

"I resent that, Ph'theri. We're going to a lot of trouble to get that brain for you."

"Where are the ordinary brain units?"

"They're all here now, Mr Sciavoni," Silverson said brightly. "The Soviets came through with theirs about half an hour ago. I guess their SST landing was what alerted Ph'theri."

"Good," said Ph'theri. "Let us get on with that transfer, at least. We have dissected the corpse. We will perform brain excision together with eyes and elements of the spinal column. Subsequent testing procedures should occupy another twenty-four hours, which will allow you time to establish the intelligibility of the data we transfer to you. If there is no sign of the Self-Embedding Brain by then, we will wait another twenty-four hours, then we shall have to leave—"

Two other Sp'thra, who must have been monitoring the conversation, appeared in the doorway of the scoutship. They carried a display screen with a small control panel down the ramp and set it on the concrete before Sciavoni.

"This is programmed with the relevant information. And now, the brain-units please," Ph'theri insisted.

Reluctantly, Sciavoni called out instructions; and shortly after that the first of six mobile stretchers with a sedated human form on it was wheeled through the glass doors.

Sciavoni hurriedly bent to inspect the data screen.

TWENTY

THE WOMAN IN the hut died, and her maka-i laden brain with her, about midday, in spite of Chester's efforts.

Yet the deformed baby still lived on after a fashion. Its ruptured organs continued to function. Its exposed brain remained conscious. Its blind head shuffled after sounds like a worm. It squealed.

The Xemahoa all went back to the village shortly after dawn, Kayapi leading the sick, confused Bruxo by the hand like a child. No one bothered to look into the taboo hut. For the baby it was plainly a case of ordeal by exposure—and Caraiba. Perhaps it didn't matter to Kayapi whether the baby was alive or dead, from the point of view of interpretation.

The Indian men retired to their hammocks to sleep their racing headaches off. Only Pierre seemed to be trying to come down from his drug trip by racing it to death—splashing back and forth along the jungle corridor between village and hut, obsessively. His behaviour reminded Sole of a shellshocked ex-submariner who used to run up and down the road outside his house when he was a boy, performing endless trivial errands.

After the mother died, they confronted the Frenchman, to see whether his exertions had induced a more lucid frame of mind yet.

But Chester was in a sour mood at his failure to preserve the Indian woman's life and Tom Zwingler was feeling sick at heart at the delay to their mission, so that the confrontation did not start off sympathetically or happily.

"Did you tell this Kayapi guy the Bruxo has to go away?" demanded Chester.

"The birds of his thought have flown off," Pierre sighed. "All lost in the forest since he saw that baby. But Kayapi will call them back—Kayapi knows how."

This faithful trust in someone who had done nothing whatever for the woman or her child was the last straw to Chester.

"Smart guy. Your Kayapi'll eat shit with the best of them—and know exactly why he's doin' it. Like us, hey? Only, more effective, hey? He'll get what he wants. Look how he manipulated you—drugs and girls and I dunno what else!"

For a moment Pierre was utterly taken aback.

"But Kayapi is a man of knowledge," he stammered. "The Xemahoa have an amazing comprehension of the world—"

"Don't give me that crap. Kayapi couldn't care a blue damn about 'the world'. He's seen where he's best off. He wouldn't cut much ice in the outside world away from this shit-heap, is all."

Pierre stared at the Negro in worried disgust.

"He is my teacher—"

"A fine baby their 'amazing comprehension' produced! They're lucky it had a mouth and a nose on its face."

Pierre fluttered his hands in agitation.

"Kayapi has suffered and learnt in exile. Now he comes home. He is the true hero figure."

"It's all so bloody accidental!" Tom Zwingler exploded. "It isn't as if he knew the water was going to go down. We blew the dam. He couldn't have known things were going to happen this way."

Pierre shook his head stubbornly.

"No. He knew—he promised me."

"Believe what you like, damn you! But to me, this monster is the real climax of the maka-i business. The one and only conclusion it would have come to without our intervention. Kayapi is just a plain lucky opportunist."

They might handle Pierre more tactfully, Sole reckoned. It was stupid putting his back up like this. He tried to shift the tenor of the conversation away from recrimination and bickering.

"That's as may be, Tom. But mightn't we still be right about these Indians? To put it in Ph'theri's words, about their high trade value? It still seems to me the Indians are tackling the same sort of problem as the aliens are tackling with their thirteen thousand years of technology. The Sp'thra found themselves confronted by something abnormal—something from outside of Nature. They built a universal thought machine to answer the challenge. The Xemahoa were faced by this unnatural flood and fought back in their own terms—not technological terms this time, but biological and conceptual ones—"

Pierre stared at Sole in bewilderment, wondering, perhaps, whether another wave of the drug-reality had just washed over him. Of course, Pierre knew nothing whatever about the Sp'thra Signal-Traders. Taking part in a discussion with him on these terms was rather like inviting an ancient Roman priest of Jupiter to discuss salvation with a couple of Jesuits!

"For crying out loud, Chris, you're not trying to suggest that that monster is any sort of answer?"

"It's alive. Let's keep it that way, is all I suggest. Maybe there's a reason why it has no eyes."

"Sure! Its DNA is so fucked up by that fungus!"

"Maybe it will see another reality outside of this. Who knows what language it may be capable of generating? What it may be able to describe? Can't we find something to feed it? It breathes. It can eat."

"They're not marching out to the manger bearing any gifts, I notice," observed Zwingler sarcastically. "They can't think much of it."

"Oh, that is explained," Pierre said briskly. "Kayapi has told them, he employs you as Caraiba Bruxos—so they keep away."

"Why the hell didn't you tell us! Let's see about gettin' some milk for that brat. Show me where, Frenchman."

Chester seized hold of his arm and marched him away towards the village.

Sole went into the hut to take another look at the maka-i child.

What flight of fancy had made him come out with that remark about an 'answer'? He was grasping at straws. This whole business of the ecology and chemistry and linguistics of the Xemahoa culture would take a couple of years' patient research to disentangle. Maybe in the end all they would find out was that these people had discovered some naturally-occurring stimulator like the one that Haddon had already synthesized, but with particularly undesirable hallucinatory and teratogenic side-effects—producing fantasies and monsters instead of more efficient thought.

The baby let out a kitten's squeal as Sole's shadow fell across its exposed brain. He experimented moving backwards and forwards. Could it sense light and shade after all?

What the hell! It would die. And be better off dead— like the mangled mother by its side, whose nine months of taboo imprisonment only led to this sorry mess.

Chester returned from the village, pulling a woman along brusquely by the hand. Her breasts were swollen with milk, their nipples fat pepper pots. Pierre splashed alongside, speaking to her in Xemahoa consolingly.

The sight of the dead mother and the freak baby made her moan with fear, but Chester kept a firm hold on her, goosed her nipples and shoved his long black finger at the baby's mouth.

"Tell her not to pick the baby up, Frenchman—she'll harm it."

The woman finally understood what was expected, bent over the baby, guided a swollen nipple to its lips. The lips closed on her and sucked her lustily.

"Christ only knows if there's any way through that thing from its top end to its bottom. Maybe it's all tied up in knots inside. That's the story, ain't it—clever snake tied himself up in knots?" Still, Chester watched the woman carefully in case she damaged any of the ruptures.

"Sorcerer's apprentice is wandering round the village looking half-demented—realized he ain't heir apparent to this shit-heap any more—"

"It isn't a shit-heap, you white Negro," growled Pierre. Chester laughed scornfully.

The woman fled back to the village after half an hour. But Pierre had told her to come again, and she said she would.

Since no one else seemed prepared to do anything about the dead mother's body—and it couldn't stay lying beside the baby—Chester finally carried it out of the hut and away into the jungle. He left it wedged in the crook of a tree. It could be buried when the water had all gone. Or the Xemahoa could burn it—whatever the local custom was. He came back to the hut and lay down on the pallet beside the monster, with a shrug of disgust, to get some rest. Nowhere else was dry.

Late on in the afternoon Pierre reappeared with some dry fish and some kind of pasty soft-boiled taproot which he handed to Sole.

Sole shared the meal with his two companions—and discovered how hungry he was. Even dry fish and boiled root seemed delicious.

When they finished eating, Pierre demanded:

"What's it all about then, Chris?" He was cold sober

now. "Am I supposed to understand that the American Government has wrecked its own dam for the sake of a few Indians? That's a pretty tall story."

Sole gathered up his courage and told him.

The subsequent confessional episode left Sole feeling limp and exhausted. He felt swarmed-over, sensitized, eroticized, and guilty—very vulnerable—as though he had become emotionally dependent on the Frenchman once again, in some dark corner of himself. As though Pierre had been reinstated in his position as Sole's conscience and superego. Which simply wasn't the case. He was clear of that hang-up now. He was free. It was just a question of proceeding by the most effective route to gain Pierre's acceptance of what was going to happen—since Pierre was the person who had influence with Kayapi. So he had to confess—to gain the right emotional leverage. Or so he reckoned, at any rate. Cold facts would not be sufficient for Pierre.

Tom Zwingler could see none of this. He regarded Sole's confessional performance with open hostility and contempt—though he was none too sure of himself, by this stage. His ruby-nudity was showing—his armour had been missing for too long.

For Sole it was excessively disturbing—this vulnerable, touchy explanation to his former friend and the one-time lover of Eileen. The man who had given life to his son.

Pierre went away to think, or to get some sleep.

Sole hunted for somewhere to lay his own tired body. His nerves felt raw with over-stimulation. Chester woke up when he wandered into the hut a second time; and Sole took his place on the straw bed. He fell asleep beside the baby.

No helicopter came.

The woman returned from the village to feed the baby when the stars came out.

Pierre held himself aloof, except for providing some more dried fish and root for them to eat. They tasted less delicious this time. He refused to talk about the Sp'thra or the brain trade. Anyway, these seemed ever more remote as the next day dragged on dampfooted into yet another dusk. And another wet dawn.

Zwingler grew progressively more gloomy. He consulted his watch mechanically from time to time. But as the American grew more saturnine, Sole's spirits began to recover. The problem of the Sp'thra became a fantasy interpolation between the secluded solidity of Vidya's world and the equally secluded and solid reality of the Xemahoa people. The two special worlds connected up with one another in his mind healthily and cleansingly.

Sole began going down to the village and looking round, watching the reviving life of the jungle people with increasing fascination. The women wove fish traps, winding the long strands of leaf fibre in and out according to traditional patterns that Pierre said were derived from the shape of the constellations—stars swam in the sky, a harvest of light trapped in imaginary lines, and so fishes were supposed to swim into the traps, attracted by these mimic lines, entangling their fins in them. Women smoke-dried the fish which the men scrupulously gutted—the dragging out of entrails being a male preserve, though as the men were untidier than the women a perpetual heap of stinking guts lay not far away from the huts, host to droves of flies—on the other hand, maybe this kept the flies away from the huts themselves.

The male children played games of marbles with small round stones and gourds with holes in the end as jackpots, the winner dancing round rattling the full gourds like maracas—and the girls tried to slip in and steal any of the stones that popped out of the hole during the boy's gyrations. Inevitably the boy lost some of his winnings, had to chase and trap the girls who snatched them up while their friends ran interference for them. This could be guaranteed to lead on to the Laughing Contest, a slap and tickle routine of sexplay and an endurance test carried on with huge high spirits.

Kayapi and the Bruxo stayed secluded till late on the third day after the birth in the hut with the mat over the door. Then the young Indian reappeared, looking tired but supremely confident, a long distance runner on his winning stretch. He called a crowd together—from the fringe of which the sorcerer's apprentice looked on, face stubbornly blank, the new mental leper.

When enough had gathered, he went back inside and led the old man out. Blood still clung to the Bruxo's lips and nose in a dry black crust that flies settled on, which he was too weary to wave off. His bodypaint had run and mixed till he looked like a mess of balled-up plasticine, with his macaw-feather pubic bush tatty and mud-stained now.

The old Shaman looked down at the mud that remained of the flood, and smiled.

Together, uproariously, the Xemahoa men laughed.

They took their laughter seriously, sending it booming round the clearing, chasing away the last gremlins of the flood. Of all the men, only the apprentice refused to laugh, keeping a stiff face and finally slinking away with his tail between his legs—Kayapi laughed volubly in the direction of his retreat, hooting him off the scene.

The Bruxo and Kayapi set off for the hut where the baby lay.

At the taboo hut, Kayapi gestured Chester and Zwingler aside impatiently, took the old man by the arm and led him in. Sole approached Pierre.

"What are they going to do with the baby? Any idea?"

216

Pierre shrugged his shoulders, contemptuously as Kayapi.

They stayed inside a long time, till the stars came out and the moon to light the clearing. Chester and Zwingler stood behind the other Indians, nervously alert for sounds, Chester fingering the dart gun and Zwingler consulting his watch—and except for the absence of bonfires on their stands of stakes in the deeper floodwater of three days before and the absence of a mother in the hut, it was a replica of the original birth scene. From within the hut after a time came a loud groaning noise, and from the women grouped outside, who hadn't participated during the events three days previously except as passive spectators, arose in response a loud groan—mimic birth pains which the Xemahoa men promptly uttered short barking laughs at.

"Fuckin' thing would have bin dead if I hadn't got it fed," growled Chester. "This whole thing's so fuckin' arbitrary—like you said, Mr Zwingler."

"They know perfectly well what they're doing," Pierre rebuked him loftily, a shade too sanctimoniously so it seemed to Sole.

After a period of groaning and laughter under the moonlight, the Bruxo appeared in the hut doorway, spoke to the tribe.

Pierre condescendingly interpreted.

"Changes are coming to pass. Let me tell you a fresh story of how the snake has come out of the stone again—how he has coiled himself round the outside of the stone. Bruxo says that the child lacks eyes because he doesn't need them. Eyes are the tunnel the brain looks through. However this child's brain is already outside of his head, watching us and knowing us without the need of eyes—the brain itself looks out..."

"I sure admire this guy's inventiveness."

"Imbecile—this is the birth of mythic thinking. A vast

change could be coming over this inbred people."

"Damn cute opportunism, I still say. Took him three days to work out an alibi—"

"If we could only explain our own culture shocks to ourselves as meaningfully," wished Sole.

"Quite!" breathed Pierre intensely, giving him the first sympathetic look for many hours.

Then Kayapi came out carrying the ruptured child into the moonlight—the baby uttering sharp kitten cries.

"Christ, be careful," hissed Chester, handling his dart gun impotently.

Kayapi held the child up high to the stars and moon, walked among the Xemahoa daintily, delicately, as the Bruxo spoke stumblingly on from the doorway.

"The thinking brain has come outside. Have dreams left the Xemahoa people then? he asks. No, for Kayapi my son from Outside, who knows the Outside World, will put dreams back inside the Xemahoa stone. How? Watch him. Water is gone from xe-wo-i—that's the tree the fungus is parasitic on. The maka-i mother has gone to lie in xe-wo-i's arms—"

The Bruxo stumbled towards the crowd which divided and fell in behind him and Kayapi, as Kayapi bore the baby out into the jungle, holding it high.

They came to the tree where Chester had lodged the mother's body—it still hung in the tree crotch.

"Hey, is that the tree?"

"How the hell do I know?" snapped Pierre. "I told you I never knew—"

"Big coincidence," sneered Chester. "Maybe he's just makin' out that's the fungus tree. Somebody must have slipped into their hut and told 'em I put her there. Everything's grist to that bastard's mill—"

"Maybe the Bruxo divined it," sniggered Zwingler.

"Shut up, he's saying she is buried in the sky—I suppose he means the air, rather than underground—so that maka-i may have room to re-enter the earth and the Xemahoa to dream new dreams—"

"He's plannin' on gettin' rid of the baby, I'm tellin' you—I can smell it a mile off!"

"Damn it, Chester, we're powerless—watch!—be an observer."

"At least until you hear your helicopter coming," Pierre smiled grimly.

"At least till that."

Kayapi knelt by the tree roots, laid the baby down on the still wet soil, began scooping at the mud like a dog with his forepaws intent on burying a bone.

Dug a hole.

Some of the yellow clay he exposed he scooped into his mouth, chewed and swallowed down.

"Bruxo says he will return to the Xemahoa people—to the inside of the tribe—bringing inside with him what was outside, the escaped dreams—"

Kayapi picked the baby up—and the women groaned in unison—and the men gave vent to guttural barking laughter.

Abruptly he brought the baby to his mouth, sank his teeth into the brain hernias. For minutes he gnawed as ravenous-seeming as a wild dog or vulture at the baby's brain hernias, while the women groaned and the men laughed, gulping that living brainmatter down till he'd peeled brain back to the smooth rifted skull.

Sole vomited as Kayapi's tongue flicked into the fissures deep as he could, slobbering at the soft baby skull in a cannibalistic french kiss.

Finally he thrust the spent body into the hole he'd dug, without touching the hernias of the guts, pressed down the soil around it, hid it; patted the soil down with a smug grin . . .

Face distorted, Pierre stared at Sole and his pool of root and fish vomit.

"You sell brains, now he eats them!" he screamed. "Oh but the universe is a filthy cannibal place—existence itself is exploitation! Don't your space monsters just prove that too. Come on Chris, tell me some more about the wonders of the galaxy—then let's get out there and eat knowledge!" Pierre jabbed a finger viciously up at the overhead leafcover, hiding the bland cold stars...

Thereafter Kayapi strutted about, while the old Bruxo lay in a state of collapse inside the taboo hut on the pallet where the baby had been born.

Chester watched over the old man sullenly—over the last remaining Self-Embedding Brain—trying to make things tolerable for him.

TWENTY-ONE

SECRET & SENSITIVE

Subject: WASHINGTON SPECIAL ACTION GROUP MEETING # 2
CONCERNING PROJECT "LEAPFROG"

7. It is remarkable to what extent the 'Brazilian Revolution' has already, *by sheer adjacency,* thrown Argentina, Uruguay and Guyana into widespread civil turmoil, and Paraguay into a state bordering on anarchy —and had serious repercussions in nations as far removed from Brazil geographically as the Republic of South Africa, Spain and Japan. In the 'supersaturated' cultural context of Planet Earth today, this kind of trigger effect is predictable, and it is worth noting that the contagion may be as much mental, as strictly geographical.

8. This 'trigger effect' has been subjected to a mathematical analysis of the psychosocial vectors involved, by the Rand Corporation. It is in no way a statement of the outmoded panic concept popularly known as the 'Domino Theory'. This is a scientific model and must be heeded as such. Even the isolationist philosophy of many senior figures in the Administration cannot reasonably baulk at acceptance of a need for exemplary action at this point— action based not upon 'political' hypotheses of dubious merit, as heretofore, but upon the psychosocial realities of Planet Earth. (See the attached Rand Corporation document on the testing out in practice of the math models involved, in Puerto Rico, and in Angola.)

9. It is evident that the events in Brazil, if not reversed, represent an immediate 50% attrition of US investment and resource potential for the whole subcontinent.

10. Attempting to control these events by applying 'conventional' pressures is unlikely to prove effective. There is considerable evidence that key elements in the Brazilian Administration, hitherto considered stable and pro-American, have abruptly polarized in the opposite direction.

11. The precipitating event in this upsurge of nationalistic and even of extreme xenophobic reactions is of course the unfortunate—and unforeseen—monitoring by a Chinese satellite of the small nuclear explosions that breached the dam codenamed 'Niagara'. The People's Republic Government's announcement of this, against a background of rising insurgency inside Brazil itself, was a propaganda stroke of the first order. The equally unfortunate and unforeseen flood devastation produced by project 'Niagara Falls' provides the final obstacle to a 'conventional' political solution to the nationalistic frenzy now gripping Brazil and much of Latin America.

12. It is vital to neutralize the snowballing set of events in Latin America; to trigger an 'anti-catalyst' to divert these events. And this 'anti-catalyst' must be *as momentous and of the same order* as the Amazon disaster.

13. It is therefore recommended that Project 'Leapfrog' should be 'shunted' along these diversionary lines.

(See attached Rand Corporation working paper, *'Transfer of Threat: an analysis of hostility transferred from an actual and internal enemy to an imaginary and external enemy'*, para 72, '... to a theoretically plausible yet statistically unlikely "Alien Menace"'.)

14. It is recommended that in order to maximize the technological payoff from Project 'Leapfrog', while at the same time diverting the South American revolutionary situation, Project 'Mulekick' should be proceeded with at speed.

15. It will be necessary to inform the Soviet Government as soon as (i.e. during) the delivery of 'Mulekick'. And to adopt a posture of national defence readiness, whilst guaranteeing equal rights to share any technical data accruing as pay-off.

TWENTY-TWO

"DON'T FRET ABOUT it, Pierre," said Sole lamely, as the long-awaited helicopter came down at last upon the village. "What Kayapi did might have been the right thing, in Xemahoa terms—he had to find some answer to the presence of that monster, damn it! I know it made me throw up. But mightn't it still have been the right thing to do? Sometimes the right thing is the thing that makes us sick—"

"Kayapi—" the Frenchman spat out.

"—may be a Xemahoa genius."

"—is a vile opportunist, a dirty little village Hitler."

"Crap, Pierre. It's like you said earlier—he's a myth-maker, a cultural strongman. And I'll tell you something else. We have to act in a ruthless manner too—not for one Indian village but for the whole damn planet."

"Words, words—"

"If what we need to do involves taking somebody's brain out of their head—"

The helicopter landed. It wasn't piloted by the Texan nor did it carry Chase or Billy—but pilot and passenger had the same clear-cut Mormon uniformity of the Soft War Corps that even the Negro Chester managed to fit, with his slick-carved souvenir features; though as he ran up now he resembled a distraught Queequeg with his eternal harpoon. Tom Zwingler emerged from Pierre's hut, rubbing sleep from his eyes.

"Zwingler?"

"Thank God for that! You're from Franklin? What happened?"

The passenger ignored the question.

"Why's the sky dark at night then, Zwingler?"

"Universe is expanding," Tom Zwingler smiled as a world of comforting certainties, codewords and organization reasserted itself for him. But an uncertain look came over his face as he took in the brusque hostility in the other man's tone.

His smile wasn't returned.

"You're to evacuate with us right away. But you needn't bring any of these Indians with you. Project 'Leapfrog' has been altered."

"But—why? Have we left it too late? Have the aliens gone?"

"Explanations while we fly, Zwingler. Right now we're in one hell of a hurry. The Brazilian Air Force are hunting for us."

"They're—doing—WHAT?" exploded Chester. "WHO are doing WHAT?"

"The Brazilian Air Force. Part of it anyhow. The past few days have seen some surprises, I may tell you! There's civil war in Brazil. And chaos spreading across half-a-dozen countries. On account of that mess you and your demolition geniuses made of things."

The man glared resentfully at the trio.

"Goddam awful mess—"

"We haven't heard anything about what happened. We've got no radio. We've just been waiting here."

"You'll hear about the hornet's nest you stirred up soon enough. Radio!—it's frightening these days. How many of you are there? I thought there were just three."

"You'll be coming, won't you Pierre?" asked Zwingler slyly.

Pierre's eyes gleamed with a sudden ray of hope.

"You said Revolution? And the Air Force are on the side of the Revolution?"

"That's about it," the mormon salesman nodded.

225

"The Revolution!" Pierre whispered gleefully. He glanced around him furtively, as though he was thinking of rushing off into the jungle and joining in the fighting there and then.

Sole caught his look and smiled his best Iago smile.

"You can't do anything about it stuck here in the jungle, Pierre—you'd better come along with us."

Sole was conscious, as he said it, that he sounded like a policeman advising the criminal to come quietly.

Pierre hung back, reluctant—and excited.

Even this small measure of delay worried the newcomers.

"Would you folks hurry up? The Frenchman can do what he pleases, but my instructions are to fly you three outa here as soon as can be. You're a helluva security risk, s'posing the Brazilians locate you. Weren't for this, you might have bin left here. Things are that touchy, folks."

Sole had to laugh.

"*We're* a security risk? My God! Things have turned on their heads."

Pierre was glancing about the village shiftily again— planning his escape.

"The Frenchman oughta be a security risk too," grinned Chester. He raised the dart gun and casually fired a needle into Pierre's bare shoulder. "Sorry, Pee-áir," he laughed, mimicking Kayapi's pronunciation.

Pierre stumbled away with a dazed expression on his face. He hadn't gone more than five or six paces when he sprawled face down in the mud and lay limp.

Chester handed the gun to Tom Zwingler and walked over to Pierre's body leisurely; hauled him upright with one hand then bore him back to the helicopter in a fireman's lift.

Presumably it was all for the best, thought Sole.

Obviously Pierre was in no condition to stay in the

jungle. His body had taken a terrible beating from flies and leeches and general strain over the past few days.

As Sole helped Chester hump Pierre's light frame on board the helicopter, he found himself shivering with a numb guilty thrill. Chester was happy too—he had fired his harpoon at last.

They flew over flat green jungle through thin rainmists and zones of rainbow sunlight. And that man in a hurry, whose name was Amory Hirsch, filled in the details of the missing days. The three men, so abruptly snatched from the timeless village of the Indians, heard with a shiver of fear of the changes in the outside world that had sprung so absurdly from their actions. They had searched for a needle in a haystack—and set the haystack on fire.

They heard of the disaster at Santarém. Of the tens of thousands drowned. The ocean-going ships washed deep into jungle, where they toppled over and their boilers burst. Assassinations of American engineers before the assassins themselves were washed away like so much jetsam. Tidal waves of anger and hatred washing over the Brazilian cities. And how in all the confusion one fact stood out. One lunatic, unaccountable fact. That fearful use of nuclear weapons by the Americans to sabotage their own Amazon Project.

They heard how the pinprick explosions were detected by the Chinese transpacific satellite, the primary role of which was now clear to everyone, a spotter guideline for the ICBM system of the People's Republic. "Two lousy kilotons!" cried Amory Hirsch, distraught at the pettiness of it—but it had been the straw that broke the camel's back, in two senses: ecological—and political. As soon as the Chinese found out, be damned to the pretence of earth sciences research. Be damned to the Chinese game of musical satellites—of soaring to the top of the charts with their latest hitsong, *Red Chairman of the Board*. With what relish they leaked this news, no matter if it blew their own cover. Leaked it? No—avalanched the world with it. Meanwhile the Soviets were lying low—suspiciously low. Then fear and suspicion rode the globe at this first fearful use of nuclear weapons since Nagasaki. American property in Rio and São Paulo was burnt and looted. One part of the Brazilian army and air force defected. The other part was paralysed and reluctant to intervene. The régime's taut control abruptly snapped. Lunatic, anarchistic episodes followed—the napalming of the US Ambassador's residence in Brasilia was one. A wave of anarchy flushed through the country from town to town. From mind to mind. The guerrilla underground proclaimed its provisional government from the liberated city of Belo Horizonte. And this wild free violent mood lapped over, in far ripples from that flash flood on the Amazon, into neighbouring countries, infecting and contaminating.

"In nineteen hundred and seventy-five all the people rose from the countryside," murmured Sole.

Amory Hirsch glared at him stonily.

"You might at least get the year right, whatever your sympathies."

"Sorry, I was thinking about something else."

"You were thinking about something else! Jesus Christ Almighty!"

"Yes, I see this situation's bad," said Tom Zwingler anxiously. "But what about the other business? Have we missed our chance of the stars then? Have the Aliens packed up and gone home? Is that why we have to go back with empty hands?"

Amory Hirsch sneered.

"There's a big announcement upcoming on that one—and it ain't at all what you think."

Helplessly, Zwingler gnawed at a fingernail.

228

"What are you talking about, Hirsch? What else is there to think except that it's the greatest chance Mankind has ever been handed on a plate!"

"On a flying saucer, you mean," laughed Hirsch.

"But we found what we came to find, I tell you. Why should this mess down here stop us taking some Indians back to the States?"

Hirsch shook his head.

"Don't worry, fella. You'll hear all about the reality scene once we get on board that airplane out of Franklin. This sickness in South America may be adjustable. Essentially it all depends what you're prepared to throw into the other pan of the scales. History—politics—mass moods —it's all a question of balances. Finding the right pressure points. The Chinese were ready enough to blow the cover on their satellite, to brew this mess up for us. We only have to up the ante in the most effective way. Amusingly, we can have the Soviets on our side in quashing this revolution."

It was several hours later that Sole and Zwingler listened disbelievingly to Canal Zone Radio, as the anti-hysteria package was launched. Archimedes had said he could move the world, if only he had a place outside of the world to stand, and a long enough lever. It seemed that the Aliens had been elected to provide that place outside of the world.

But what lever would be used?

"... Big news at this nine o'clock nightly newstime. The joint US—USSR declaration one half-hour ago that hostile extraterrestials from another star system are operating in Earth's near vicinity. It is now reported that the giant satellite visible over the Pacific Ocean and Siberia and Iceland, reported to have been launched last week by the Soviets—was a cover story agreed between the two major space powers to avoid world alarm."

"Unbelievable," muttered Zwingler, fumbling at his throat.

"...Hostility is now certain since the destruction of a joint US-Soviet spacecraft with the loss of three astronauts' lives, and the destruction of unmanned satellites crossing the path of the alien ship. The flooding of the Amazon basin caused by the destruction of a key dam by a nuclear weapon, reported by a Chinese satellite, is now definitely established in the joint communiqué as tallying with reported sightings of Unidentified Flying Objects in the area—"

"Damnable!"

"Take it easy, Zwingler," shrugged Hirsch. "You're a passenger now. Just along for the ride. It was naïve to put your trust in unhumans, when you can't trust human beings. Wouldn't you say, naïve?" He thrust a polished marble face bluntly at his fellow passengers. "Unhumans sounds pretty much like inhumans to me, eh?"

"...Urgent consultations between the Soviet and American governments via the Hot Line taking place for several days now. The joint communiqué says it has been thought advisable to reveal the presence of this alien spacecraft, now that it is definitely proven hostile—in view of the widespread panic that might result from any further nuclear sabotage of major engineering works—"

"What stupid lies! Don't they think of the stars at all?"

"...Emphasized strongly in the communiqué, that any nuclear detonations should not be seen as indicators of any Soviet-American hostilities. Consultations are under way with other members of the Nuclear Club to avoid possible misinterpretations—"

"Surely the Sp'thra can't still be in Nevada!"

"Oh but they can," crowed Amory Hirsch. "The inhumans can!" He smiled a waspish smile.

"...From Stateside meanwhile, news that the president will address the nation in one half-hour's time simultaneously with the Soviet Premier addressing the Russian people—"

"It's madness!"

"No madder than the madness riding Latin America right now. We reckon it's the proper antidote. The R base X for this revolution—the prescription."

"It's criminal," sputtered Zwingler. "It's the biggest mistake. What does the whole of Latin America matter beside the million worlds out there! We buy a stinking little peace by sacrificing the stars, when we could have bought the stars with half a dozen brains. It's so STUPID. *Stupid!*"

The jet passed high over Panama in the dark of the starry night, and on out over the Caribbean.

And so the sanity filters were selectively removed, one by one. Excited American—and Russian—voices told about the immensity of the interstellar globe orbiting the Earth. UFO sightings were reported from Los Angeles and Omsk, from Tashkent and Caracas. Mysterious charred holes in superhighways. Jets crashing unaccountably. Brought down by who knows what?

Their jet veered out over the Gulf of Mexico towards the American South.

"The Russians?" Amory Hirsch retorted to Zwingler's persistent, peevish questions. "Well, for one thing they're implicated with us right up to their necks in this brain trading business. And two, it was the Chi-Coms who scooped all the political kudos by detecting that nuclear blowout at the dam. And three; well, frankly the trading didn't go too well after you left. Sure, we traded, they traded. But the return in technological data was shaping up as inadequate. The addresses of a few mangy stars. A few crutches to help us hobble round the solar system a bit faster. But not nearly fast enough to escape our own death sentence from any number of exponential causes. Crumbs from the rich man's table! Hell, Tom, don't you see, we're the HUMAN RACE. Soviets and Americans alike. Screw this stupid revolution. How could we be bothered to jockey for influence over a few hundred million miserable gauchos or whatever you call 'em? Maybe the Chinks can be bothered to. Call themselves the 'Middle Kingdom'? They're bloody earth-bound peasants, is all! But Soviets and Americans, we're both of us frontiersmen at heart. We're not donkeys to be lured a few idiot steps by hanging a carrot before our noses. We turn right round and KICK the carrot out of the hand that mocks us with it."

"I still don't see it," Zwingler moaned.

Amory Hirsch leaned forward patronizingly.

"Tom, you and Leapfrog—that's the short term view. A new spacious view is in order."

"Short term!" Zwingler clutched for his lost ruby moons as though for prayer beads, but didn't find them. There were no adequate prayers.

Flying towards the gulf ports, they picked up more of the progress of the crusade of hysteria from KCTA in Corpus Christi. Amory Hirsch laughingly revealed the codename of the operation—a farrago inspired by memories of the Orson Welles terror broadcast of 30 October 1938—and Sole winced as he remembered his own instinct about the alien TV broadcasts. This was destined to be a much more sophisticated and professional performance than the Welles broadcast back in the Stone Age of media awareness—for this tragic farce they had some actual aliens as actors.

It seemed, though Sole couldn't swear to it, that the jet was flying more leisurely the closer it got to the USA —maybe they flew slower so as not to trigger any missile sequences set to the superspeed of flying saucers. But there were no flying saucers—they were a myth, a lie. Only one scout ship existed, and that still on the Nevada airstrip, if Amory Hirsch's word was to be trusted. With one great globe in space with its crew of sad haunted travelling salesmen.

So the Globe had shot down Russian and American satellites with laser beams?

"Has it shot down any?" clamoured Zwingler.

"Course not," smiled Hirsch, though even as he said it a cloud of doubt passed over his face, as if Welles Farrago was too realistically scripted for him to doubt. Then he winked superciliously. "This is all cereal packet stuff strictly for the kids. The real difficulty is synchronizing our retaliatory blows—not using the hammer to stun the fly—on the other hand not using the fly swat to zap the elephant with—"

"It's disgusting," Zwingler shouted at him, losing control. "All I know about flies and elephants is this, Mister Hirsch, I might have swallowed a fly or two in my time, but I do most strenuously strain at this elephant of dishonesty and deceit!"

"Sorry you feel that way, Tom," smirked the other man, "but it's policy."

The President talked about:

The coming together of Earth's people—in the face of the inhuman adversary. Impossibility of comprehending the intentions or the powers of the truly alien. Their proven hostility attested to publicly by the United States and Soviet Union standing shoulder to shoulder as brothers. By the wanton destruction of the Amazon Development Project with atrocious loss of life and property damage—immediate aid to be rushed to the survivors through the agency of the United Nations, since the Brazilian people had been taken in by irresponsible Chinese lies and propaganda. The assassination in space of two Americans and one Soviet cosmonaut, to whose bravery all homage—write them down in the roll of honour of Planet Earth, Colonel Marcos Haigh, Major Joe

Rohrer, Major Vadim Zaitsev. The lasering out of orbit of Earth Resources Satellites—the sabotaging of Earth's efforts for betterment by a superior and haughty technology—like vicious children pulling the wings off flies...

"Those names," cried Zwingler. "I remember them. From Nevada."

"Nonsense, Tom," Hirsch laughed. "You're hallucinating. Take any of those Indian drugs?"

On the final approach, as they watched the sprawl of Houston coming up below them, KTRH announced the detonation of a one-kiloton tactical homing missile upon a 'flying saucer' temporarily grounded in the Nevada desert...

While the wheels jolted down upon the runway, Amory Hirsch laughed triumphantly and polished his hands.

A moment later, word came of the Soviet orbital bomb that wrecked the Unhumans' transpolar globe, cracking it open like an egg and spilling its yolk across the sky above the Solomon Islands...

"Bastards—dumb fucking bastards—vicious stupid shits..." cursed Tom Zwingler monotonously while the jet slowed to a halt, till the NO SMOKING sign blanked out.

TWENTY-THREE

"WE'LL WALK FROM here on."

"Sure?"

Sole nodded.

They got out of the lowslung blue Ford car with the legend USAF stencilled on its front doors. The toothy Negro sergeant who'd been driving them backed into a gateway then sped off back the way he'd come, negotiating the country lanes with a faint squeal of tyres.

"Over there, that's Haddon."

Sole pointed at the Unit half a mile away on top of the rise, backed up against its own dense mini-jungle of fir trees.

"My little Indians—" he shrugged.

He indicated the straggle of the village across the barren fields behind them.

"That's my place—with the blue VW. You head on over there, Pierre. Eileen'll be waiting. I—I'll catch you up."

His own home?

Containing a woman Eileen whom he happened to be married to—yet her voice over the comsat telephone link the other night had sounded like such a cleverly personalized answering service! Containing a boy, Peter, who more closely resembled the looks of this other bitter empty man he stood with on the country lane...

Sole pushed Pierre gently towards the stile leading on to the field path. It wasn't an affectionate push, however —there couldn't be any affection any more. But it was gentle.

Pierre gave Sole a puzzled look, but climbed the stile without asking any questions, and set off along the stiff mud track.

And Sole was alone.

The English countryside seemed as blank and stripped-bare as the face of the Moon, after the Amazon rain-forests. The sky with all its empty dry air rubbed its nothingness over him coldly. He set off towards Haddon Unit, through the dead fields.

He had never felt quite so nervously aware, as he walked, under the clear empty eggshell sky, of being located on the surface of a gross statistical accident—as well as of being encompassed by the ghosts of billions of casualties who might have lived, but never had—of other Soles who might have been born, but weren't—and whose exclusion bracketed his own existence about till it too seemed unreal—a life lived in brackets. He was filled with a haunting consciousness of every twig and stalk of grass crisp and clear in their total arbitrariness—bracketed into existence by the exclusion of so much more, infinitely more. Every clod of earth shaped itself into a grinning hunch-back gargoyle as he walked. The blue of the sky behind barren branches became stained glass in some empty cathedral of the void—a fan of peacock plumes courting nothingness.

He swung a carrier bag stuffed with clothes, conscious of many other Soles carrying out different projects and making different choices in this dead random zone.

Beyond that peacock blue that Sole saw as a stained-glass window and a display of plumes, in the blackness which that blue had become by the height of a thousand miles, Major Pip Dennison floated in his michelin-man suit—veteran of five hundred South-East Asian combat sorties and a duty tour in Skylab, author *cum laude* of a PhD thesis on the math of orbital trajectories. His faceplate reflected the blue disc of Earth with its white whorling streaks of cream meringue—a soda fountain in space.

His umbilical tether snaked away, reflecting the harshest of sunlights, towards the hanging shuttle craft from which other gossamer lines also spun away to other rubber blobs of humans. Half a dozen spacemen had landed on different parts of this vast rent metal fruit whose segments had sprung apart through the rumpled rind, bursting deep black-shadowed canyons and crevasses down into it. Like wasps they had flown out to suck the juice from the spoilt fruit.

Flies to a hunk of rare venison hung up there to mature, in the icebox of space.

Pip consulted the Roentgen counter strapped to his wrist. The rate of rotting of this venison was subject to an inverse law: only when the radioactive rot had ceased would the whole carcass be ripe for the picking. What a feast in the sky it would be—this split orange, burst egg, hunk of venison.

First they would pick over this north side of the fruit. Later, they would head round it to the hole punched in the south side three hundred feet deep by five hundred wide—that million-degree axeblow that had split the enemy's skull— watching their Roentgen counters as they worked.

Yet a thought daunted Major Dennison, as he looked down the steel crevasse. Could some alien beast have survived the axeblow and loss of air—and still be alive somewhere down there?

The pit yawned darkly. They said, didn't they, that a spaceman was only a deepsea diver keeping the pressure in, instead of out? What octopus tentacles might reach for him out of the injured darkness? Pip shivered in his well-heated suit as he unclipped his tether and clamped it magnetically to the metal rind. Elsewhere on the ruptured surface, half a dozen Americans and Russians belayed their tethers too...

Pip angled his light down and snapped a holograph of the chasm with fat buckled tubing gleaming at the bottom of it. He let the camera hang loose and checked for a second time the handiness of the improvised weapon they had all been issued with—an explosive pellet thrower powered by compressed gas.

"Dennison about to descend," Pip told his throat mike.

"Good luck, Pip," a voice buzzed in his ear. "Good hunting."

Pip swung his body round and started climbing upward. The change of orientation put Earth's soda fountain a thousand miles below his feet, blue oceans whipped with cream.

Sole's intentions were as ice-sharp as the winter day, as he pushed the main door open and walked into the heat inside.

The Christmas tree was gone. Balloons gone. Streamers gone.

No one saw him as he fitted his key into the first security door and passed through to the rear wing.

He took the lift down and stepped out into the corridor, hurried to the first window.

Inside the Embedding World the wall screen was dead and the four children lay sleeping on the floor in a neat row.

Gulshen's leg was encased in plaster. Rama's hand was wrapped in bandages. Vasilki's brow was bandaged and her face badly bruised.

Vidya was the only unblemished one. Yet he did not sleep quietly. Even through the tranquillizers and barbiturates his lips moved. Muscular tics twisted them.

Sole barely registered the peculiar circumstances. A glance showed him that Vidya was safe and that was all he cared about. He walked through the airlock ignoring the speech mask hanging up, dropped the carrier bag beside the boy and bent over him.

"Vidya!" he called tentatively.

The boy moved fitfully and his lips twitched but he didn't open his eyes.

Drugged, Sole noted with distaste. He glanced at the video pickups. Possibly they weren't switched on, and if they were switched on nobody would be watching, as there was nothing to record.

He emptied the clothes out of the carrier bag and began dressing Vidya. Amusing to think of the boy waking up fully dressed for the very first time—maybe feeling bound up in a bit of a strait jacket at first—then the huge enlargement of his vistas dawning on him . . .

Pierre's footsteps crumpled the gravel as he skirted the blue Volkswagen and went round the side of the house.

He looked in through a window, saw a boy wriggling about in an armchair before the TV set—crossing and uncrossing his white matchstick legs under him restlessly. The boy's face shocked him. The soft foxy features. His own childhood face, from a green buckram photograph album.

But Chris had never said anything. Hadn't even hinted. How long was it since that time in Paris? It was possible.

His own child? It might explain Chris's ambivalent attitude—the sense Pierre had ever since he become conscious of Chris there in the jungle, that Chris had been thrashing out some private dilemma that had nothing to do with Indians or Aliens or even his experiments at the Hospital.

Another window brought him face to face with Eileen.

For a moment she failed to recognize him, he looked so thin and worn, then she flew to the kitchen door.

"Pierre! But Chris said nothing on the phone—"

239

"No?"

They kissed lightly. Pierre held her by the shoulders to look into her eyes—which seemed older and cooler now.

He gestured uncertainly at the other room, where the TV was playing hurdy-gurdy music.

"I never knew—Chris didn't mention anything. I—I am right, aren't I?"

"Yes—his name's Peter. My Chris doesn't seem to have said much—"

"Ah—Chris has gone up to the Hospital for something. Maybe to give us a moment together?"

Pip floated into a corridor which carried cable-bearing pipes around the inner skin of the Globe—now they were buckled and ruptured. Further along, the corridor was pinched together by the shock wave of the explosion and its roof scraped the floor like a coalmine gallery squashed flat by subsidence.

Nearby, a hatch had sprung open. A ladder with metre-wide spaces between the separate rungs led down to a lower level. Blocking the view drifted the body of one of the angular aliens, surrounded by a frozen pink haze.

Pip bounced himself cautiously upward from rung to rung till he reached the dead unhuman floating in the nebula of its blood. He hauled the corpse aside. Its grey clothes—or was that stuff skin?—tore away from the chilled metal leaving a frozen layer behind.

Pip pushed himself into a high, vaulted corridor more spacious than the first corridor had been. He shone his light around. The corridor led off in one direction along a buckled curve, vanishing out of sight. In the other direction it opened into a hallway of idle, dead machines. A second alien body hung midway between them, turning very slowly end over end. Fingers splayed out like tree twigs. Ears had burst open into grey streamers from its skull. Pip swung his body round so that the roof became the floor again, then pushed his way by gentle shoves towards the machinery. Ambassador from the world of whipped cream, he inspected these first pickings of the meal of Mind. He snapped holograms, checked his Roentgen counter.

After ten minutes, when he couldn't make out the function of the machines, he drifted down a long rumpled ramp to a lower level still...

Sole carried the sleeping Vidya up in the lift and along the corridor. Outside the hairmesh security glass, the green barbed woods pressed a corset round the building. It was quiet.

He unlocked the first door.

In the interface between the two doors, Lionel Rosson stood waiting for him. He didn't seem surprised to see him, or the boy in his arms.

"What are you up to, Chris? Sabotage? Or is it sentimentality? I suppose I ought to say welcome home to Haddon. But let's get that boy back to his proper place first, hmm? Oh, I would have wanted you back here so desperately, a week ago! But now ... well—it's different, isn't it?"

Sole whispered furiously:

"I'm taking Vidya out of here. To live a real life. I'm sick of bogus science and lying politics. Projects for the advancement of Mankind! Codename after codename for bestiality—their Leapfrogs and Mulekicks. And Haddon's just as bad—"

"What's a Leapfrog, Chris? What's a Mulekick?" Rosson asked, humouringly, keeping a wary eye on the sleeping boy, and keeping his own back to the outer door.

"Hasn't it all been on the telly then? Flying saucers. Alien menace. All that crap. I hear it knocked the wind out of the sails of revolution in South America!"

"You've been involved in that then, Chris? Ah well!

241

Time enough to tell me. You've seen the injuries? You realize the boy is tranked? And needs to be, damn it!"

"I've had my fill of needs. Political needs. Scientific needs. Humanity's needs. Bugger all needs!"

"You don't understand the situation, Chris. Let's take Vidya downstairs again. We'll work out a strategy, hmm?"

"Who wants a 'strategy'?" sneered Sole.

"We do, Chris. Things reached crisis point—"

"You've ballsed things up, you bastard—you didn't look after Vidya!"

Sole put the boy down on the floor gently.

"For Chrisake, Chris, listen to me—the language programme broke down. The kids accepted the overload on short term memory up to a certain point. But it's broken down now like a dam bursting."

Sole growled at the foggy figure before him.

"Bloody well leave dams bursting out of it!"

"Sure, Chris. Anything you say. But listen, will you? The kids reverted to babbling. Not baby babbling. It was concepts, ways of thinking—"

"Get out of my way, you. Fuck your ways of thinking."

"The thing is, your embedding has—"

Sole hit Rosson in the stomach.

"—taken place," gasped Rosson. Sole caught hold of his mane of hair and swung his head against the wall violently till Rosson crumpled up and sagged to the floor.

He picked Vidya up again and unlocked the outer door.

Pip floated into what would later be known as the First Chamber of the Brains.

His light fell on many crystal life-support boxes—row upon row towering up to a vaulted dome. Tendrils of wires led up to them, like jungle creepers climbing trees, from the instrument panels below. Wires led into the plastic jelly that filled the boxes, where they split into a million filaments, that touched every part of what those boxes contained: naked brains—set in the jelly like fruits in a trifle.

There were brains of many forms and sizes. Some resembled fungi. Some, corals. Some, rubbery cactus plants. Sections of spinal columns jutted below the brains, some as straight as ram-rods, others curled like drawn bows, others ripple-form like waves. Sense-organs stood out, attached to the brains on muscular cords and bony rods. A few were recognizable as eyeballs; others ambiguous. Were they for seeing light at all—or some other form of radiation?

Pip gazed up in a mixture of awe and disgust. The set-up reminded him of a biology lab in school—pickled sea creatures drained of colour, floating in alcohol.

None of the life-support boxes had ruptured, though, when the Globe burst.

He wondered—could their minds have survived inside that protective gel of theirs—quick-frozen so fast that they had no time to die, but only hibernated?

There'd been no vital organs to rupture, no lungs to burst. The life support systems had just suddenly cut off —and the brain had already been plunged to a temperature where all functions were suspended.

Could cryogenics engineers from Earth restore any sort of consciousness to these creatures? Was there any chance they could reactivate the life support systems? Warm the brains up? Bring them back again?

Maybe the shock of pseudo-dying when the cold rushed in would have been too massive for the mind to come through intact, even if a trace of consciousness still lingered.

Yet if there was the slightest chance! Surely Humanity owed it to these prisoners, to bring them back again. And owed it to itself. As many mental sciences could stem from the contents of this chamber, as physical sciences from the machinery of the Globe.

Such thoughts exalted him—eagle scout, PhD *cum laude*, veteran of the crusade for Asian freedom—as he hung there among the brains of beings from across a thousand light years, and whispered a prayer.

Lord, may these brains be resurrectable.

May they be raised to a new life by Ettinger Foundation engineers. To a true mind alliance, which those ghouls denied them—as they would have denied Humanity—rushing in here to pick our brains and fly off again. Please, Lord, for Humanity's sake.

God bless the Ettinger Foundation, whispered Pip into his helmet. Bless them and help them to bring the frozen body back to life and cure it.

It was a prayer he'd whispered many times before—his own four-year-old niece had been frozen in a tube of liquid nitrogen, dead of terminal cancer, the summer before.

Pip wept into his helmet tenderly, from sheer compassion. His torchbeam danced over the frozen brain aquarium.

Sole carried Vidya through the frozen fields by the same route as he'd come. Though it was the longer way round to his house, it was less public. He was less likely to meet anyone. As he walked, the cold air began to penetrate Vidya's sleep. The boy had never felt such cold before. His lips tasted it and twitched. His cheeks blushed with it. His skin crawled.

Sole crossed the road where he'd parted from Pierre and set his eyes on the blue car parked by his house. The Volkswagen spelt mobility. Escape.

He held the boy tight, loving him and hating all else, as the child's lips began to mumble sounds.

Vidya's eyes opened, and he stared blankly at the great blue vault of sky and towering skeletons of trees.

*   *   *

Eileen and Pierre came out to meet him, Pierre catching hold of her arm to stop her when he saw the boy.

"Chris—what sort of game is this?"

She stared at Vidya and the boy stared back, locking on her eyes disconcertingly.

"You've brought an Indian boy back from Brazil?"

"Chris brought nothing but himself and me. That's one of their experiments from the Unit. They usually keep them under lock and key—Chris must have flipped his lid bringing him here—"

Inside the house, a telephone bell began to jangle.

Pierre took his hand off Eileen's arm, belatedly.

"Shall I answer? I can guess what it is. You mightn't realize it, Eileen, but your Chris has just torn his precious career up and thrown the pieces in the air."

She stared at the Frenchman in bewilderment.

"What—?"

"Chris has just committed a huge breach of security. Though God knows why. It doesn't look like he does—"

Chris hugged the boy, and gazed down at him.

"Fortunately he's healthy," he said, as much to himself as to Eileen or Pierre. "There's nothing physically wrong with him. He's bright. Look at him taking it all in, cunning little bugger—"

Pierre gestured questioningly at the house, where the telephone kept on ringing. But Eileen wasn't paying attention. She stared from her husband to the child in its ill-fitting clothes. Pierre shrugged and went indoors to take the call.

"Do you mean this kid is yours, Chris?"

"Why yes! Who's else?"

"But ... when? How? Is this what you dragged Pierre here to witness—this shabby domestic intrigue? This petty tit for tat. After you've been away such a time you can only produce this gesture—you petty hateful nobody!"

Vidya stared at her face twisted by anger. His fists

245

balled up inside his gloves. His body arched against the restraint of clothes. He writhed about like a snake in Sole's embrace as the cold air stung his face.

Sole stared at his wife. Her outburst puzzled him. It seemed so paranoid and irrelevant. He hadn't even been away 'such a time'—it was less than two weeks.

"I didn't screw some bitch foreign nurse if that's what you think! Vidya is the child of my—my mind."

"So Peter isn't a product of your precious mind? A cruel trick, Chris, bringing Pierre here to rub it in."

"That's an accident, Pierre being here. Honestly. My God, why should it be a trick?"

"Can I see into your heart any better than you can yourself? Do I know why your subconscious needs a setpiece like this?"

"Setpiece? What the hell are you talking about!"

"Pierre arriving. Then your dramatic entry with your 'real' child in your arms. That's a child of the mind is it? I can't compete with that. What on earth is a child of the mind!"

The boy's eyes flashed from Sole to his wife and back again. The electricity of words flowed between them, and he fed on it greedily. Sole had to hold him tighter as his limbs flexed and he twisted about in his arms. It was all emotional nonsense Eileen was talking. It didn't make sense. The idea of bringing Pierre here hadn't been that at all. It had been—generosity. An attempt to give her something, not take something away, or humiliate her.

"I don't suppose I can stay here anyhow. Have you got the car keys? I'll have to take him somewhere else."

"This is beyond me. You just ... simply ... amaze me."

Sole began to feel a curious light-headedness.

Eileen was receding into the background. The house, the car, the landscape were all changing subtly. Still there, but—different.

He was still seeing familiar things; but seeing them

as though this was the first time he had set eyes on them. The familiar things were at the same time infinitely strange and fresh. They had taken on an unsettling double life. Their colours were faded and at the same time bright. Their shapes fitted in neatly to his customary picture of things—and simultaneously were oddly distorted and foreshortened as though the rules of perspective were being interfered with.

The house, as well as being a house, was now a giant red box of plastic bricks. The car was a Volkswagen saloon—and also a great plastic and glass spheroid of no very obvious function.

Eileen stood before him—a flat figure posturing on a screen suspended in mid-air.

Beyond, a barren plateau stretched out into infinite distance, unable to terminate itself with any solid boundary. Panic mounted in him as he searched for the boundaries that ought to be there, and were not. The most he could locate was a circular zone of confused light, very far away. Or was it very far away? Or very near? He couldn't tell—and when he tried to concentrate on the problem, the world flashed in and out at him, frighteningly, growing alternately very large and very small. In that confused zone far off, lines of sight broke down and vanishing points stubbornly refused to vanish. He tried to fashion a wall out of that medley of lights and darks far off—but the wall, half-completed, flowed in at him and out again, flexing and contracting about him, as though he had been swallowed by a soft glass stomach he could see through—and the stomach walls pulsed in and out while its acids nibbled at his bare skin, licking it with a harsh invisible tongue.

From this unbounded, menacing plateau sprung at intervals stiff towering giants, balanced upon great solitary legs, waving their hundreds of arms and thousands of fingers slackly overhead.

Above their reach was more of the great opaque stomach—its foggy depths were coloured blue, up there. They fled away and raced towards him, compressing him to a tiny spot, then inflating him till it seemed his head would burst with thinking of it.

Then he did an impossible thing.

He twisted about, in fright, in his own grasp; for an instant, saw both himself holding, and himself being held—saw the Self that held him, and saw the Self he held; the two sights superimposed on one another. Almost as soon as it formed, this double vision fell apart, and the two states began to alternate separately before his horrified eyes.

Rapidly, the two versions of Himself speeded up their substitutions of one another—quickening pace till they were flashing before his gaze like a film and producing a sickening illusion of continuity—but continuity in being two separate places at once.

Soon the visions fused again—and he was holding on to himself, and struggling against himself, not knowing which was the true state.

As before, the double vision shattered. He was Sole the Man staring in fear and nausea into the Boy's eyes. But these eyes swelled into deep pools. Mirrors. Saucers of glass. He could see himself reflected in them, at the same time as he saw himself *through* them.

In their depths a whirlpool spun frantically on its own axis, sucking everything in to a vanishing point that never vanished but only grew fearfully dense with light—with all the sights it was seeing yet couldn't find a way to discard from attention.

He wore the sky close as a hat. He knew the moil and coil of wisp clouds barely visible in the blue, intimately. His fingers branched the branching of the trees. His tongue tasted one by one the rows of brick teeth in that closed red mouth of a house that would swallow him, swallow him. And, at the very same time, he knew he was already swallowed, by the pulsing translucent stomach of the outside world.

This world flipped, into a new state of being.

It fell apart from lines and solids into a pointillist chaos of dots. Bright dots and dark dots. Blue dots, red dots, green dots. No form held true. No distance held fast. New forms making use of these dots in entirely arbitrary, experimental ways, sprang into being among the overwhelming debris of sense perceptions outside of him—fought to impose themselves on the flux of being—failed. Fell apart. And new forms rose.

A new creation was struggling to build itself out of the flood of information pouring at him. A new meaning. But all the sane, functional boundaries had dissolved and this chaos was saturated with meaning to such an extent it had lost all possibility of meaning any one thing or set of things. All appeared as of equal value.

A terrible, physical pressure was building in him, to crystallize this saturated world out into meaning—at all costs.

Where was the third dimension, that kept reality spaced out? This world seemed two-dimensional now—pressing tight about his eyes and ears and nose like a membrane, as packed with matter as the heart of a collapsed star. A flat sphere of dots of sense data pressing directly on to his brain, bypassing even his eyes and ears. It bound his thoughts about like a hungry womb.

The pressure in his head became an urgent need to smash his way through this membrane—to force things to become three-dimensional again, and absorb the vast excess of data.

And yet he was aware, instinctively, that the world he was seeing already was three-dimensional—that this two-dimensional quality was merely an agonizing illusion. Aware that he was trying to force something upon the world that could not be there in any rational universe—a dimension at right angles to this reality: somewhere to store the sheer volume of information flooding his brain and refusing to fade away.

He was watching a movie—but as the new scenes arrived, the old scenes refused to yield and pass on. They too continued to be screened. He had to find somewhere to put them, where he could forget about them.

'A dimension at right angles'? The image stung him to awareness of where he was, and who. The Man holding the Boy. And he realized with horror that these thoughts and emotions were largely Vidya's—and how he was now trapped by them.

Reason—rationality—is a concentration camp, where the sets of concepts for surviving in a chaotic universe form vast, though finite, rows of huts, separated into blocks by electric fences, which the searchlights of Attention rove over, picking out now one group of huts, now another.

Thoughts, like prisoners—imprisoned for their own security and safety—scurry and march and labour in a flat two-dimensional zone, forbidden to leap fences, gunned down by laser beams of madness and unreason if they try to.

Vidya's concentration camp had bulged at the seams. The fences fell over from sheer pressure of bodies. The outermost fence—the boundary beyond which lay the inarticulable—had snapped too. And this was unfortunate—for the concentration camp is the survival strategy of the species.

Vidya's thoughts spilled out—into Sole's mind, and into that chaos beyond, 'whereof we cannot speak', dragging him after them.

Sole grew vaguely aware of a flat ghost of a figure parading before his eyes, and gesticulating.

A man's voice, with a French accent, cried:

"For God's sake get away from him, Chris—leave him alone! The boy's mad. He can infect you with it, if you're too near him. They said on the phone, a projective empath. And mad. They're coming for him with an ambulance. Put him down and walk away—"

The flat, posturing ghost of dots pulled a second ghost figure back into the brick-toothed mouth that had wanted to gulp him and swallow him up in the flatness of its walls. But he was beyond boundaries, flying high.

"You don't see any vision of truth, Chris—my God, you've created a monster worse than that Xemahoa beast!"

The world flowed around him more demandingly again —a million bits of information. His present awareness, however much it distended, still ached with the strain of finding room for all this fearful wealth. The world was about to be embedded in his mind in its totality as a direct sensory apprehension, and not as something safely symbolized and distanced by words and abstract thoughts. The Greater was about to be embedded in the Lesser. Frantically he searched for adjacent dimensions of existence to receive this spill—the spill-water from a flooded dam. Yet the pressure could only discharge back into the same dimensional framework as the brain that perceived it. His fear of the coming discharge grew—a wild panic as the Embedding coiled within him.

"Come away, Chris. The boy has to be kept sedated. They'll have to operate on him. They'll have to cripple his brain, to save him. Put him inside the car, shut the door on him."

But Vidya is my mindchild. How do I leave my mind?

Sole-Vidya had no way to leave himself.

All sensory information about the situation flowed the other way.

Inwards. Sucked into the whirlpool—occupying mental space without being able to oust what had already flowed in.

The spring would overwind—would burst and fly apart.

"Please come away," begged Eileen. "Leave him."

Leave Vidya? Leave himself?

Vidya's limbs thrashed about in a mechanical dance as Sole held him tighter in his arms, and loved him, agonizing with him...

"Kid snapped his own neck," Rosson told Sam Bax bitterly as a male nurse lifted the dead boy into the back of the ambulance. He rubbed his own skull tenderly beneath the mop of hair.

"Injuries weren't nearly so bad with the other kids. You might say this boy was the ringleader. I can't say I didn't warn you, Sam."

"How does this affect the use of PSF in general, Lionel?" the Director demanded in a testy tone. "Is this the first sign of a general breakdown? God, what a mess if it is. All those people we've treated and let go home."

"Not necessarily, Sam. PSF is being used in conjunction with straightforward language procedures in the main part of the Unit. It can only do good there. Dorothy and I are working with logical patterns. There's not this saturation effect. Richard's world might give us some trouble soon, I dunno... I'm just astonished by the form this particular breakdown took—the projective empathy factor. Now that's really a fascinating byproduct. If Chris had damn well listened to me we might have had a chance to explore it instead of a snapped neck. We still have a chance with the other three kids. For God's sake let's be careful."

"A kind of telepathy, is it, Lionel?"

Rosson looked doubtful.

"I think what was happening in Vidya's brain was an overload of data that his mind couldn't switch off. It was forced to go on processing it. Couldn't filter it out. The brain circuits must have fused open—repeating and repeating. And this amplified the voltage flow far beyond what the brain machine is designed for. In fact, the current got so strong that it was able to transmit some kind of echo of itself that other brains could detect. That must be how this projective empathy works—and I suppose other parapsychological phenomena. Some sort of field is laid down that another brain can pick up, which disturbs the chemical balance of the corresponding sets of neurons in the other brain and stimulates them to a ghost firing. That's your telepathy for you—such as it is. Not genuine communication of ideas from mind to mind. Not dialogue—but a domineering influence, a sort of electrochemical hypnosis. Frightening—and not very useful. Since the boy was effectively insane—and broadcasting his insanity. I felt the same effect myself, when I was close to the boy, before we sedated them. When Chris comes out of shock, perhaps he'll be better qualified to comment—he's been dragged deeper into it than me."

Sam Bax stared irritably at Sole's body lying sedated on a second stretcher.

"With this little escapade I rather fear our Dr Sole has cooked his goose."

Rosson looked at Sole too. His head was hurting him.

"He's been under strain. Let's not make too much fuss about it, Sam. We'll all need to pull together to clear this mess up," he said generously—though he cursed Sole for a bastard and a fool.

Sam shrugged, unimpressed. He looked round for Eileen.

"Ah—Mrs Sole. Your husband will have to go into the Unit for observation, you realize. I'll see you're kept informed. It might be as well if you didn't visit him immediately."

"Quite," she answered dryly.

Shortly after, the ambulance drove away.

"Unless Sole's mind is cracked as bad as the boy's," Sam

Bax purred at Rosson, ushering him impatiently towards his own car.

Rosson tossed his mane of hair, winced as it tugged at his broken scalp.

A thousand miles over the Solomon Islands, travelling northward, minds weren't cracked at all, but deepfrozen—to a degree above absolute zero...

To the north of Las Vegas, beside the Atomic Energy Commission testing ground, minds weren't cracked at all, but dispersed in lightly radioactive debris drifting slowly south before settling into the desert.

The casinos were far enough south for nobody to need worry. The gambling went on. Minds reckoned the odds.

Five thousand miles further south, a Xemahoa Indian named Kayapi wasn't much worried either.